DEADLY DANCING AT THE SEAVIEW HOTEL

By Glenda Young

Helen Dexter Cosy Crime Mysteries
Murder at the Seaview Hotel
Curtain Call at the Seaview Hotel
Foul Play at the Seaview Hotel
Deadly Dancing at the Seaview Hotel

Saga Novels
Belle of the Back Streets
The Tuppenny Child
Pearl of Pit Lane
The Girl with the Scarlet Ribbon
The Paper Mill Girl
The Miner's Lass
A Mother's Christmas Wish
The Sixpenny Orphan

The Toffee Factory Girls
Secrets of the Toffee Factory Girls

DEADLY DANCING AT THE SEAVIEW HOTEL

Glenda Young

Copyright © 2025 Glenda Young

The right of Glenda Young to be identified as the Author of the Work has been asserted by her in accordance with the Copyright, Designs and Patents Act 1988.

First published in 2025 by
Headline Publishing Group Limited

1

Apart from any use permitted under UK copyright law, this publication may only be reproduced, stored, or transmitted, in any form, or by any means, with prior permission in writing of the publishers or, in the case of reprographic production, in accordance with the terms of licences issued by the Copyright Licensing Agency.

All characters in this publication are fictitious and any resemblance to real persons, living or dead, is purely coincidental.

The Seaview Hotel and the Vista del Mar in this story are fictional hotels and are not based on any hotels in Scarborough.

Cataloguing in Publication Data is available from the British Library

Hardback ISBN 978 1 0354 1554 0

Typeset in 12.6/16.8pt Adobe Garamond Pro
by Six Red Marbles UK, Thetford, Norfolk

Printed and bound in Great Britain by Clays Ltd, Elcograf S.p.A.

Headline's policy is to use papers that are natural, renewable and recyclable products and made from wood grown in well-managed forests and other controlled sources. The logging and manufacturing processes are expected to conform to the environmental regulations of the country of origin.

Headline Publishing Group Limited
An Hachette UK Company
Carmelite House
50 Victoria Embankment
London EC4Y 0DZ

The authorised representative in the EEA is Hachette Ireland, 8 Castlecourt Centre, Dublin 15, D15 XTP3, Ireland (email: info@hbgi.ie)

www.headline.co.uk
www.hachette.co.uk

To Scarborough, my happy place

Acknowledgements

Thank you to the ladies at Pure Bliss Spa, Sea Road, Fulwell, Sunderland for helping me carry out the most intriguing research I've done for any of my books! Thank you to Martin Atterbury of Scarborough TV News for sharing his love of playing music for others to dance to. Thank you to Angie Pearsall and her rescue greyhounds Carla and Rudy for teaching me everything I know about rescue greyhounds and helping bring Suki to life. Thank you to Elaine Davies of Scarborough for her insider knowledge of the hotel industry, to Joe Parkinson for invaluable story advice, to dance teacher Julie Venton and amateur dancer Louise Hardy for their insights into the world of dance. Thank you to Lisa Piercy for crime advice, and to Steve Ritchie of the Headlands Hotel in Scarborough, whose dad really was once crowned 'Best Pub Pianist in Britain'. Thank you to Elvis fans Paul and Kristie Lanagan. Thank you to Michael and Gemma of the *Conversation Street* podcast; you can listen to their weekly *Coronation Street* fan podcast at conversationstreet.podbean.com or wherever you listen to podcasts. Thank you to my agents, Caroline Sheldon of Caroline Sheldon Literary Agency and Safae El-Ouahabi of RCW Literary Agency. Finally, love and thanks, as always, to my husband Barry.

Chapter 1

On a warm summer's day, two women dressed in black sat on a bench on a Scarborough clifftop. The younger woman was Helen Dexter, owner of Scarborough's Seaview Hotel. The other was Helen's right-hand woman, Jean, the hotel's cook. Ahead of them was a crescent-shaped bay where the blue sea sparkled. Behind them stood the hotel. It was Helen's home and her business, her life. It had ten rooms and three storeys and was her pride and joy.

Helen pushed her bobbed brown hair behind her ears and listened to the waves below and the seagulls overhead. She unbuttoned her black jacket but noticed that Jean kept hers firmly closed. Jean turned her face to the sun and squinted through her big round glasses.

'It'd be a perfect Scarborough day . . . under different circumstances,' she said with a crack in her voice.

Between the women stood a bottle of champagne and two glasses. And on the ground at Helen's feet, in the shade of the bench, lay Suki, her rescue greyhound. Suki's caramel limbs spilled on the ground and her lead was tied to the bench. Helen looked at Jean.

'Are you ready?' she asked.

Jean took a deep breath and nodded, with tears in her eyes. Helen picked up the champagne bottle and twisted the cork, which came out with a subdued pop. Jean held out her glass, which Helen filled. Then she filled her own glass and set the bottle down.

'To your mum,' she said.

Jean clinked her glass against Helen's. 'To my mum. She's no longer suffering from the pain in her legs,' she said, wiping away a tear.

Both women turned to the sea as they sipped their drinks.

'It was a lovely funeral,' Jean said quietly.

'The vicar did her proud,' Helen agreed. 'And the care home staff put on a delicious spread afterwards.'

Jean opened her handbag and invited Helen to peer inside.

'I took enough ham sandwiches to last me all week.'

Helen couldn't help but smile. It was typical of Jean, letting nothing go to waste.

They sat in silence for a moment, sipping champagne. Then Jean raised her glass again.

'Here's to living life to the full, like Mum used to do.'

'I'll drink to that,' said Helen. She took a sip, then lowered her glass and looked at Jean. Her friend was clearly tired, done in; her mum's death had hit her hard. Jean had never been one to show her emotions, but Helen knew she was suffering, no matter how much she said otherwise. She gently placed her hand on the older woman's arm. 'If you need me, I'm here.'

Jean pushed her glasses up to the bridge of her nose, then sat up straight in her seat.

'I'll be fine,' she said briskly. 'Aren't I always?' But then her face clouded over. 'Mind you, life will take some getting used to now that Mum's gone. I used to walk up and down Filey Road to visit her care home three times a week. I'm not sure how I'll fill my time now.'

Deadly Dancing at the Seaview Hotel

Helen thought for a moment.

'Well, when you feel ready, you could think about starting a new activity in town. There are art classes, for instance.'

Jean shook her head. 'I can't draw to save my life.'

But Helen wasn't about to give up.

'There are yoga lessons in the South Cliff Gardens. I could go with you.'

'Yoga? Me? Pfft!' Jean huffed. 'You'll not catch me doing a downward dog with my backside in the air, or standing on one leg pretending to be a tree. I'm not daft.'

'You could learn how to upcycle furniture,' Helen continued, undeterred.

'Upcycle? What's that when it's at home?' Jean sniffed, then took another swig of champagne. A misty look came into her eye.

'Mind you, there is one thing I fancy doing.'

'Oh?' Helen said, intrigued.

Jean rolled the stem of her glass between her fingers, watching the liquid move in the flute.

'I wouldn't mind picking up my ballroom dancing again.'

Helen raised her eyebrows. 'You used to dance? Just when I thought I knew everything about you, you go and surprise me like that! You know, the guests we've got coming in today are ballroom dancers. They're taking part in a dance competition at the Spa. You could ask them for some tips.'

A faint blush came to Jean's cheeks. Helen wasn't sure if the champagne had gone to her head or if it was just the warmth of the sun. But when Jean began to speak, Helen realised it was the rush of memories that was making her animated for the first time since her mum's death.

'I was a young girl when Mum made me take dancing lessons. I hated it at first. I was a right little madam, stamping my feet and bawling my eyes out when she left me at the dance class. But do you know what? In time, I began to love it. It was the dresses I loved most, the pretty colours, pink and lemon. Frills on my socks. T-bar dancing shoes. Oh, the clothes were gorgeous.'

Helen was intrigued to hear more about this side of Jean's life that she'd never been aware of.

'I danced for years, until I was a teenager,' Jean said. She patted her ample stomach under her black mourning jacket. 'That's when I started to pile on the weight and became self-conscious about the way I looked. So I stopped dancing. No matter what I did to get the weight off, nothing helped. I had to accept my body shape, accept I wasn't going to change it no matter how much I jived or jitterbugged. I tried diets, but, well, you know me, I enjoy my food too much. That's why I've spent my lifetime working in catering. I love cooking and baking. Anyway, I soon realised I was the wrong shape for being a dancer back then. Nowadays, it's different, and people of all sizes are welcomed into the world of dance.'

'Oh Jean,' Helen murmured.

Jean took another sip of champagne and shrugged. 'It's all water off a duck's back. I accepted long ago that I'm a dumpy little woman. I take after my mum.' Tears filled her eyes again, and she swallowed hard. 'Oh Mother, I'll miss you,' she called out to the sea. 'But here I am, doing exactly as you told me in your will. Sitting on the seafront in Scarborough, raising a toast to you with champagne.'

They sat in silence for a while. At Helen's feet, Suki slowly pulled herself to standing on her long, skinny legs. The dog looked out to sea and Helen gently stroked her head.

Deadly Dancing at the Seaview Hotel

'You're welcome to join me and Suki on our beach walks each morning,' she offered, but Jean shook her head.

'I've got my morning routine and I'll stick to it, thank you. You know I like to make an early start on cooking breakfast at the Seaview. I don't have time for dog walks.'

Suki looked at Jean with imploring eyes. Helen lifted the champagne bottle and refilled the glasses. Jean raised hers again.

'Another toast,' she said. 'This time to my future.'

'To you, Jean,' Helen said, clinking her glass against her friend's.

'What time are the guests due to arrive?' Jean asked, snapping back into business mode. Helen looked askance at her.

'Now, Jean, I've already told you that you're not working today. This morning we buried your mum after her long illness. The last thing you need is—'

'To be stuck at home with too much on my mind,' Jean said firmly.

Helen protectively laid her free arm around Jean's shoulder. 'Are you sure you want to come to work?'

'I'm certain,' Jean replied quickly. 'I can't be on my own. Not today.'

Helen bit her lip. 'You could have stayed at the hotel tonight, but our guests coming in have booked all the rooms on an exclusive-use contract.'

'All ten rooms? But you told me I'll only be cooking for six guests,' Jean said.

Helen counted on her fingers. 'That's right, we've only six guests, but one of them wants a separate room for her office – she called it her HQ – so that's seven. Another wants a room to do his podcasting from, so that's eight.'

'Podcasting? What's that?' Jean said.

'Well, in simple terms, it's a way of broadcasting over the internet on a particular subject. In this case, the subject is ballroom and Latin American dance. Podcasts are dropped live online—'

'They're *what*?' Jean complained.

Helen smirked. 'Sorry, Jean. Podcasts are made available in bite-sized chunks, usually once a week, but you can listen to them any time you like. Anyway, the podcaster is just one of our guests. The rest of them are dancers, and they've asked for the biggest room we've got to house all their costumes – dresses, shoes and so on – so that's nine. I guess they'll be bringing a lot of luggage. However, I don't mind asking them if you can use the room that's left, if you'd like to stay. I'll offer them a discount if they grumble. The main thing is that I don't want you to feel as if I'm sending you home if you'd prefer company. I'm sure the guests would understand, given the circumstances.'

'No, thanks, love. A group booking the whole place sounds too noisy for my liking,' Jean muttered.

Helen turned her head to look at the Vista del Mar, the hotel next door to the Seaview. It was run by Miriam, a difficult woman who thought herself and her hotel a cut above Helen and the Seaview.

'Miriam might have a quiet spare room; you could always stay there if you'd like to be close by.'

Jean almost choked on her champagne. 'Me, stay at the Vista del Mar? You must be kidding, lass. Miriam's too snobby by half. I can't think of anything less pleasant than staying with her. Plus, she's got her "No Vacancies" sign in the window, although I haven't seen anyone going in or coming out for a few days. I wonder what's going on.'

Deadly Dancing at the Seaview Hotel

Helen shrugged. 'Can't say I've noticed much about Miriam or her hotel lately. Anyway, you'd be welcome to stay on my sofa. It's yours, Jean, any time you need company, or a place to stay, or a shoulder to cry on.'

'I've got shoulders of my own,' Jean huffed.

Helen took a sip of champagne. Jean patted her hand.

'Thanks, lass. I appreciate everything you've done. The last few weeks have been rough. But Mum had been ill a long time. She lived in the care home for years. At least she's not suffering now, and I'll take heart from that.'

At Helen's feet, Suki began to move, straining against her lead. Something had caught her attention.

'Steady, girl,' Helen said, stroking the dog's ears.

Tourists were walking along the clifftop, admiring the stunning view of Scarborough Castle and the beach. Close by, a man leaned on the railings, looking out to sea, and Helen couldn't fail to notice that he wore the most remarkable shoes. They were black, well polished and looked expensive, but it was the heels that caught her eye; they were built up at least two inches. The front of the shoes curved up and away, and there were large silver buckles on the sides.

'Cuban heels,' she muttered under her breath. 'Don't see many of those these days.'

'What's that, love?' Jean said.

'Nothing,' Helen replied.

A little boy ran by, chasing pigeons. Cars pulled up at the kerb to unload holidaymakers with buckets and spades, windbreaks and picnics. Helen watched as families meandered down the cliff path to the sea. Then she noticed that Suki's ears were up on alert; the dog was watching the man in the Cuban heels.

'It's just a man,' she told the dog softly. 'Nothing to worry about.'

Warmed by the sunshine, Helen took off her jacket, then topped up their glasses. Jean gave a long sigh.

'Of course, now I'm going to have to think about what to do with all the money.'

Helen placed the bottle on the ground. The champagne bubbles had gone to her head. She didn't normally drink so much when she was working, but today, after the funeral, was an exception to her rule.

'What money?'

Jean's brow furrowed. 'My inheritance, of course. The money Mum bequeathed me in her will. I've been left a small fortune that I don't know what to do with. It was tied up in stocks and shares, payable to me on Mum's death. I knew nothing about it until I was called to see her solicitor. Mum always was a dark horse.'

Was Helen mistaken, or had the man at the railings moved closer to her and Jean? She shook her head to remove the daft notion. The emotion of the funeral and now the heat and champagne were making her see things that weren't there. And what if he *had* moved closer? There was no law against it. Perhaps he was trying to get a different view of the beach.

'I don't know what to spend it on, Helen. Or should I reinvest it? I haven't a clue where to start. I know nothing about finances and money.'

Suki pulled on her lead, causing Helen to turn and look again at the man in the Cuban heels. This time, she was certain he had moved closer and must have been able to hear every word Jean had said. She eyed him cautiously, wondering if she knew him, but she didn't recognise him. She guessed he was in his late sixties. He had

Deadly Dancing at the Seaview Hotel

a kindly face and wispy white hair, and was dressed smartly in chinos, a crisp white shirt and the unusual shoes. But he was now invading their space and she felt uncomfortable.

'It's time you were going indoors, love, to get ready for the guests coming in,' Jean told her.

Helen glanced at her watch. Jean was right, as usual. She lifted the bottle from the ground, untied Suki's lead and stood.

'I had no idea it was so late. Will you join me?'

Jean raised her champagne. 'My glass is still half full,' she said with a smile. 'I'll stay here to finish it, for Mum. It's what she would have wanted.'

'I'll pop the bottle in the fridge in case you want to finish it later,' Helen said.

She walked across the road with Suki. Before she entered the Seaview, she paused and turned to take one last look at her friend. Jean was sitting with her back to her, and Helen could see her cropped blonde hair, her black jacket and her hand holding her champagne glass. But then a chill ran down her back as she realised that the man in the Cuban heels had moved away from the railings and was talking to her.

Chapter 2

Inside the Seaview, Helen let Suki off her lead. She never usually brought the dog in through the front door, but today she felt too hot and bothered after sitting in the sun in her funeral garb to go all the way round to the back. As she walked into the lounge, she couldn't resist peeking outside again to see what Jean was up to. She grew concerned when she saw she was still chatting to the man in the Cuban-heeled shoes.

In the corner of the Seaview's lounge was a small bar, and on the wall behind it was a framed photo of Helen's late husband, Tom. She turned to the picture and spoke to Tom, as she often did when she had something on her mind.

'Who is that man with Jean?' she muttered, but as ever, Tom didn't reply.

Helen watched as Jean stood from the bench. She was smiling and looked happy as she headed across the road to the Seaview. Helen jumped back from the window, not wanting her friend to think she'd been prying. She walked out of the lounge as Jean came around the corner from the hallway, and they almost collided with each other.

'I've been chatting to a nice man out there,' Jean said brightly.

Helen raised her eyebrows. 'Oh?'

Deadly Dancing at the Seaview Hotel

'Yes, what a lovely chap. So interesting. He's involved in the dance competition that's going on at the Spa.'

'Is he a dancer?' Helen asked. The Cuban heels might make sense if he was, although he didn't seem to have a dancer's physique. Weren't dancers supposed to have great posture? She remembered the man's rounded shoulders and the way he was slumped against the railings.

Jean shook her head. 'No, he's something to do with putting the show on; a financial backer, he said.'

'Is he a Scarborough man?'

'Oh yes, he's local. Lives on Paradise Mews. Can't say I've met him before. He's a few years older than me. Been in the army, he said. Divorced twice and he's got a son.'

Helen laughed out loud. 'My word, Jean. You found out a lot about him in such a short time.'

'What can I say? When I like someone, I like to know all about them. You should know that about me by now.'

Helen shot her a look. 'And did you tell him much about you?'

'I told him why I was drinking champagne on a weekday afternoon. He seemed nice and I felt I could trust him. It's been a long time since I had such a connection with a man. We had a good chat.'

Helen looked her hard in the eye. 'What *exactly* did you tell him?'

Jean started. 'That's my business. What's got into you, Helen? Why are you looking at me like that?'

Helen took the empty glass from Jean's hands and put it on the bar. This gave her a second to think about what to stay next.

'Jean, you're in a fragile state. You've just buried your mum and now you've got her will to sort out, and from what you've told me, there's an awful lot of money due to come your way . . .' She glanced nervously out of the lounge window. She was relieved to see the bench empty and no sign of the man. 'I wouldn't want anyone taking advantage of you.'

Jean waved her hand dismissively. 'Pfft! No one takes advantage of me, love, you should know that by now.'

She turned towards the door that led down to Helen's apartment. When she reached it, she paused.

'You've nothing to worry about, Helen. I'm as tough as old boots. Always have been. Now, come downstairs and I'll put the kettle on. We'll have a pot of tea and some biscuits.'

Downstairs in Helen's apartment, the sun flooded into the open-plan kitchen and lounge. The heat was stifling, and Helen opened the patio doors that led out to a small paved area. Suki padded outside to lie in the shade. Jean immediately went to the kettle and Helen tried to stop her.

'Jean, no. Sit down, please, and let me look after you. After the morning you've had, the least I can do is make tea for you.'

But Jean wouldn't hear of it.

'No, love. Let me do this. I need to. If I sit down and do nothing, I'll start thinking about Mum and getting upset. It's my way of coping, do you understand?'

Helen knew Jean well enough to know that no matter what she said, it wouldn't change her mind. She sank into a chair at the dining table, watching her friend as she pottered in the kitchen, reaching for mugs, plates, biscuits and milk. Jean pulled a tray from a drawer and arranged things just so, then suddenly, without warning, she stopped. Her head dropped. Her shoulders slumped. The teaspoon in her hand clattered to the floor. Helen leapt from her seat and threw her arms around her. In silence, she led her to the sofa, where Jean's tears of heartbreak over the loss of her mum finally began to flow.

Half an hour later, Helen and Jean were sitting at the dining table with a pot of tea and a plate of biscuits. Helen had changed out of her black funeral dress and tights and was now dressed in jeans and a T-shirt. Suki was lying under the table, hoping for biscuit crumbs. There was a knock at the door, then the sound of a key in the lock. Helen knew exactly who it was, as there were only two people she trusted with keys to her apartment, Jean and Sally. Sally was the Seaview's cleaner, and one of Helen's closest friends. Married to Gav, she had a six-year-old daughter, Gracie, and was five months pregnant with twins.

Sally breezed into the apartment, her long blonde hair tied in a messy bun. She headed straight for Jean and wrapped her in her arms.

'I'm sorry I missed the funeral, Jean. I had my accountancy exam at college this morning. How did it go? How are you? I had to come and see you as soon as I could.'

Without waiting for Jean to answer, she looked at Helen.

'How is she, Helen? Is she OK?'

Then she looked back at Jean.

'Are you coping all right? Is there anything I can do? People always say that, don't they, after someone dies, but I mean it, Jean. If there's anything I can do, you must tell me.'

Jean pulled away from Sally's embrace.

'There is one thing you can do for me, love, and that's to sit down and shut up. Oh, and stop cuddling me, both of you. If I need a hug, I'll ask.'

Sally and Helen shared a look. Sally bit her lip.

'I was only trying to be nice,' she said softly.

Jean patted her hand. 'I know, love, and I didn't mean to snap. I'll be my old self again soon, you'll see. Mum wouldn't want me to be miserable. Tea?' She lifted the teapot.

Sally pushed an empty cup towards her. 'Please.'

As Jean poured, she looked at Sally. 'How did your exam go?'

Sally crossed her fingers. 'It was tricky, but I think I did well. If I pass and get my accountancy qualification, I could help you with the hotel accounts, Helen.'

Helen was about to speak, but Jean chipped in first. 'You could help *me*,' she said.

Sally perked up. 'With what?'

'I'm coming into some money. Mum left me everything in her will. I haven't a clue what to do with it. I need investment advice.'

Sally's face fell. 'Oh, I don't think I can help with that, Jean. It's not my area of expertise. I could ask Gav; he knows a lot of financial advisers.'

'How is Gav? We haven't seen him or little Gracie in ages,' Helen said.

Sally smiled widely. 'Well, Gracie is a handful, and Gav, as always, is working non-stop. He adores being Gracie's stepdad and he's excited about being dad to the twins.' She gently placed her hand on her growing stomach. 'Mind you, there's no slowing him down. He's opening a new business in town soon.'

'Another one?' Helen cried. 'How many will that make?'

Sally began counting them off on her fingers. 'Well, he's got his taxi firm, Gav's Cabs; his plumbing business, Gav's Baths; his security business, Gav's Cams; the sandwich shop in Filey, Gav's Grub. Plus there's Gav's Garden Services in town and Gav's Go-Karts on the seafront, and he's also a partner with Marie at Tom's Teas vintage tearoom. So the new one will be number eight. He's a creature of habit. Once he's got a business up and running and it's successful, he likes to open a new one.'

Helen was intrigued. 'What's the new business going to be?'

'I can't say. It's a surprise. But it's opening this week and you'll be given a VIP invitation. You too, Jean.'

'Can't you give us a clue?'

Sally mimed zipping her mouth closed and shook her head, then gave a mischievous smile. 'I could tell you . . . but then I'd have to kill you.'

Jean bristled in her seat. 'Let's have no talk of murder, Sally, not even in jest. We've had quite enough of dead bodies connected to the Seaview.'

Sally dropped her gaze to the table, chastised.

'It's all right, Sally, don't worry,' Helen said brightly, trying to lift the mood. 'More tea, anyone?'

She refilled the cups and offered the biscuits again, but Jean shook her head. This worried Helen, because Jean never refused a biscuit.

'You all right, Jean?' she asked, but Jean simply nodded, then looked away.

Over chocolate digestives, Helen turned the conversation to more cheerful matters. They were discussing the new Alan Ayckbourn play showing at the town's prestigious Stephen Joseph Theatre when her phone rang. She glanced at the screen, hoping it'd be a call from Jimmy, the tall, dark, handsome Elvis impersonator who'd become increasingly important in her life. She was surprised to see it was Jimmy's daughter, Jodie.

She swiped the screen. 'Hi, Jodie, it's Helen. Is everything all right? . . . Your dad's done *what*? Really? Of course, yes. I'll have a word with him. I understand, Jodie. Don't worry. I'll take care of it.'

She hung up to find both Sally and Jean staring at her.

'Jodie's having a problem with her dad,' she explained. 'Jimmy's interfering, thinking he knows what's best for her. He sometimes forgets she's a grown woman. Anyway, I said I'll speak to him next time I see him.'

Jean raised an eyebrow. 'And when will that be? If you ask me, you don't see him often enough. If he was *my* boyfriend, I'd keep him on a short leash.'

Helen tutted. 'He's not my boyfriend. We're too old to call each other girlfriend and boyfriend. He's just a friend, that's all.'

'He so is your boyfriend,' Sally teased.

'Well, whatever you want to call him, Jimmy Brown is a good man,' Jean said sagely. 'You should hang on to him, Helen. Don't keep him dangling, he won't wait for ever.'

Helen crunched into another biscuit to stop her from saying something she might regret. She was still taking her relationship with Jimmy slowly. Too slowly for Jean's liking, clearly, but at a comfortable pace for herself. She'd met him when he'd stayed at the Seaview with his troupe of twelve Elvis impersonators, Twelvis. Later, he'd moved to Scarborough after falling in love with the place, and with Helen. He'd bought a comfortable semi-detached house off Falsgrave Road and was now taking evening classes in IT at college as well as finding work around town singing as Elvis.

Deadly Dancing at the Seaview Hotel

Jimmy was the first man Helen had developed feelings for since her beloved husband had died. Some days she wrestled with how things were developing with him. It felt like she was being unfaithful to Tom, or at least to his memory. She was relieved when talk turned to the upcoming dance competition instead.

'I might pop along to watch,' Jean said. 'I quite fancy taking to the floor again, if only I could find someone to dance with. Your Tom used to be a good dancer.'

Helen smiled fondly. 'I wouldn't have said he was great, but he loved to jive. I was never as good as him, but I learned a few steps and we performed our party piece at the Elvis parties we used to run upstairs.' She sighed. 'That's all in the past now.'

'Doesn't Jimmy do the jive? He's a big Elvis fan,' Sally said.

'Do you know, I've never seen him dance,' Helen replied. Then she took a deep breath. 'It's our anniversary this month.'

'Yours and Jimmy's? What are you doing to celebrate?' Jean said.

Helen shook her head. 'No, I mean me and Tom. It's our silver wedding anniversary, or at least it would have been. Tom always dreamed of making a pilgrimage to celebrate our special day.'

'A pilgrimage? Like those people who walk barefoot across northern Spain? I didn't know Tom was religious,' Sally said.

'He wasn't. There was only one idol he worshipped, and that was Elvis. We'd planned to make a pilgrimage to Elvis's home, Graceland, but Tom died before we got to live out our dream. I don't want to go on my own and it wouldn't be right going with anyone but him.'

'I heard it's cursed,' Sally whispered.

'What? Graceland?' Jean said.

Sally leaned forward confidentially. 'No, the dance competition. I read about it online. It used to be held in Blackpool, but after what happened last year, different organisers were brought in. The new people hope a change of location will get rid of the curse. That's why it's being held in Scarborough.'

Helen opened her eyes wide. 'A curse? Tell us everything you know.'

Chapter 3

Jean pushed the plate of biscuits towards Sally. 'Come on, love. We want all the details.'

'Well, when the dance competition was held in Blackpool last year, one of the judges was almost killed. A glitter ball fell and smashed at his feet. They say if it'd fallen on his head, he wouldn't have survived.'

'Sounds like a health and safety matter rather than a curse,' Helen said.

Sally took a biscuit and snapped it in half. 'Wait, there's more.'

She popped half the biscuit into her mouth and slowly chewed, then pulled a face.

'Since I got pregnant with the twins, food doesn't taste as nice as it used to,' she complained.

Jean patted her hand. 'You've not long to go. Only four months.' She leaned in close. 'Tell us the rest. We haven't got all day. There are guests due in soon and there's still the bar to stock upstairs.'

Sally put the uneaten half-biscuit back on her plate.

'Well, the online article I read said there'd been a feud between one of the dancers and a judge. Now, the article could have been a load of nonsense, of course, but there are plenty more posts saying the same on social media, though some people have brushed it off as a conspiracy theory.'

Jean sat back in her seat and crossed her arms. 'And what do they say, these conspiracy theorists?' she huffed.

'That the dancer tried to bribe the judge to ensure they and their partner won the competition. When the judge wouldn't budge . . .' Sally smiled. 'Hey, I'm a poet. Anyway, when the judge refused to have anything to do with bending the rules, the dancer took revenge by loosening the glitter ball, intending for it to fall on the judges' table, right at the end where this particular judge always sits.'

Helen shook her head. 'Sounds a bit far-fetched to me. The glitter ball mustn't have been fitted properly; there was probably a fault. The judge was lucky he wasn't underneath it when it fell.'

Sally's eyes widened. 'He was lucky, yes. But the dancer standing next to him wasn't. When the glitter ball fell and smashed on the floor, she was knocked backwards in shock. She hit a table behind her, broke her ankle and had to be rushed to hospital. She hasn't danced since. She blames the curse for putting an end to her dancing career.'

Helen's hand flew to her heart. 'That's dreadful; the poor woman. I didn't know about this. I've been so busy, I haven't had time to read the local paper or check social media lately. I don't like the idea of a curse coming to Scarborough. What if our dancers bring it with them and it ends up here at the Seaview?'

Jean tutted. 'That's enough talk about curses and people getting hurt. Today's been difficult enough.'

Helen gently laid her hand on her friend's arm, but Jean shrugged her away, then clapped her hands twice.

'Come on, girls, it's time to get our backsides into action. Sally, take the mixers and crisps upstairs to the bar. Helen, you need to make a list of shopping to pick up at the cash and carry. Meanwhile,

Deadly Dancing at the Seaview Hotel

I'll prepare sandwiches for the arrival of our guests. They should be here soon.'

'You don't have to do this, Jean,' Helen said gently. 'You don't even have to stay. If you want to go home, I'd understand.'

But Jean was firm. 'I've already told you, I'd rather be here with you and Sally. It gives me something to do and makes me feel useful. If I go home, I'll end up thinking about Mum and the funeral. It won't do me any good. I want to stay and that's that. I won't hear another word about me shirking my duties.'

At this, Suki stood, walked across the room and laid her head on Jean's knee.

'Not now, Suki. There's work to be done. Helen, pass me my apron.'

Helen pulled a clean apron from the drawer. She held it with both hands, unwilling to pass it to Jean.

'Are you sure you feel up to this?'

Jean took the apron from her. She unfolded it and placed it over her ample bosom, which was straining under her black blouse, pulled it across her wide hips, clad in a black skirt, then tied the strings behind her back.

'I'm certain.'

As she bustled away, busying herself with plates, bread, smoked salmon, cheese and salad, Helen watched her with a frown. In all the years she'd known her, nothing had ever fazed her. However, after such an emotional morning, at her mother's funeral, Jean was acting as if everything was normal, and Helen was worried. Reluctantly she left her to her work.

'I'll help you carry the bottles up to the bar. I don't like you lifting heavy things in your condition,' she told Sally.

'I'm fine, Helen, really, don't fuss,' Sally replied.

As Helen prepared to head upstairs, she paused at the door, wondering how best to help her friend. As if reading her thoughts, Jean turned around. In her hand she held a butter knife, which she pointed at Helen with a wan smile.

'Go on, get yourself to work, lass. I'm fine. And please stop asking how I am. I'm the same Jean I've always been. I'll cope, you'll see. Stand there any longer gawping and I'll butter you as well as this bread!' She gave a cheeky wink.

Helen climbed the stairs carrying a bottle of spirits in each hand. When she reached the lounge, Sally was laying beer mats on the small round tables. She looked up when Helen walked in.

'I'm worried about Jean,' Helen said.

'Me too. She's normally so tough. But we both know she won't thank us if we start mollycoddling her. She'll accuse us of treating her like a child.'

Sally's words prompted Helen to recall Jodie's phone call.

'Speaking of which . . .' she said, pulling her phone from her jeans pocket.

She pressed Jimmy's name on her screen, and he answered immediately.

'Jimmy? Fancy meeting up for a drink tonight?' she asked. 'Oh, nothing special. How about the Scarborough Arms, seven o'clock? . . . OK, see you then . . . What? . . . Oh, um, yeah . . .'

She glanced at Sally and was unhappy to see her moving tables around to make the most of the view of the North Bay beach from the window. She'd told her umpteen times not to do any heavy work during her pregnancy, but Sally could be as stubborn as Jean.

'Love you too,' she whispered, then hung up and pocketed her phone. Behind the bar, Tom looked at her from his picture, frozen in time with a smile on his lips and a twinkle in his eyes. Oh, what she'd give to see that smile again. She pushed her shoulders back. Life had moved on, and she had to move with it.

'Sorry, Tom,' she mouthed to the photo.

'Helen, they're here!' Sally called excitedly.

Helen spun around to see three bright orange taxis, all sporting the Gav's Cabs logo. Sally stepped close to the window, peering at their guests as they clambered from the vehicles. Helen gently pulled her back.

'Don't make it look like we're watching them, love. I want to give them a friendly first impression, not make them think we're spying on them.'

'Sorry, Helen. Shall I go downstairs to let Jean know they're here?'

'That'd be great. They've asked for afternoon tea on arrival. Let Jean know she can send the sandwiches up as soon as they're ready.'

Sally disappeared downstairs and Helen walked out of the lounge, preparing to meet her guests. In the hallway, she paused in front of the mirror. She pushed her bobbed hair behind her ears, straightened her shoulders and set her face to greeting mode with a relaxed, professional smile.

'You're not looking too bad for fifty, Mrs Dexter,' she told her reflection.

She was preparing to open the door to greet her guests when through the wall from next door at the Vista del Mar came an ear-splitting, blood-curdling scream.

Chapter 4

Panicked, Helen yanked the door open, ready to run down the path and into the Vista del Mar. While she didn't much like her snobby neighbour, she hated to think of her in danger. As she hared out of the Seaview, in full view of her guests, who were unloading their cases from Gav's Cabs, the door to the Vista del Mar flew open and Miriam came running out. She looked red in the face and flustered, but, Helen was relieved to see, unharmed.

'Miriam? Are you all right?' Helen called.

Miriam turned to her and smiled through gritted teeth. 'Everything's perfectly all right, Helen dear. Why shouldn't it be?'

'Because I heard you scream!'

She held up a hand and gave a nervous laugh. 'It was nothing. I've, er . . . joined the . . . um . . . operatic society. Yes, that's it. I was practising my scales.'

Helen was puzzled. It certainly hadn't sounded tuneful.

'I'll keep the noise down from now on,' Miriam said quickly.

Helen looked at her, trying to work out what was happening. With Miriam, you never knew. Her neighbour was a handsome woman of indeterminate age — perhaps sixty-five, although Helen had never been sure. She wore her years well, with her long greying hair tied in a loose plait that fell down her back, and her oversized smoked glasses gave her the look of a gracefully ageing Yorkshire

Deadly Dancing at the Seaview Hotel

Brigitte Bardot. She always dressed smartly. Today she wore a flattering navy two-piece trouser suit and a white blouse with flouncy sleeves. She was breathing heavily as she retreated towards her front door.

Helen leaned across the stone wall that separated their hotels. 'Are you sure you're all right? That was some noise I heard coming through the wall just now.'

Miriam flicked away her concern as if getting rid of an annoying fly. 'I'd have thought you'd have better things to do with your time than listen to other people's business,' she said sharply.

She glanced towards the gate at the end of the path, where the new arrivals were chattering excitedly, carrying brightly coloured suitcases, suit carriers and large boxes.

'I see you have guests arriving, dear. I expect you'll need to show them to their rather standard rooms inside your humble abode.'

And with that, she flounced back inside the Vista del Mar, slamming the door shut behind her.

'How rude,' Helen said, glaring at the closed door. Then she turned and braced herself to meet her guests, beaming and issuing a cheery hello.

Often when people arrived at the hotel, they were tired after travelling, but these guests were buzzing with an infectious energy that Helen picked up straight away. There were three men and three women, all dressed in jeans, hoodies and sneakers. But despite their casual attire, they were the most attractive, well-groomed guests the Seaview had ever received . . . all except one.

'Welcome, everyone. Please come in,' she said. 'I'm Helen Dexter, owner of the Seaview. It's a pleasure to meet you.'

She stood by the front door, greeting the six guests as they walked inside. Heavy cases were humped up the steps and over the threshold. Helen helped with each one. A shiny suit cover was thrust into her hands.

'Be a darling and take this.'

The command came from a short woman with vivid curly orange hair. Helen obliged and laid the suit carrier over a case. The hallway was already crowded with a small mountain of boxes, garment carriers and holdalls, and there was a sharp tang of perfume in the air.

'Please, everyone, go into the lounge. I'll check you all in, then Jean, my . . .' It was on the tip of her tongue to say the word *cook*. For decades, that had been Jean's title, one she'd worn with pride. But as the Seaview had recently been awarded four-star status, Helen decided to go up a notch. '. . . my *chef* will serve the afternoon tea you've requested.'

She went to a small table in the hallway where she kept details of her incoming guests, then she took the keys for their rooms from the key box and walked into the lounge. The guests had already settled themselves, some looking out of the window at the stunning view, others checking their phones or reading tourist leaflets they'd picked up in the hall. At a table in the middle of the room, a man with bad posture, wearing a shapeless black anorak and scuffed shoes, sat tapping furiously into his phone.

She tried to work out who was who. She had a married couple on her list, Mr and Mrs Curzon. She looked at the short woman with the orange hair. It was too orange to be natural and was curled and lacquered to within an inch of its life. The woman was sitting at a table with a man with a round, pleasant face who looked familiar to Helen.

Deadly Dancing at the Seaview Hotel

'Have any of you stayed at the Seaview before?' she asked, wondering if he'd been a previous guest. But they all replied that this was their first time at the Seaview, and their first time in Scarborough.

She returned her attention to her list. She suspected that this familiar-looking man and the orange-haired lady were the married couple, but there was only one way to find out.

'Mrs Curzon?' she asked.

'That's me, darling. I'm Carla,' a voice called from the bay window. Helen looked up, surprised that her experienced landlady antennae had proved wrong. She hoped she wasn't losing her touch. The woman sitting by the window was, she guessed, in her mid thirties. She was slim and petite, with dyed red hair cropped in a severe bob, which swung under her chin when she moved.

'And Mr Curzon?' she asked, glancing around, wondering who Carla's other half was.

'Please, call me Monty,' replied a handsome, charming man from the opposite side of the room.

Helen's heart skipped a beat when she took in Mr Curzon's movie-star looks. Jet-black hair was swept back from his smooth face, and he looked as if he'd stepped out of a 1940s film, where he would have played the lead role of a dashing aviator, perhaps called Rex. He'd have a dog called Laddo, who'd wait bravely while his master was away fighting in the war. He'd win medals and return home a hero, where his mother would have a freshly baked apple pie waiting for him. With double cream.

She pulled herself back to reality as the man stood and walked across to shake her hand. He brought with him a musky aftershave scent.

'Nice to meet you,' Helen said.

'Delightful, isn't it?' he replied.

He returned to his seat without glancing at his wife, who was looking out of the window, where surfers were riding the waves.

'My husband and I requested separate rooms, Helen. I hope that request will be accommodated,' Carla said, without turning around.

Helen glanced at her sheet. 'Yes, of course, Mrs Curzon. It's all in hand.'

'Call me Carla, darling,' Carla replied, still gazing out of the window.

Helen returned her attention to the older woman with the orange hair. She couldn't take her eyes off it. She marvelled at the confidence it must take to wear such a vivid colour, and felt like giving the woman a round of applause.

'Are you Mrs Cassidy?' she asked.

The woman nodded, and the orange curls moved forward and back, then stood rigid again.

'I'm Bev – or Ballroom Bev, as I used to be called back in the days when I danced. Now I work as an agent, getting dancers work and making sure they're paid. I trust you've booked me a spare room to use as my HQ? I need an office to work in because I've got people to call and emails to send. I need a desk, a chair and good natural light. I hope the phone signal's strong, because there's an important call I'm waiting for.'

She turned to the man sitting at her side.

'And this is my brother, Tommy.'

Tommy grinned sheepishly at Helen. There was an innocence about him, she thought. He was younger than his sister, who Helen guessed was in her fifties, but the similarity was definitely there in their looks. They shared the same thin facial features and almond-shaped eyes. However, where Bev's hair was orange and rock solid with lacquer, Tommy's was more sensible, brown and cut short. When he smiled, his face lit up, and Helen was struck by how white his teeth were. He caught her looking at his mouth and beamed more brightly.

'It's nice to meet you,' she said.

There was a sharp burst of laughter from a seat by the door. The woman sitting there was slim and petite, like Carla, and Helen began to feel like a carthorse, overweight and lumpen in the company of these lithe dancers. She pulled her T-shirt down over her hips.

'Nice?' the woman said, adding another sarcastic laugh. 'Oh, it's always nice to meet Tommy, all right. Everything about Tommy is *nice*.'

'Rosa, shut it!' Bev snapped.

Helen watched the exchange with interest. Rosa looked to be in her twenties, the youngest of the group. Her long auburn hair fell in waves to her shoulders, like a commercial for expensive shampoo. She was very pretty, with beautifully smooth, clear skin, making her look as if she'd been airbrushed. Everything about her was immaculate. Her eyebrows and lips were plucked and painted with expertise.

'Helen, I don't want Tommy and Rosa to have rooms on the same floor,' Bev said sharply.

'Noted,' Helen said with a forced smile. She scribbled the requested change on her sheet of paper, then looked around the room. Carla was still gazing out of the window. Monty was lifting his phone at angles to his face, taking selfies. Helen watched as he smiled at the camera while ignoring everyone else. As instructed, Rosa had remained quiet, her long, slim legs crossed at the ankle. There was only one person left to meet. The man in the black anorak. The only one in the room who was slouched. The only one in the room who wasn't groomed to perfection. As she only had one name left on her list, the dots were easy to join.

'You must be Paul Knight,' she said kindly.

He was still tapping into his phone, fully absorbed.

'Paul, don't be rude. Speak to the landlady,' Bev ordered.

He put his phone down, turned to Helen and smiled. He was in his thirties, she guessed. His face was sweaty, his body odour sour and he looked like he needed a shave.

'Paul's our podcaster,' Bev chipped in before he could say a word. 'He needs a spare room for his editing equipment, laptop, tablet, iPod, microphone, that sort of thing.'

'All the rooms are ready,' Helen replied. 'But I'm intrigued. Why does a dance group need a podcaster?'

The room fell silent. Not even Bev put herself forward to speak. Helen waited for someone, anyone, to respond, and when no one did, she got to her feet and began handing out keys, feeling embarrassed and irritated with her guests for blanking her.

'Afternoon tea will be served soon,' she explained to the silent room.

'Thank you, darling,' Carla said as she took her key.

'Much obliged,' Monty said, giving Helen a cheeky wink.

'I'll look after Tommy's key and both of mine,' Bev said, and Helen handed over three keys. 'And you've put us in rooms next to each other, I hope.'

'Yes, as requested,' Helen replied with a forced smile. 'I did note your request for interconnecting rooms, but that's something we don't have at the Seaview.'

She handed Paul his two keys.

'I'll let you choose which room you'd prefer to stay in and which one you'd like to use for your, er, podcasting.'

Paul looked at her, giving nothing away. 'Cheers.'

Finally Helen gave a key to Rosa, who snatched it from her hand. Then she stood and leaned towards Helen, whispering in her ear.

'I'd be careful what you say to Paul. Don't tell him anything unless you want the world to know. He'll broadcast anything juicy if he thinks it'll pull in listeners to his precious podcast. Paul knows all our deep, dark dancing secrets. The podcast's called *Dancing Knight & Daye*; you should listen to it online.'

She turned and walked out of the room. Immediately Paul stood to follow, but Bev caught his arm.

'Paul, leave her!' she said, but he shrugged her hand away.

Helen watched as he left the room. She saw him catch up with Rosa at the bottom of the stairs and start to whisper to her, so she stepped forward a little, pretending that she was making sure they knew where they were going. But when she heard the words *Blackpool*, *judge* and *glitter ball*, a chill went down her spine.

Chapter 5

Helen was curious but didn't have time to think about Paul and Rosa's whispered exchange. Her other guests were beginning to move, gathering handbags and holdalls from the hall. She stepped towards the suitcases and suit carriers.

'Please, let me help you with your cases.'

'I'll manage fine,' Tommy said, beaming a bright white smile.

'Bev, could I help you?' Helen offered.

Bev nodded, and her orange curls moved forward, then back.

'That'd be great,' she replied.

As Helen lugged cases to the bottom of the stairs, ready to carry them up, Carla and Monty pulled their bags from the pile.

'Darling, would you be so good as to take this upstairs?' Carla purred, indicating her case to Monty, who took it from her slim, manicured fingers. Meanwhile, Paul the podcaster was picking up a large suitcase.

'I can help you with that,' Helen said, but Paul shook his head and said he'd prefer to carry it himself as it contained an expensive laptop that he used for podcasting. There was now only one case left, with a suit carrier draped across it. Helen guessed it must belong to Rosa, who'd swanned upstairs empty-handed.

When Helen reached the first floor, she indicated rooms 1 and

Deadly Dancing at the Seaview Hotel

2 for Tommy and Bev. 'Room 3 could be your office. It depends on which room you'd prefer,' she told Bev.

'Which room has the sea view?' Bev asked.

'Rooms 1 and 2 are at the front and look straight onto the North Bay. Room 3 is at the back, with a view over the town. You can still see the sea from the back, but it's the South Bay beach.'

Bev pushed open the door to Room 2. 'Tommy, you're in Room 1,' she barked, and he disappeared inside.

'Does he always do what you tell him?' Helen asked lightly. She was stunned when Bev turned to her with a face full of thunder.

'Always,' she said darkly.

Inside Room 2, Bev marched straight to the window and stood with her hands on her hips, looking out.

'It's a beautiful view,' Helen said enthusiastically.

But Bev whipped the curtains shut. 'I don't want anyone to know I'm here,' she muttered.

'No one can see into the room. You're on the first floor,' Helen tried to reassure her.

'It's best to be on the safe side,' Bev said. 'Has anyone been in touch with you to ask if I'm booked to stay here?'

Helen's curiosity was piqued now. 'Is there any reason why they would?'

Bev shook her head, and Helen marvelled again at how the orange curls stayed put. Then she turned back to the window, putting an end to their exchange.

'Come down for tea any time you're ready,' Helen told her, exiting the room backwards, wondering what was going on. Her guests had arrived at the Seaview only ten minutes ago, and already she could feel tension brewing. Oh, why weren't there some straightforward families and tourists booked with her this week instead of this highly glamorous yet unusual troupe of dancers?

From the landing upstairs, she could hear Carla's voice.

'Monty, be a darling and drag this case onto my bed, would you?'

And then Paul came puffing and panting his way up the stairs, carrying his heavy black suitcase. Helen stood to one side to let him pass.

'Are you sure I can't help bring anything up to your room?' she offered.

'Thank you, but no,' Paul said. 'This case contains precious equipment and I'm the only one insured to handle my laptop. I wouldn't want you incriminated if anything went wrong.'

He took a moment to gather his breath on the landing and set the case at his feet. Helen looked at him.

'Are you expecting things to go wrong?'

Paul stared at her. 'When I'm on tour with these dancers, I can never be sure.'

She waited for him to say more, but he picked up the case and continued on his way, leaving a stench of stale sweat on the landing.

'Come down for tea any time you're ready,' Helen called after him.

She walked downstairs, happy to see Jean and Sally laying out plates of sandwiches in the dining room.

'Are the guests settled in?' Jean asked as she moved flasks of hot water.

Helen sank into a chair. 'Well, they're in, that's about as much as I can say. They seem a bit . . .' she struggled to find the right word, 'tense. Maybe they'll relax when they come down for tea. You'll meet them all then.'

'You can have the pleasure of meeting me now,' a man's voice boomed from the doorway, and Helen started when she saw Monty standing there, tall, strong and handsome. He walked straight to Jean, took her hand and kissed it.

'Monty Curzon, how wonderful it is,' he said. Jean's mouth opened, but nothing came out, which surprised Helen, as her friend was never lost for words. Then he walked to Sally.

'I'm Monty, how lovely,' he said, kissing Sally's hand too. Sally's face went bright pink. Both women were struck dumb, staring at Monty as he filled a plate with food.

'Come on, girls, back to work,' Helen chided, although she fully understood why Sally and Jean were taken in by Monty's movie-star looks. He really was an astonishingly handsome man.

Jean pushed her glasses up to the bridge of her nose. Sally smoothed her hair away from her face. But neither of them moved.

'Pull yourself together,' Helen whispered into Jean's ear.

Jean began to bustle around the table, arranging plates and cups. Helen gave Sally a nudge, and she too returned to work, placing tea bags and coffee in front of the flasks. The doorbell rang and Helen went to answer it. Her heart lifted at the sight of her best friend, Marie. Behind her, parked on the street outside, was Marie's open-topped red sports car.

'Hey, I wasn't expecting to see you today. What's up? Come in,' Helen said.

Marie stepped into the Seaview in her stiletto-heeled black leather boots, bringing with her a cloud of subtle dusky perfume.

'You look gorgeous,' Helen said as she kissed her friend on her powdered cheek. Marie was, as always, dressed up to the nines, making Helen feel even more dowdy in her jeans, T-shirt and ankle boots.

Marie reached her hand to Helen's hair and wrapped a strand of it around her finger. 'I wish you'd let me do something with this. You're not making the most of yourself.'

'I haven't got time to make the most of anything other than the Seaview,' Helen said, trying not to get snappy.

Marie strode confidently along the hallway. 'Just thought I'd call in to see you and—'

She stopped dead as Monty appeared at the bottom of the stairs.

'Oh my giddy aunt,' she whispered. 'You didn't tell me Adonis was here.'

He caught her staring and stretched his hand towards her. 'Monty Curzon, what a pleasure it is.'

Helen might have been mistaken, but it looked like Marie dropped a curtsey.

'Marie Davenport,' she replied coolly, holding on to Monty's hand for longer than was necessary. 'I used to be Marie Clark, when I was married. But now I'm divorced and I'm free and single. *Very* single, for someone like you.'

Helen positioned herself between the two of them. 'And Mr Curzon is happily married. His wife is upstairs.' She ushered Marie into the dining room. 'Stop flirting with my guests, it's unprofessional.'

'He started it.' Marie pouted, turning to look at Monty again, but he'd already gone into the lounge.

Deadly Dancing at the Seaview Hotel

'Look, Marie, we're about to serve tea. Was there something you wanted?'

There was a misty look in Marie's eyes. 'What? Oh. Yes,' she said, snapping back into the here and now. She delved into her designer handbag and pulled out a Jiffy bag. Helen tried to peer at it, but Marie handed it to Sally.

'Fresh from the printer. Gav asked me to deliver them straight to you. I bumped into him when I was picking up the new menus for Tom's Teas. You're looking well, Sally. Pregnancy suits you; you're blooming.'

Sally acknowledged the compliment, then ripped open the Jiffy bag and pulled out a bundle of coloured flyers. She handed one to Helen.

'Gav's Tans?'

Sally beamed with pride. 'It's Gav's new business. He's opening a tanning salon next to Boyes on Queen Street. Oh, I've been dying to tell you for ages, Helen, but Gav wanted the news kept secret. Now that he's had flyers printed, it's all systems go and I can spread the word.'

'I must dash,' Marie said. 'I've got a spa treatment booked at the Crown Hotel.'

Jean bustled out of the dining room into the lounge. 'Mr Curzon, would you like a drink?' she said.

Helen gave Marie a wry smile and leaned close to her. 'I think Adonis has caught Jean's eye. She never offers to work in the bar if she can help it.'

Marie inched towards the door to the lounge, where Jean was standing beside Monty at his table in the window.

'It was lovely to meet you, Monty,' she said with a warm smile.

'It always is,' he replied.

Helen followed Marie to the front door, and they embraced quickly before Marie left. Helen waited by the door, watching her friend as she stepped elegantly into her sports car and set off with a cheery wave, her long hair flying behind her in the wind. She was about to close the door and return to help Jean when a young man outside the Seaview caught her eye. He was tall and skinny, with swept-back fair hair, and he wore a smart grey suit. He was looking at the hotel, staring directly at it and filming with his phone.

'Hey, you!' Helen called. 'What do you think you're doing?'

The man stopped filming and began talking into his phone. Helen heard every word.

'She's here. I've found her,' he said, then he quickly walked away.

Chapter 6

Helen ran down the path. 'Oi! You!' she yelled, but the man jumped into a black 4x4 with tinted windows, revved the engine and sped off.

She clocked the number plate, desperately trying to keep it in her head, repeating the numbers and letters as she stomped back to the Seaview. As soon as she returned indoors, she'd write it down and . . . then what? What on earth would she do? Call the police and tell them someone had been filming her hotel? If so, would they take her seriously? She knew how stretched the local police were and she wouldn't want to waste their time with a paranoid phone call. For heaven's sake, people walked past her hotel all the time, every day, at all hours. She doubted there was little the police could do, but still, the numbers and letters went through her mind like a mantra.

As she pushed the front door open, she bumped straight into one of her guests. The number plate flew out of her mind as she came face to face with Ballroom Bev's fresh-faced brother, Tommy.

She recovered from the shock of knocking into him, and they both apologised to each other. Tommy hadn't said much since he'd arrived, letting his sister speak for him, and Helen was glad she now had the chance to say a personal hello. However, she wished it had been under different circumstances. Bumping into her guests in the hallway was not usually how she made their acquaintance. She stepped back, not wanting to invade Tommy's space. Her heart was already beating fast after the incident with the man in the black car outside. She took a moment to gather herself.

'Hello, Tommy, have you settled in?'

Tommy beamed a smile. His whole face lit up with those gleaming white teeth.

'Bev says her room is great, thank you, Helen.'

'And do you like yours?' she asked, noting he hadn't answered on behalf of himself. She wondered if this was just how he and his sister had always been, a habit too hard to break.

'It's got a great view of the beach,' he replied. 'Bev's happy, that's the main thing. She's setting up her office in the room across the landing. She'll be glad once she can start work.'

Helen eyed him keenly. 'Sorry, were you leaving when I bumped into you just now? I wouldn't want to keep you.'

But Tommy shook his head. 'I wasn't going anywhere. I was practising new dance steps along your hallway. There wasn't enough space upstairs in my room.'

'Oh, how wonderful,' Helen said. 'I've never had dancers staying here before, never mind practising in my hall. I feel honoured. You can use this space any time you like, but keep a watchful eye on the door so you don't bump into anyone else.'

Tommy bowed gracefully, performing just for her. 'You're too kind,' he said as he straightened. He peered around the door of the dining room.

'Oh good. Bev hasn't come downstairs yet for something to eat. We're still fine to talk for a few more minutes.'

'Does she keep you on a short leash?' Helen asked. She'd meant

Deadly Dancing at the Seaview Hotel

it as a joke, a tease, but the way Tommy's face fell suggested she'd overstepped the mark.

'She's my agent as well as my sister. She has my best interests at heart.' Another mega-watt smile beamed from his pleasant face.

Helen surveyed his features. There was definitely something about him that looked familiar, but she couldn't put her finger on exactly what it was.

'Bev's looked after me since our parents died when we were kids. Of course, she had her own dancing career until . . . well, she doesn't like to talk about it, so I'd rather not say. She might tell you herself if she thinks she can trust you. Now she works flat out securing dancing work for me all over the world. Or at least, she tries her best. Not everything works out as planned.' A sad look clouded his face for a split second, then he smiled again and it was gone.

Helen nodded to the dining room. 'Please, help yourself to food,' she said.

'Would you care to join me?' he asked. 'I'd like to sit with you to talk, if that's all right. Until Bev comes downstairs, of course.'

'Of course,' Helen said.

She followed Tommy into the dining room, where Jean and Sally were serving sandwiches and making tea. When she peered into the lounge, she saw Carla and Monty with dainty amounts of food on their plates. Paul the podcaster had piled his high with egg and cress sandwiches and two slices of Jean's coffee and walnut cake. Rosa was sitting in the seat by the door again, distancing herself from the others, nibbling a smoked salmon and cucumber sandwich.

Tommy was helping himself to a slice of cake, and Helen kept glancing at him curiously. When she'd spoken to him, his voice had brought back a hazy memory from her childhood. Just then, Jean looked up from the sandwiches and stopped dead.

'I don't believe it!' she cried, staring straight at Tommy. 'It's you, isn't it? It's little Tommy Two Shoes! I'd recognise that smile anywhere!'

Helen looked from Jean to Tommy, trying to make sense of the name, the voice, the beaming smile on Tommy's face.

'You've got me! Yes, it's me!' he laughed.

Her brain went into overdrive as the memories flooded back. Saturday mornings on the sofa, watching children's TV. And then everything slotted into place.

'Tommy Two Shoes!' she gasped. 'My word, that takes me back.'

Tommy rolled his eyes. 'Just think what it does to me!'

'I used to watch you all the time, every week. You had your own TV show as a child, *Tommy's Tunes*! All the dancers would come on, all the children. It was wonderful.'

Jean nodded in agreement. 'My word, lad. You've grown up to be a right bobby dazzler. So, have you been dancing all your life?'

'Every day,' Tommy replied in a sing-song voice.

'It's an honour to have you staying here,' Helen said. She was trying not to gush, but they'd never had a celebrity at the Seaview before.

'But I'm not Tommy Two Shoes any more,' Tommy said politely. 'That was the name I was given when I danced on TV as a boy. Now that I'm an adult professional dancer, I go by the name of Tommy Ten Dance.'

Deadly Dancing at the Seaview Hotel

'Ten Dance?' Helen asked, puzzled.

Jean tutted and shook her head. 'Surely you know about the ten dances, Helen?'

Helen shook her head. The only thing she knew about ballroom dancing was what she'd learned from watching *Strictly Come Dancing*.

Jean began counting on her fingers. 'I learned them when I used to dance as a girl. There are five ballroom dances: waltz, foxtrot, quickstep, tango and Viennese waltz.'

'And five Latin American dances,' Tommy chipped in. 'Rumba, samba, paso doble, cha-cha-cha and jive. And I dance them all, whatever the occasion, wherever the place, as long as I'm paid. In our business, a ten dancer is known as a jack of all trades but, sadly, a master of none. And that about sums me up. That's why I need Bev, you see. She gets me exhibition dance work on cruise ships, in holiday parks, anywhere they need someone reliable, someone with a bit of sparkle. Would you like to see my sparkle?' He shook his hips from side to side.

'Ooh!' Jean cooed.

'This is my chef, Jean,' Helen said.

Tommy offered Jean his hand.

'I don't know whether to shake it or kiss it,' Jean teased. 'You were a lovely lad to watch on TV. I felt ever so proud of you when you hosted *Tommy's Tunes*. Didn't you have a sister who danced too? Oh now, what was her name . . .'

'Bev,' a voice barked from the doorway.

Helen spun around to see orange-haired Bev striding into the dining room.

'My name *was* Ballroom Bev,' she said confidently, heading

towards the table. 'But now it's just Bev. I don't dance. I won't waltz. I've forgone the foxtrot and terminated my tango.'

Helen watched, incredulous, as Bev continued.

'I had an accident that ruined my rumba and knocked my samba out of sync. And don't even get me started on what it did to my cha-cha-cha.'

She sidled up to Tommy and slid her arm around his waist.

'Now I work for my brother, putting him first, getting him work by whatever means possible. That's why he's here in Scarborough for the dance competition. It's time to put Tommy Two Shoes back on the map.'

Tommy's smile faltered. 'Oh Bev,' he whispered.

'Shush, little brother. Everything will work out just fine. You won't be a jack of all trades for much longer. I intend to see to it myself that you get the recognition you deserve. I'll put you back in the spotlight with a new show on TV if it's the last thing I do.'

She turned to Helen.

'We're waiting for a call from a TV production company to confirm they've signed the contract for Tommy's new show.'

Tommy looked hopefully at his sister. 'They still haven't called?'

Bev shook her head, and her orange curls remained firm. Tommy moved away from her and continued helping himself to food.

'Not too much cake, Tommy, you know you've got a sweet tooth. All that sugar goes straight to your stomach,' Bev warned.

Tommy walked off to the lounge with his plate. Helen and Jean watched him go.

'He moves so gracefully,' Jean sighed. 'I hope he'll get the TV show.'

Deadly Dancing at the Seaview Hotel

Bev's eyes narrowed. 'Oh, so do I, more than anyone knows. However, there's a fly in the ointment. Another dancer has been earmarked for the same show, and the final decision on who gets it has yet to be made. It could be Tommy, or it could be her.'

Her face darkened, and she clenched her fists. Helen followed her gaze, out of the dining room, across the hall to the lounge, to where Rosa sat by the door.

Chapter 7

Bev walked off to join Tommy in the lounge, where they sat with their heads together in hushed conversation. Only Helen, Jean and Sally were left in the dining room. Sally was on her phone, scrolling through social media.

'Everything's up and running and it's all systems go for Gav's Tans!' she cried.

'That's great,' Helen said. She was a little distracted, as Jean had flopped onto a seat and was now sitting with her head in her hands. She sat next to her, and Jean sighed loudly.

'I'm starting to feel done in, love. I think it's the champagne, making me feel sleepy.'

Helen gently patted her hand. 'I'm surprised you've lasted this long; you've had one hell of a day. Take tomorrow off, Jean, have as long as you need. And you can take the rest of the champagne with you. There's still some left in the bottle.'

Jean sat up straight. 'No need to give me the day off. I'll be back tomorrow as usual, bright and early, to make breakfast.'

She stood and began to collect plates and cups from the table. Helen stood too and took hold of her hands.

'No, Jean. Sally and I will clear this away. There's no need for you to do it.'

Reluctantly Jean moved away.

Deadly Dancing at the Seaview Hotel

'Are you sure you don't want to stay downstairs tonight with me? You could have my bed; I'll take the sofa,' Helen offered.

But Jean shook her head. 'I'm going to have a tot of rum when I get home, raise a glass to Mum and have an early night. I'll see you tomorrow.'

She kissed Helen on the cheek, then walked to the door that led down to Helen's apartment. Helen turned to Sally, astonished.

'Blimey. In all the years I've known Jean, she's never kissed me before.'

'Make the most of it. I won't be doing it again!' Jean called.

That evening, Helen walked the short distance to the Scarborough Arms, her favourite pub. It was a large, historic place on North Terrace that catered for residents and tourists alike, serving great food and real ale. When she walked into the bar, Jimmy was there with a pint of locally brewed Wold Top ale in front of him and a glass of red wine for her. She kissed him full on the lips, then sank into the seat next to him and raised her glass.

'Cheers,' she said, taking a long sip.

Jimmy was tall, handsome and slim. He was fifty years old, with dark hair turning grey around his ears. He often dyed the grey to black for his job as an Elvis impersonator, which took him all over the country and beyond, to wherever the work was. Sometimes, if Helen was lucky, he'd be singing in Scarborough at one of the hotels and they'd spend time together, time she always enjoyed. Other times, they spent weeks apart while Jimmy was working in Spain at Elvis-themed bars. She breathed in his lemon spice aftershave and felt comforted by his presence after such an unsettling day.

'How did Jean's mum's funeral go?' he asked.

'It was as heart-rending as you'd imagine. Jean tried to be stoic, you know what she's like, but she faltered a little. She even gave me a kiss before she left this afternoon.'

'Crikey,' Jimmy muttered. 'That doesn't sound like Jean.'

'She's emotionally wrung out. I told her to take time off, but she refused. She says she wants to be at work, not sitting at home. I can relate to that. It's what I went through when Tom died. Jean was the one who helped me cope then. The least I can do is be there to support her when she's going through her grief.'

'I'm sorry I couldn't be at the funeral. I had an audition I couldn't get out of. Unfortunately, it didn't go well. I gave them everything in my repertoire, even Hawaiian Elvis and 1968 Comeback Elvis, but nothing hit the spot. Turns out they were looking for a gimmick, not an Elvis tribute artiste. They're putting on a pantomime, *Snow White and the Seven Elvises*.'

Helen bit her lip to suppress a giggle, as she could tell how upset he was.

'They didn't like my style,' Jimmy said, then he kicked the table leg in frustration.

She started; she'd never seen him so angry before.

'Sorry, Helen, I'm upset about what happened today.' He tucked his feet away under the chair. 'Anyway, I sent a donation to the care home, as Jean requested.'

Helen raised her glass. 'To Jean's mum.'

They clinked glasses, then sat in silence a moment as Helen decided how best to broach the subject that had been on her mind since Jodie's call. She wondered what Jean would do, and decided that whatever it was wouldn't be subtle. But she had to be careful, as Jimmy was already upset over his failed audition.

'Jodie called me,' she said gently as he took a sip from his pint. He almost choked and began to splutter.

'Steady on there,' Helen said, waiting for him to compose himself.

'Why?' he asked when he could finally speak.

She put her glass down and turned to face him. 'I'm going to come right out and say it, Jimmy, with no prevarication. Jodie's a grown woman with her own life.'

'She's vulnerable,' he began.

Helen held up her hand. 'She's in a good space after getting help to beat her addictions. She earns her own money now. She's not a little girl any more.'

Jimmy sank back in his seat. 'What did she want?'

Helen took a deep breath. 'She asked me to speak to you to . . . Oh Jimmy, I'm sorry, but she wants you to back off and stop interfering in her life. She said you'd turned up at the hostel demanding to see her and that you caused a scene when she said she was too busy to chat.'

'She lives in a hostel for the homeless, Helen. I've a right to check on her, haven't I?'

'She doesn't just live in the hostel, Jimmy, she manages it,' Helen said calmly. 'You can't just turn up when you want to. Ring her first, show her respect. Show the others who live there respect too.'

Jimmy downed what was left of his pint and stormed off to the bar. When he came back, he banged the fresh pint on the table, then sat down, crossed his arms and put his chin on his chest, like a petulant child. Helen wondered if she'd gone too far. But all she'd done was pass on his daughter's message.

When he finally spoke, his tone was grumpy. 'Jodie couldn't tell me this herself?'

Helen knew he was hurt.

'She said she'd tried, a few times, but you wouldn't listen.'

'And so she gets you involved,' he muttered. 'Well, Helen, as you're so experienced in matters involving my daughter and my life—'

She held her hands up in mock surrender, trying to lighten the tone. 'Hey, don't shoot the messenger.'

Jimmy stood. 'I'm not taking lessons from you in how to treat my daughter.'

Helen was confused. 'Jimmy? I was only passing on what Jodie asked me to.'

'The two of you are taking sides against me.'

'Jimmy, no. Sit down and we'll talk.'

He loomed over her, shaking his head. 'No. I'm not sitting here listening to you judging me for the way I treat my daughter. I think . . . I think it might be best if we have a break from each other for a while.'

'I'm not judging you. And I don't want a break,' she said, aware now that people around them were watching. Jimmy put his jacket on, then stuffed his hands in his pockets before storming out of the pub, leaving his pint on the table.

'Jimmy!' Helen called. She picked up her bag and ran after him, catching him by his arm. When he swung around to face her, she saw tears in his eyes.

'I've had a rotten day, Helen. I didn't get the job I auditioned

Deadly Dancing at the Seaview Hotel

for, and now this . . . You're telling me that I'm not a good father, and my own daughter's too scared to tell me to my face. I'm sorry, I need to be on my own.'

Resigned, Helen let him go. She knew he'd need time to cool down. Slowly she began to walk back to the Seaview, going over in her head the words she should have said instead of the ones she had, wondering if she could have been more subtle. She wondered if she'd been too uncaring, letting him walk off without trying to placate him, and pulled her phone from her bag, ready to call him, to apologise and explain, but then stuffed it back.

'Ah, what the heck! If he wants a break, let him have one,' she muttered as she walked, but she kept checking her phone, in case he called.

Her mind turned to her guests, and to Jean, Miriam, Sally and Gav's Tans – anything that would stop her from thinking about Jimmy. She remembered the podcast Rosa had mentioned, and thought about listening to it when she got home. Maybe it would shed light on what was going on with the guests. It might help explain the strange, cool relationship between Carla and Monty, and give her insight into Bev's tension about her brother's TV comeback being thwarted by Rosa.

When she reached the Seaview, she saw a Gav's Cab waiting outside the Vista del Mar. At first she thought it was guests arriving to stay there, but then she saw Miriam locking her front door. At her feet were two suitcases.

'Would you like me to help you with those?' she asked.

Miriam lifted her chin as she struggled with the cases. 'No, thank you, dear. I can manage.'

'Are you leaving?' Helen asked.

'Always prying into other people's business, aren't you?' Miriam sniffed.

'No, I was just asking, that's all,' Helen said, determined not to let Miriam get to her. She felt emotionally wrung out after the funeral, her guests' arrival and now her argument with Jimmy. She was in no mood for more. 'Will you be away long?' she asked.

The taxi driver leapt out of his seat to place Miriam's suitcases in the boot. Miriam paused with one hand on the cab door, then leaned close to Helen.

'I've closed the Vista del Mar for a few days,' she began. 'There's a . . . let's call it a slight problem with my hotel, dear. It's why I haven't taken guests for a while. I thought things might resolve themselves, but they haven't, so I'm off to stay with my sister in Bridlington. I'll be gone a short while. There'll be, er . . . people coming and going while I'm away. You might hear some noise. But rest assured, I'll be back.'

'A slight problem . . . what problem?' Helen asked.

Miriam's face crumpled. She looked left and right to ensure no one was listening, then leaned closer and whispered something in Helen's ear.

'You'll have to speak up, Miriam, I can't hear,' Helen said.

Miriam's face flushed pink. 'Oh, the shame of it,' she said, a little louder this time. 'I've got bedbugs, Helen. My poor hotel is infested.'

Helen shuddered. It was every landlady's nightmare.

'What if they're in my hotel too?' she said, but Miriam had already jumped into the cab and slammed the door. She waved her hand regally in Helen's direction as the taxi drove off.

Helen bit her lip. She hadn't noticed any sign of bedbugs in the

Deadly Dancing at the Seaview Hotel

Seaview, and none of her guests had complained. However, if there were bedbugs at the Vista del Mar, well, who knew? The last thing she needed was to have to close her hotel as Miriam had closed hers and call in a pest control company to fumigate the place.

She let herself into the Seaview and was relieved to see the lounge empty. She didn't feel like making small talk with her guests after her run-in with Jimmy and now the bad news from Miriam. She checked her phone again to see if Jimmy had called, but there were no missed calls or texts. She felt a mix of relief at not having to deal with his bad mood and a desire to help make things all right. She put the phone away. She'd speak to him when she was ready, and when he'd cooled down.

She went down to her apartment and greeted Suki with a scratch behind her ears. The night was warm, so she opened the patio doors to let in the night air. Suki immediately went to lie down outside, keeping her watchful gaze on Helen indoors. Helen swiped her phone into life and searched for the podcast. She thought Rosa had said it was called *Dancing Night and Day*. A close match appeared: *Dancing Knight & Daye*. She knew Paul's surname was Knight from the information he'd provided when he'd checked in, so she assumed it was the right one.

She poured herself a glass of red wine to replace the one she'd left in the pub, then made herself comfortable on the sofa. There were many episodes of the podcast, but she decided to listen to the most recent one, called 'Scarborough Dance Competition'. It began with a jingle, a catchy little tune, then Paul's dulcet tones oozed into her ears, his smooth, suave voice at odds with his down-at-heel, scruffy appearance. He spoke about how excited he was to be travelling to Scarborough for the first time in his life and

Glenda Young

visiting the UK's original seaside town. This made Helen smile. Then he said he'd been booked into a bog-standard bed and breakfast called the Seaview Hotel. Her smile turned upside down.

'Bog standard? How dare you!' she muttered darkly. Suki looked at her with concern.

Paul spoke with passion about his love of ballroom and Latin dancing. He sounded knowledgeable and confident, and Helen soon fell for his spellbinding voice. He talked about the dancers he'd be travelling to Scarborough with, referring to Monty and Carla as the 'Magnificent Curzons' and Ballroom Bev Cassidy as 'the tenacious agent all dancers want to have fighting on their side'. He spoke of Tommy Two Shoes in almost reverential tones, highlighting the illustrious career of a man who'd had his own TV show as a boy.

And then he came to Rosa, and Helen heard a wobble in his voice. She learned that Rosa had trained as a ballet dancer before turning to ballroom and Latin dancing, where she was required to showcase the standard ten dances. He talked about her dream of getting on TV with her own show. However, the show was still at the stage of being an offer that hadn't come to fruition. Up against her was Tommy Two Shoes. Ballroom Bev, Paul explained, was pushing the TV execs hard for the show to go to her brother and would go to any lengths to make sure he got it.

The podcast was short and sweet, lasting ten minutes, and it ended with the same catchy jingle. Helen scrolled down the list of past episodes, and her heart stopped when she saw one named 'The Curse of the Dance'. She remembered what Sally had said about what had happened in Blackpool, something involving attempts to bribe a judge and a smashed glitter ball. She took a sip of wine, then pressed play.

Deadly Dancing at the Seaview Hotel

As Paul's words reached her ears this time, Helen's eyes opened wide in surprise. He sounded less sure of himself in this podcast. He kept faltering, and the editing wasn't as smooth. The latest episode had been his personal, first-hand account of preparing to travel to Scarborough, looking forward to spending time with the dancers and sharing his love of their world. But this one was different. His voice was guarded, careful as he reported on conspiracy theories he'd read online. When he mentioned Blackpool and the smashed glitter ball, Helen sat up straight and listened carefully.

Her heart began to pound as the story unfolded. She detected a wobble in Paul's voice when he described how the glitter ball had smashed, causing a dancer to fall in shock. She already knew this from what Sally had told her, but the way he delivered the news to her now, direct to her ear pods, made her shiver. He carried on, saying that the injured dancer had been rushed to hospital, where she swore she'd never dance again. Helen's eyes widened further when Paul revealed that the injured dancer was none other than Ballroom Bev.

Chapter 8

The next morning, Helen woke to a bright, sunny day. She could hear Jean in the kitchen, singing along to the radio. Having Jean in her home, and in her life, made Helen feel safe and secure. She showered quickly, then threw on jeans, trainers and hoodie and walked into the kitchen. She went straight to Jean, ready to hug her, but Jean backed away, holding a spatula up like a weapon.

'I'm fine, love. You don't need to ask me how I am, kiss me or hug me. Got it?'

'Got it,' Helen replied. 'But the minute you feel you need to take time out . . .'

'I won't,' Jean replied sternly. 'Now, take the dog out for her W.A.L.K.' If she'd said the word, rather than spelling it out, Suki would have rushed to the door before Helen had had time to put on the dog's collar and lead.

Within minutes, Helen was walking out of the back door of the Seaview with Suki at her side. She breathed in the fresh sea air as she turned the corner onto King's Parade and walked down the cliff path. Before she reached the beach, she saw one of her guests heading towards her, wrapped in a changing robe. She was carrying a large beach bag with a wet towel poking from the top. Carla's shock of red hair was hard to miss even when it was wet and pushed back from her face. Helen yawned. She was feeling tired of late because she wasn't sleeping well. Everyone told her this would happen when she hit her menopause years, and now their words were coming horribly true. She tried to focus as Carla approached her.

'Morning, Helen, I've been sea swimming. Is it something you do?'

Helen shook her head. 'No chance. It's far too cold. Did you enjoy it?'

Carla looked across the beautiful bay. 'I loved it. It helps calm my mind, stops me thinking about . . . Well, I shouldn't say any more really.'

'Oh, you should. You can trust me,' Helen said, breaking her rule about not being nosy about her guests. There was no one around to overhear her, so she had nothing to lose.

Carla turned her brown eyes on her and appraised her. 'Yes, I think I can. There's something about you. You're ordinary.'

'Oh, thanks very much,' Helen said with a forced smile.

'You're hard-working, and I admire that. Running the Seaview single-handedly must be difficult.'

'I have staff who help me. I could never do it on my own,' Helen said, thinking fondly of Sally and Jean.

'Teamwork makes the dream work, that's what everyone says. Monty and I are a team. We dance together, of course. We're the Magnificent Curzons on the dance floor – that's what everyone calls us. Did you know that?'

'Yes, I listened to some of Paul's podcasts last night.'

Carla grimaced. 'Those podcasts will be the death of me,' she hissed.

Helen raised her eyebrows. 'Really? The ones I listened to

seemed innocent. Paul is a genuine fan whose passion and dedication to dance really comes through.'

Carla glared at her. 'It's what he *doesn't* say that makes me nervous, darling. He knows us all too well. He knows our secrets, and we live in fear that one day he'll broadcast them. Some of us would be ruined if that ever happened.'

Helen cleared her throat. 'Surely things can't be that bad?' she dared ask.

'There are a lot of dark things going on in the dance world underneath the spangle of a salsa or the whirl of a waltz,' Carla said.

Helen didn't like the sound of that. 'Then maybe it's for the best if I don't get involved.'

'We're your guests and living under your roof, so perhaps you already are,' Carla replied.

Helen felt a chill run down her back, despite the sunny morning.

'Did you listen to the episode where our prickly rose, the prima ballerina, was mentioned in relation to Tommy's hopes for a TV comeback?'

'Prickly rose? Do you mean Rosa?' Helen ventured.

Carla smiled. 'Ah, so you did listen to it. Well, Rosa's agent in London is working flat out to win her that show and stop it from going to Tommy. In addition, Rosa has already thwarted my own plans here in Scarborough.'

'In what way?' Helen asked, intrigued.

'Well, Monty and I were due to strut our stuff with an exhibition tango to kick off the competition and open the show. We'd planned our routine for months and had it down to perfection. But last night Rosa told me the programme had changed at the last minute. It means that Monty and I aren't dancing our party piece after all. You can guess who's now topping the bill.'

Helen didn't need to reply.

'They say this dance competition is cursed, Helen. And in my opinion, that curse is Rosa.' Carla lifted her chin. 'Anyway, enough of my ramblings. I'll see you at breakfast. But please, darling, don't seat me anywhere near that woman, or I'll scream blue murder.' She shook her head, and her wet hair splattered seawater against Helen's cheek.

'Don't you ever wear a bathing cap?' Helen asked, wiping away droplets with the back of her hand.

Carla shook her head again, and more water landed on Helen's face. 'Never!' she laughed. 'I love to be in touch with nature. I want to feel the wind in my face and salt water on my skin.'

Helen carried on down to the beach with much on her mind. Her encounter with Carla had left her shaken, and her legs felt wobbly as she descended the path. Her mind kept returning to Carla's hair: how red it was, how slicked back it became when wet. She turned her face to the sun and let the sound of the waves calm her.

Her walk on the sands with Suki by her side was as peaceful as ever, and the solitude helped restore her. Every few minutes, she pulled her phone from her pocket, but there was still nothing from Jimmy. She didn't know if she should call him, or even whether he'd want her to. She also felt unsettled thinking about the strange man in the 4x4 who'd she caught filming the Seaview. She sighed and carried on.

After she'd walked the length of the beach, she retraced her steps up the cliff path. She planned to go back in through the door that led straight to her apartment. It didn't do to take Suki through the front door while she had guests. It wasn't fair on those who didn't like dogs. She was striding along King's Parade, thinking about Miriam and her bedbugs, reminding herself to ask Jean about pest control, when she heard voices coming from the other side of the road. Glancing across, she saw Monty and Bev sitting together on the wooden bench where she and Jean had sat the previous day to raise a champagne toast to Jean's mum. The pair had no clue she was there, and she could hear their raised voices.

'Rosa knows all about it,' Bev was saying angrily. 'She's threatened to tell Paul for his podcast. She's going to tell him everything.'

'It'll ruin me if the truth gets out about what happened in Blackpool,' Monty replied.

'Then we have to stop Rosa from talking,' Bev said.

Chapter 9

Helen returned to the Seaview mulling over what she'd just heard. After learning from the podcast the previous night that it was Bev who'd been injured in Blackpool when the glitter ball fell, she wondered if Monty was involved too. She also mused on how close Monty and Bev really were.

As she let Suki off her lead and opened the patio doors to the warm day, Jean called to her.

'I'm going dancing tonight.'

It took Helen a moment to register what she'd said. She looked across the room to see Jean opening a catering-size tin of baked beans.

'Sorry, what?'

'I said I'm going out dancing. At the Spa. With that man.'

Helen's blood ran cold.

'What man?' she asked, although she had a horrible feeling she already knew. A pair of Cuban-heeled shoes sashayed through her mind.

'That nice chap I was talking to yesterday on the bench. I reckon it's fate, Helen. There I was saying goodbye to Mum, and he walked into my life just when I needed a friend.'

'You've got plenty of friends. You've got me and Sally,' Helen said quickly.

But Jean carried on as if she hadn't heard.

'I bumped into him again yesterday on my way home. He was walking down Columbus Ravine. I said, "Well, what a coincidence" and he said, "Yes, it is." He's got lovely manners, Helen, he's a real gent. And he wears gorgeous shoes. Anyway, he asked me if I'd like to go dancing and I said to him, "Now that's another coincidence," because yesterday I'd been saying to you, Helen, hadn't I, that I'd like to take up dancing again. It's as if he knows me inside out. I feel like I've known him for years. Isn't it strange how some people can make you feel like that?'

'Be careful,' Helen warned.

Jean waved the tin opener in the air. 'Be careful about what? What's so wrong with a fella wanting to take me to a dance? I'm in my prime. Mum's death has made me realise a lot of things, not least that I should make the most of every minute while I'm still on this earth.'

Helen walked into the kitchen and sat on a stool. Jean was standing at the stove. Helen looked at the back of her friend's short blonde hair.

'Remember when Tom died?'

'How could we forget, love,' Jean said gently, glancing at her.

'Well, you'll remember how confused I was, especially about running this place on my own. I didn't know whether to sell up and move away or carry on to see if I could manage alone.'

'Of course I remember,' Jean said as she began to slice mushrooms.

'Then you'll remember how you helped me through those difficult days. I was vulnerable and not myself. I found it hard to make decisions, and sometimes I made the wrong ones.'

Deadly Dancing at the Seaview Hotel

Jean turned to her with a knife in her hand and sighed deeply. 'What are you trying to say, love?'

'I'm trying to say that I'm worried about you. Yesterday you told me you'd come into a lot of money from your mum's will. And now you've got this chap who's turned up out of the blue. He was listening to our conversation when we were sitting on the bench, and each time you spoke about your inheritance, I noticed that he inched closer. He might have heard you talking about wanting to start dancing again. Don't you see, Jean? He could be a con man, after your money. That's why I'm worried.'

'Pfft!' Jean turned her back on Helen and resumed slicing mushrooms with more vigour than before.

'Well, don't say you weren't warned,' Helen said. 'Anyway, what's this fellow's name?'

'Bobby Tanner,' Jean said without turning around.

The name meant nothing to Helen. Resigned, knowing only too well that Jean was her own woman, older and more experienced than herself, she wondered if she was overreacting and decided to change the subject.

'By the way, Miriam's closed the Vista del Mar and gone to stay with her sister in Bridlington.'

'Why?' Jean asked.

'Bedbugs, apparently. The place is infested. The pest control people are coming in while she's away.'

Jean's brow furrowed. 'That's odd. She didn't have to leave to have the hotel fumigated. Some of the pest control companies can be in and out within a day. She could have had it open again tomorrow.'

'Maybe the infestation is a lot worse than that, and it will take a few days,' Helen said. 'Anyway, we both know how precious Miriam is. If there's one tiny bug left, she'll be screaming blue murder and shutting up shop. I think she probably wants to be on the safe side – close down, get pest control in and leave it for a few days. It's probably what I'd do, to guarantee all the bugs had gone. I bumped into her last night. She was getting into a taxi. I don't know when she'll be back.'

'I reckon she'll be back sooner rather than later,' Jean said darkly. 'You know how difficult and snobby she is. My guess is that her sister won't put up with her for long.'

'You don't think *we've* got bedbugs, do you?' Helen asked.

A noise behind her made her turn, and she saw the door to her apartment open and Sally breeze in. Her long blonde hair was tied in a ponytail.

'Morning, Helen, morning, Jean, morning, Suki!' she called as she took off her jacket and picked up her Seaview Hotel tabard. The tabards were blue with the hotel logo in white, exactly as they'd been since Helen and Tom had first taken on the Seaview, and Helen saw no reason to change them.

Sally pulled the tabard over her baby bump.

'I'm going to need a bigger one,' she said.

'Wear one of Jean's old ones for now. It should be big enough. I've ordered a new set, including some larger ones, and they should be arriving soon,' Helen said.

Sally slid onto the stool next to her.

'How are you, Sally? You look a bit peaky.'

'Things aren't great at home,' Sally replied with a grimace.

Jean spun around with a look of concern on her face.

'It's not the twins, is it?' Helen said, alarmed.

Deadly Dancing at the Seaview Hotel

'Is little Gracie all right?' Jean asked.

Sally smiled. 'Don't worry about me and the twins, we're doing just fine. And Gracie's well too, although she's a lively handful, as always. No, it's Gav who's the problem this time. He's been on cloud nine for months, excited about the twins coming and the opening of Gav's Tans. However, yesterday something happened that wiped the smile off his face. And you know my Gav, it takes a lot to upset his sweet and sunny nature.'

'He's resilient, I'll give him that,' Jean said approvingly. 'So what's happened?'

'An old school friend of his, Frankie, is in town. Frankie and Gav haven't seen each other in months and Frankie wants to meet up, but Gav doesn't want to see him.'

'Why not?' Helen asked.

'Well, there are two reasons. The first is that Frankie's always been jealous of Gav's success. Gav's tried many times to offer him advice, but Frankie has no business sense and hasn't been able to make a go of things on his own. Gav gave up on him years ago as he felt he was wasting his time. Each time he offered advice, Frankie went and did the opposite of what he suggested. Frankie now works with his dad, something involving financing gigs. And the second reason Gav's upset,' Sally's face flushed pink, 'is that Frankie and I had a bit of a thing, years ago, before I met Gav and before I met Gracie's dad. I dumped him when he started losing his temper. He used to lash out with other people and I was terrified he'd hit me, so I left him. Anyway, Gav gets extra protective whenever Frankie's in town.'

'Frankie sounds like a bad 'un, and you did the right thing getting rid of him. What sort of events does Frankie finance with his dad?' Helen asked.

'Concerts, gigs, sports . . . and they're backing the dance competition at the Spa.'

Jean's eyes grew wide. 'What's Frankie's surname?'

'Tanner. Frankie Tanner.'

Her hand flew to her heart. 'It's kismet.'

'No, it's Tanner,' Sally replied.

Jean placed both hands on the kitchen counter. 'Well, there's a coincidence! I've just met a new man and his surname's Tanner.' She cast a cautious look at Helen. 'And he's involved in backing the dance competition at the Spa.'

'Is he called Bobby?' Sally asked.

Jean nodded.

'Then he's Frankie's dad. What a small world!' Sally cried.

'I hope Bobby controls his temper better than his son,' Helen noted.

'So do I! Frankie's got a new girlfriend too, and you'll never guess who she is,' Sally continued.

'Go on, tell us,' Jean said, eyes wide.

Sally raised her eyes to the ceiling. Helen and Jean followed her gaze.

'Is her name written in the plaster?' Jean joked.

Sally leaned forward, eyes sparkling with mischief. 'Frankie's girlfriend is one of our guests.'

Jean tutted loudly. 'It's not the little woman, Bev with the orange hair, surely? She's old enough to be his mum.'

Sally shook her head, then looked at Helen, waiting for her to guess too.

'Then it's got to be either Carla Curzon or Rosa de Wolfe,' Helen said.

Deadly Dancing at the Seaview Hotel

'Rosa de what?' Jean asked.

'De Wolfe, that's her surname.'

'That's her,' Sally said with a smug smile. 'Frankie and Rosa have just got together. He's already made her top of the bill at the dance competition. She's doing an exhibition dance to open the show with her dance partner, Tommy Two Legs.'

Helen smiled widely. 'It's Tommy Two Shoes, but you were close.'

She was surprised to hear that Rosa and Tommy were dancing partners. After Bev had told her that Tommy was up against Rosa for the TV show, she'd pegged the pair as rivals. Plus, there was already something niggling her about Rosa. Carla had revealed that she and Monty had been shunted out of the slot to open the show. Had Rosa used her connections to Frankie and his dad to bump Carla and Monty off the programme and place herself in the opening dance instead?

She clapped her hands. 'Come on, ladies. Let's have breakfast, then we'll get to work.'

Right on cue, Jean set two perfectly cooked bacon sandwiches on soft white bread in front of Helen and Sally, with two mugs of steaming-hot tea. Suki wandered in from outdoors and sat at Helen's feet, hoping for crumbs.

After breakfast, Jean shooed Helen and Sally upstairs to serve breakfast to their guests. The two women, both adorned in blue tabards, waited by the dumbwaiter in the hall. It was old and creaked (just like Jean), but it still worked a treat to take food upstairs. Standing shoulder to shoulder, they greeted the guests as they walked into the dining room. Bev was first, talking nineteen to the dozen on her phone, barely acknowledging them. Tommy followed, beaming his bright white smile. Rosa was next, her long glossy hair draped around her shoulders. She managed a polite exchange with Helen, who asked if she'd slept well.

'I slept like the dead, as always,' Rosa replied.

Monty Curzon arrived clad in smart black trousers and a white shirt open in a deep V to show off his smooth, tanned chest. Helen had trouble pulling her gaze away and had to give herself a stiff talking-to. She straightened her shoulders and pushed her feet to the carpet.

'It's a beautiful morning, isn't it?' she said, just as he raised his phone in the air, turned it at an angle and took a selfie.

'Beautiful,' he muttered. Then he walked into the dining room.

'He's gorgeous, but strange,' Sally whispered.

Helen gave her a gentle nudge. 'Never talk about our guests while they're in earshot, Sally. You know my rules.'

Monty's wife Carla was next, looking far more glamorous than Helen had seen her earlier, after her swim in the sea. Her severely bobbed red hair had been blow-dried and now swung under her chin as she walked into the dining room to sit, not at the table with Monty, but at the one next to him.

'How odd that a married couple choose to sit apart,' Helen muttered, to which she received a nudge in the ribs from Sally along with a reproving look.

Finally Paul the podcaster ambled downstairs. In contrast to the dancers, who were groomed and well dressed, he was sporting an unironed T-shirt with stains down the front, and a pair of baggy tracksuit bottoms. His feet were clad in brown slippers with holes at the toes. He was unshaven and bleary-eyed.

Deadly Dancing at the Seaview Hotel

'Morning, Helen. Could I have double everything for breakfast, please? I'm starving,' he said. He scratched his belly, then walked into the dining room and fell into the nearest chair.

Helen watched as he raised his gaze, looked across the dining room and smiled shyly at Rosa, who ignored him.

Chapter 10

As Helen served breakfast in the dining room, Bev's phone started to ring, and she leapt up from her chair in excitement.

'It's the TV company!' she yelled excitedly, but in her haste to answer it, she dropped the phone. It clattered to the floor, its ringing insistent and loud.

Everyone in the room stopped what they were doing, put down their knives and forks and looked at Bev, who scrabbled around on the floor searching for her phone, which continued to ring. They all seemed to be waiting with bated breath to find out what would happen next. Finally, someone snapped as the tension grew too great.

'Just answer the bloody thing, darling!' Carla yelled.

Bev stood with the phone in her hand, swiped it into life, then walked quickly out of the room.

Once Helen had finished distributing plates of Jean's award-winning full English breakfast, she had no reason to stay in the dining room. Bev had gone into the lounge to answer the call and pulled the door closed behind her. Helen lingered in the hallway, loading up the dumbwaiter, and when she heard Bev mention Rosa, her ears pricked up.

'What if Ms de Wolfe fell ill, say, or . . . I don't know, let's say for argument's sake she went to live overseas, that sort of thing. Would the show then go to my brother by default?'

Deadly Dancing at the Seaview Hotel

The phone call was short, and Helen was almost caught eavesdropping when the other woman stormed out of the lounge. However, Bev didn't seem to notice as she strode back to the dining room. Tommy sat up eagerly in his seat.

'Well? What did they say?' he asked, almost bouncing up and down in his chair.

Bev shook her head, then shot daggers across the room at Rosa. 'They're still not ready to make a decision. Don't worry, little bruv. No news is good news, for now.'

After breakfast was over, Helen and Sally began to clear the dining room. Bev was the last to leave; she was sitting at her table furiously tapping into her phone.

'You can stay there as long as you need, Bev,' Helen said. 'Would you like more tea or coffee?'

Bev looked up, startled, then quickly covered her phone screen with her hand.

'No, I'm fine. Got to get back upstairs to my office. I've got phone calls to make, work to do, people to schmooze,' she added with an attempt at a smile.

'Would you like me to clean the room you're using as an office?' Helen asked.

'There's no need. I won't be making use of the bed in there. I just need the space to spread out my paperwork and files.'

Bev picked up her phone and sauntered out of the room, leaving Helen and Sally to finish their work. All done, they walked downstairs to Helen's apartment, where Jean was in the kitchen, slicing a lemon drizzle cake.

'I bought this at the bakery stall on the market on my way into work this morning. I'm still not up to baking cakes, not since

Mum died,' she explained. 'Fancy a slice each with a mug of coffee?'

The women took their seats at the dining table and Suki walked in from outdoors to lie at Helen's feet. Suki lifted her paw to Helen's knee and Helen looked at Jean. 'She's been giving me her paw a lot lately.'

'Is there something wrong with it?' Jean asked.

Helen thoroughly inspected the paw. 'Nothing I can see. Greyhounds can be the strangest dogs. Little things can bother them, depending on what mood they're in.'

Jean poured coffee from the cafetière into three blue mugs and handed one each to Helen and Sally. Then she passed round plates of cake. Helen bit into her slice.

'Oh Jean, it's nowhere near as good as yours,' she said.

'Sally, how's your slice?' Jean asked.

Sally couldn't reply as her mouth was full of cake, but when she stopped chewing, she swallowed, then gulped water from a glass.

'Pregnancy has changed my sense of taste,' she moaned. 'I used to love cake, but I can't seem to enjoy it any more.'

'Poor love,' Jean said. She turned her attention to Helen. 'You'll finish yours, Helen, won't you?'

Helen agreed that she would.

'Are our guests rehearsing today?' Jean asked.

'Yes, I heard them talking about heading to the Spa. The dance competition's just a few days away and they need to prepare.' Helen sipped her coffee. 'Where's Bobby taking you dancing tonight?'

Jean popped a piece of cake into her mouth and chewed. 'The Spa,' she eventually replied.

Helen was determined to find out more.

Deadly Dancing at the Seaview Hotel

'What time does it start?'

'Seven p.m.'

'Can anyone go?'

'Oh yes, everyone's welcome,' Jean replied. 'I'm meeting him inside the Ocean Room just after seven.'

Helen raised her eyebrows. 'Inside? You mean he hasn't even offered to pay your entrance fee?'

Sally laughed out loud. 'Come on, Helen, it's not like Jean's going on a date, not at her age.'

Jean sucked air through her teeth. 'It *is* a date, young lady. I like Bobby Tanner and I'm hoping I'll see him again after tonight.'

Helen put her hand on her friend's arm. 'Be careful, Jean, take it slowly and remember what I said.'

Jean brushed her hand away and stood, gathering the empty plates, then walked away to the kitchen.

Later that day, Helen's phone rang with a call from Marie.

'How's that hunky guest of yours, Monty Curzon? I've been googling him. He's done some modelling as well as dancing.'

'That might explain his vanity,' Helen said. 'I've lost count of the number of selfies I've seen him take. I don't know what he does with them all.'

'He puts them on his Instagram.' Marie began to laugh. 'Or so I've been told.'

'Listen, Marie, what are your plans for tonight?'

'Painting my toenails, face mask, bubble bath, Cillian Murphy on the telly, early night. Why do you ask?'

'Fancy coming to the Spa to watch ballroom dancing?' Helen asked.

There was a pause, and she bit her lip. She could just imagine the look of horror on Marie's face. Dancing at the Spa was not her best friend's cup of tea.

'Since when were you interested in ballroom dancing at the Spa?' Marie said.

'Since Jean came into an inheritance after her mum died, and now she's met a fella who I think is after her money. He's taking her dancing tonight.'

'And you want to spy on her,' Marie said sternly. 'If she finds out, she'll be furious.'

'She won't know,' Helen said firmly. 'But if she spots us, we'll tell her we're there to watch the dancers rehearse. Some of them are my guests, so it won't be weird for us to be there. Come on, Marie, what do you say? I need some support. Please come, if not for my sake, then for Jean's.'

'Well, I've got a pair of black sparkly sandals that I haven't yet worn. It's time I took them for an outing, and what better place than the Spa,' Marie said.

'Thanks, Marie,' Helen said gratefully. 'That's great, love. I'll meet you outside the Ocean Room at seven.'

She hung up and walked into her bedroom, with Suki following. She opened her wardrobe door, and the dog stood at her side.

'Well, Suki, what shall I wear to the dance tonight? Trousers or a dress?' She pulled out a pink, floaty summer dress from the back of the wardrobe. 'This one?' She held it up in front of her body and turned to the dog, who stared blankly back.

That evening, Helen and Marie were seated at a round table inside the Ocean Room at the Spa. There was a sprung dance floor where couples were parading by in a slow waltz as the organist played. He had his back to the floor and on either side of the organ were mirrors, much like wing mirrors on a car, so that he could see what was happening behind him. Helen caught sight of Tommy dancing with Rosa. Knowing there was no love lost between them, she thought how hard it must be for them to dance together. However, the rictus grin on Tommy's face gave nothing away, and Rosa's expression remained impassive too, as if she was lost in the rise and fall of the waltz and nothing else mattered.

The dancers weren't wearing their exhibition clothes that Helen had seen hanging in their rooms. The men were in smart suits, and Carla and Rosa both wore cocktail dresses. Carla's was baby blue, and Monty, Helen noticed, wore a tie of the same colour. She wondered if the Mighty Curzons colour-coordinated often. It was effective, she'd give them that. They looked for all the world like a couple deeply in love with each other, instead of Monty being in love with himself. Bev was sitting in a chair at the side of the dance floor, dressed in a white catsuit with sparkling blue crystals emblazoned down each leg. Her phone was clasped firmly in her hand. Paul the podcaster was next to the organist, recording the music.

'It sounds so dreamy and romantic,' Marie sighed as she swayed from side to side.

'Where's Jean? Have you seen her?' Helen urged, scanning the dance floor for Jean's short, stocky figure.

Marie rolled her eyes. 'Calm down, love. You're acting like an overly protective parent. I'm sure Jean can look after herself. Stop treating her like a child. She knows what she's doing. She's a capable woman, not the sort to be taken in by a con man – she's got too much sense. I don't know what you're worrying about. What's his name anyway, this bloke she's seeing?'

'Bobby Tanner,' Helen said, still scanning the crowd.

Marie froze in her seat. 'No . . . please don't tell me it's the guy who's bankrolling the dance competition?'

'Yes, that's him,' Helen said.

'Then that's the same Bobby Tanner who's just been released from prison after serving two years for fraud. His son, Frankie, is often in trouble too, and has been handy with his fists in the past.'

'Sally mentioned something about that today,' Helen said, her heart sinking. 'Oh Marie, I need to warn Jean.'

She stood, ready to rush to the dance floor, but Marie grabbed her arm and firmly encouraged her to sit back down.

'You can't go storming over there with all guns blazing. Jean would be mortified, and you don't want to fall out with her again. Remember what happened last time?'

Helen shuddered at the memory of when Jean had gone to work for Miriam at the Vista del Mar and she thought she'd lost her for good.

'Who knows, Bobby might have turned over a new leaf in prison,' Marie said.

Helen was about to reply when there was an almighty clatter on the dance floor. The organist stopped playing and dancers moved away. Amid shouting and chaos, two men were fighting, and Helen recognised both. The younger man was pale-skinned, tall and skinny, with fair hair swept back from his face.

'I've seen him before, he was filming the Seaview on his phone,' she told Marie.

Deadly Dancing at the Seaview Hotel

The other man was shorter and older and wore Cuban-heeled shoes.

From out of nowhere, two Spa security officers waded into the fight and pulled the two men apart. Helen was horrified to see Jean caught up in the affray. She watched as Jean walked to Bobby and dabbed his cheek with a handkerchief that she pulled from her handbag.

'The show's over, everyone, you can return to your dancing,' one of the beefy bouncers said.

The organist struck up a lively tune, hoping to encourage dancers back to the floor. However, most people returned to their tables or ordered a stiff drink from the bar. The bouncers led the two men out of the room. Jean followed, as did Rosa. Intrigued, Helen decided to follow too.

'Watch my handbag, I'll be back in a minute,' she told Marie.

Keeping her distance so that Jean didn't see her, she trailed behind the little group out to the foyer. There, she hid behind a pop-up banner advertising an upcoming gig by a folk group she'd never heard of. She peered around the edge.

'Get out, Frankie, and don't come back. You're barred,' one of the bouncers said.

'You can't bar me! I've invested money in the dance competition,' the younger man spat.

Helen gulped. So *that* was Frankie Tanner, Gav's no-good mate from school, Sally's violent ex-boyfriend and Bobby's son.

'Rosa's not worth it, son! You're better off without her!' Bobby yelled.

'Shut up, Dad. You've already said too much,' Frankie snarled. 'Speak ill of my girlfriend again and I'll knock you into next week.'

Helen retreated behind the banner. After a moment, she dared herself to lean forward again, keen to see what would happen next. More than anything, she was worried for Jean. However, when she peered around the banner, she saw the foyer was empty. Frankie, Bobby, Jean and Rosa were outside. Frankie and Bobby were still yelling at each other, while Jean was trying to pull Bobby one way as Rosa pulled Frankie the other.

Paul ran outside with his microphone in his hand. 'Rosa! Wait!' he called.

The two bouncers followed him to the entrance, their hefty frames blocking the doorway.

'He's a wrong 'un, Frankie Tanner,' growled one of them. 'He's turned out as bad as his old man.'

'The Tanner men are lowlife scum. I wish we could bar both of them, Pete.'

'Aye, but we can't, Stan, not when they've put money in the dance competition.'

Then the pair stepped forward to pull Frankie and Bobby apart again as their fighting resumed.

Chapter 11

When Helen stepped out from behind the pop-up banner a few moments later, the burly bouncers were standing in front of her with their arms crossed. Both glared at her.

'And what would a lady be doing hiding behind there, Stan?' one of them asked the other.

'Do we think she was up to no good, Pete?' Stan replied.

'Possibly, Stan. Shall we ask her?'

Both men stepped forward, and Helen shrank back, almost knocking the banner over.

'I was just . . .' Her mind scrambled to find a believable lie, and when it failed, she blurted the truth. 'I was worried for my friend, the older lady who was with Bobby Tanner. I was hiding, listening, trying to work out how I could help her.'

The bouncers uncrossed their arms and stood back.

'Stan, should we tell her the best way to handle Bobby Tanner?'

'Yes, Pete, I think we should.'

Stan beckoned Helen forward with his meaty paw. Helen leaned in, her heart going like the clappers.

'The advice Pete and I would give your friend is to leave Bobby Tanner alone.'

'He's bad news,' added Pete. 'Now why don't you run along and forget you ever met us, and we'll do our best to forget we saw you hiding behind this banner. Won't we, Stan?'

'We will, Pete.'

Helen turned on her heel and walked as fast as she could back to the Ocean Room. By now there were couples dancing again, this time to a marching song that had them parading in unison. She collapsed into her seat, lifted her glass of red wine and took a very long drink.

'Steady on!' Marie said, alarmed.

Helen held out her hand, palm down. 'Look, I'm shaking. I need another drink.'

'What happened?' Marie asked.

'Bobby and Frankie Tanner have been thrown out for fighting.'

'See, I told you Bobby Tanner was bad news,' Marie said.

'You were right. And his son's no better. I suspect that when he filmed my hotel, he might have been scoping the place out, confirming to his dad that it was where Jean worked.'

Marie raised her perfectly plucked eyebrows. 'I think you're surmising too much. It sounds like you're getting paranoid,' she said.

Helen sat back in her seat, wondering if Marie was right. She began to watch the dancing, letting the music and rhythm calm her. There was something hypnotic about a room full of people dancing the same steps at the same time. She couldn't see Bev or Tommy anywhere, and Carla and Monty had disappeared too.

'My heart rate's going back to normal,' she said at last, taking a long breath.

'What you need is something to take your mind off all of this. You need a good night out,' Marie said firmly. 'You're getting yourself too wound up over Jean.'

Deadly Dancing at the Seaview Hotel

'It's not only Jean on my mind, Marie. There's something strange going on with my guests.'

Marie leaned in close. 'Then tell me.'

Helen looked around to ensure that no one was within earshot, then she told Marie all she knew.

'The young woman who was with Frankie and Bobby is one of my guests, Rosa de Wolfe. Bobby and Frankie were fighting because of her. Rosa is Frankie Tanner's new girlfriend.'

'Well, Frankie's not a good person, Helen. When I was married to Darren, I remember him talking about the Tanner men. Darren knew all the villains in Scarborough. He was barely on the right side of the law himself. He told me that Frankie was involved in all sorts of crime around town. I wonder what Rosa sees in him.'

'It could be the power that he holds in this dance competition,' Helen said. 'Rosa's put another of my guests' noses out of joint, a dancer called Carla Curzon. She's married to the hunky fella, Monty, that you went all goo-eyed over at the Seaview.'

'Ooh, he's gorgeous!' Marie gushed.

'Oh, stop it. It's not becoming for a woman your age,' Helen laughed. 'Although I agree he's something special to look at. Anyway, Carla told me that she and Monty were supposed to be top of the bill at the dance competition. They were going to open the show with an exhibition tango. But now Rosa's opening the show with Tommy Two Shoes, and Carla's not happy, as you'd expect, especially as it was changed at the last minute.'

Marie's eyes opened wide. 'Tommy Two Shoes... didn't he have a TV show when we were kids?'

'That's the one,' Helen replied. 'Not only is Tommy Rosa's dance partner, but he's up for some dancing show on telly and Rosa's up for the same one, but only one of them can have it. I overheard Ballroom Bev tell Monty—'

Marie smirked. 'Hang on a minute. Ballroom Bev and Tommy Two Shoes. It sounds as if you've got the cast from a kids' TV show staying with you, not a troupe of dancers. Who's Ballroom Bev?'

'She's Tommy's sister and his agent. She's working hard to get this TV show for him. She's expecting a phone call from the TV production company any day. In fact, she thought the call had come this morning, but it wasn't the news she was hoping for. Anyway, I heard Bev tell Monty that Rosa has information about what happened in Blackpool and she's going to tell podcaster Paul all about it.'

'Whoa! Slow down. What's Blackpool got to do with any of this?'

Helen filled her in about the dancer attempting to bribe a judge, the glitter ball smashing to the dance floor and Bev being injured. Marie listened in silence.

'My word, there's a lot to unpick there,' she said.

'Tell me about it,' Helen sighed. 'And there's more. When I overheard Bev and Monty talking on the clifftop bench, Bev said that Rosa had to be silenced.'

Marie let out a long, low whistle through her teeth. 'Crikey, Helen. I don't envy you having to look after that motley bunch. The whole thing is weird.'

'What's even more weird is the way Rosa keeps to herself at the Seaview,' Helen said.

'Lots of people do that; there's no law against it,' Marie said.

'I know, but there's something odd about her, Marie. Something cold and calculating, despite her glamour and her gorgeous hair.'

Their conversation was cut short when Helen spotted Bev and

Deadly Dancing at the Seaview Hotel

Tommy walking alongside the dance floor. With her orange hair, Bev was an arresting sight as she shimmied in her white catsuit, the turquoise crystals sparkling under the lights. Tommy wore a flattering grey suit with a matching waistcoat and pastel pink tie. He stayed two steps behind his sister.

Helen pointed them out to Marie. 'That's Tommy and Bev. Look out, they're coming over. At least I've got one fairly normal guest in Tommy. He really is a nice man. Gorgeous white teeth.'

She steeled herself as the pair drew near, but Bev didn't acknowledge her and walked straight past. Tommy, however, slowed down.

'My sister's going back to the Seaview, but I'm not ready to leave,' he said, looking from Helen to Marie. 'I think I've got another few dances left in me if either of you ladies would like a whirl around the floor?'

Marie made to stand, but Helen got there first.

'I'd love to, Tommy, thank you. But I must warn you, I've got two left feet.'

'Then we'll get along fine, because I've got two right ones.'

She winked at Marie as Tommy led her to the dance floor. She had no clue what she was doing; the only dance she knew was the jive, which she'd learned to do with Tom. However, the music the organist was playing now was a different kind of beat. Tommy explained it was a cha-cha-cha.

'Just follow me and you'll be fine,' he said.

She tried her best, putting her right foot forward, then back, then to the side, twisting and turning, trying to copy him, but she knew she looked a sight. However, her reason for getting up on the floor with him wasn't to learn to dance. It was to find out a little more about Rosa. She hoped it might give her information about

Frankie Tanner and his dad. The more she knew about Bobby, the better she could help steer Jean out of trouble.

'I saw Rosa was involved in that awful fight,' she said.

'And cha-cha-cha,' Tommy replied. 'Shoulder to shoulder, Helen.' She turned her body as he indicated.

'I'm glad that Rosa's left,' he said. 'And now for the Alemana turn.'

'The what?' Helen tried to move her arms and legs the way Tommy was leading her. 'But Rosa's your dance partner. Wouldn't you rather be dancing with her?'

'And two, three, cha-cha-cha, one, two, three, cha-cha-cha. Close right foot to left foot.'

She really had no clue. All she could do was trust Tommy's capable, experienced hands to manage her as best he could.

'Rosa and I don't get along. We haven't got along since . . . two, three, cha-cha-cha . . . since we both went up for the same TV show. Oh Helen, I want that show more than life itself. It's been my dream to get back on telly. Rosa's not really interested in being on TV; it's something to do until another opportunity comes along. Having to dance with her . . . hold on, Helen, step right and cha-cha-cha . . . dancing with Rosa now is difficult, we're hostile to one another. However, we're professional to the last and so we keep smiling and . . . cha-cha-cha . . . smiling and dancing. And turn and cha-cha-cha . . . But do you know, I can't help thinking that my life would be so much better if Rosa was . . . and three, cha-cha-cha . . . if Rosa was no longer around.'

Chapter 12

When Helen climbed into the passenger seat of Marie's small red sports car for the drive back to the Seaview, she shared Tommy's words about Rosa.

'You don't think he's planning to get rid of her, do you?' she said, worried.

Marie kept her gaze ahead as she pulled out of the car park and onto the main road.

'Don't be daft. There's bound to be professional rivalry between the dancers. Carla wants to be top of the bill, Monty wants to be cock of the north, Tommy Two Shoes wants to be on TV and Rosa wants the best for herself. You can't blame any of them for being ambitious. Mind you, I'm still surprised that Rosa's going out with Frankie Tanner. I wouldn't go anywhere near him, or his dad. You will warn Jean to be careful, won't you?'

Helen cast her a sidelong glance. 'Earlier, you said I was being paranoid.'

'I've had time to think since then,' Marie said with a smirk.

Helen sighed. 'I'll keep trying to speak to Jean. But you know what she's like. Once she's made up her mind about something, it's difficult to get her to change it.'

Marie flicked the indicator to turn left.

'How's Jimmy these days? Is he still doing his IT class at college? Seen much of him lately?'

Helen was silent, thinking of what had happened in the pub.

'Well?' Marie prompted.

'We had an argument, and he hasn't been in touch since,' Helen admitted.

Marie spun the car around the corner of King's Parade just a little too quickly for Helen's liking.

'Oh Helen, no!' she cried. 'Why did you argue?'

'It was about his daughter, Jodie. It's a long story and I won't bore you with it, but I caught him at a difficult time. He'd had a bad audition and the news from Jodie hit him hard. We had a bit of a set-to, and he stormed out on me. I've been waiting for him to call to apologise, but he hasn't.'

Marie pulled her car to the kerb outside the Seaview. There was a man knocking at the hotel's front door, a man Helen didn't recognise. She peered up.

'I wonder what he wants so late at night.'

'He can wait a minute, can't he? Listen, I'm worried about you and Jimmy. Why don't you make the first move and call him?' Marie suggested.

Helen looked at her. 'Ever since I met him, it feels like our relationship has been going one step forward and two steps back.'

Marie smiled. 'Stepping forward, stepping back, who cares, as long as you're dancing together in the right direction.'

'But we're going around in circles!' Helen said, exasperated.

'Look, love. It takes two to tango and he's a smashing bloke. Give him a chance. He won't wait for ever. Keep him hanging on too long and he'll waltz off with someone else. He's a good-looking fellow, a real catch. You could do a lot worse.'

Marie looked at the man on Helen's doorstep.

'Do you want me to wait here until you've dealt with him?'

'No, I'll be fine. He's probably after a room and hasn't noticed the "No Vacancies" sign.' Helen kissed Marie on the cheek and clambered out of the car.

'Call me!' Marie cried, then roared away.

Helen called out to the man as she climbed the steps. 'Can I help you? I'm the hotel owner.'

His face was illuminated by the light above the door, but she didn't recognise him.

'I'm afraid we have no rooms left,' she said. She pointed at the sign in the window.

He looked pleasant enough, she thought. He was tall and stocky, with thick brown hair, narrow eyes and a thin mouth. He wore a black leather jacket, jeans and trainers. He didn't have luggage, she noted, so perhaps he wasn't after a room.

'Is there something you want?' she asked.

'Is Mrs Cassidy staying here? Or Ballroom Bev, as she used to be known.'

'I'm afraid I can't divulge information about my guests. And who might you be?' she asked coolly.

The man thrust his right hand inside his jacket and pulled out a business card. 'I'm Mike Skipton. I've got my own building company. I've been doing work on Mrs Cassidy's home and, er . . . well, I don't really want to discuss Mrs Cassidy's business with someone I don't know, but I'd be obliged if you'd hand her my card and tell her I'm looking for her. There are a few things I'd like to discuss.'

Helen took the card. It looked professional, genuine, advertising all kinds of building work. There was a landline number, a mobile number, email, website, social media, the works.

Helen watched Mike walk away down the path. When he reached King's Parade, he turned left, where there was a white van with *Mike Skipton, Builder* emblazoned in blue with the same phone numbers and website as on the card. She waited until he drove off, then turned and stepped into the hotel.

It was quiet inside, and she headed straight down to her apartment. She knew Suki would need a quick walk along the back lane before she turned in for the night. Once they'd returned, Helen sat on the sofa and Suki laid her head on her knee.

'What do you think, Suki, should I call Jimmy?'

Suki cocked her head to one side, then raised her paw, the same paw she'd given Helen before. Helen lifted it and inspected it again but could find nothing wrong. It looked intact, with nothing stuck inside, no broken skin or inflammation.

'It's fine, Suki, really. I think you're just after attention.'

Suki padded away to lie under the kitchen table, her caramel limbs spilling to the floor. Helen took her phone from her handbag, mulling over the idea of sending Jimmy a text. It would be a short one, friendly, to ask how he was, to let him know she still wanted to be with him. But when she looked at her phone, there was a long message from him. This both surprised and cheered her. She tapped to open it, but when she read Jimmy's words, she fell back against the sofa in shock.

I'm sorry about the other night, Hel. I wasn't in a good head space

Deadly Dancing at the Seaview Hotel

after the audition. I've made up with Jodie and promised not to interfere. Now I want to make up with you. In fact, I want to do more than that, if you'll let me. I want us to go away on our own, to see if we have a future. And if you want to be with me as much as I want to be with you, please say you'll come. It's on me, I'll pay. I've already checked with Jean and Sally (sorry for being presumptuous, but if I'd asked you first, you'd have used the Seaview as an excuse not to come), and they'll look after the hotel. It's ten days away, Helen. Only ten. The Seaview can survive without you for that long. However, I'm not sure if I can. I don't want to take second place to the hotel for the rest of my life . . . our lives. Anyway, here's the link to where I've been thinking of taking you. It's been a lifelong dream of mine to go. Let me know what you think. I love you and want you, Helen Dexter, more than life itself. All my love, Jimmy xx

Puzzled, Helen clicked on the link. When she saw the website it opened, she felt sick. Her hand began to shake, and her heart sank. Jimmy was planning a ten-day trip to Elvis's home, Graceland, in Memphis, Tennessee. Mixed emotions bubbled up as she tried to process what was spinning around her head and clutching at her heart.

'Oh no, anywhere but Graceland,' she murmured.

Suki stood, walked to her and rested her head on the sofa. Helen stroked the dog's head and looked into her steel-grey eyes.

'Oh Suki. Graceland was Tom's dream. We'd planned to go for our silver wedding anniversary. I swore I'd never go with anyone else. It was his special place, a pilgrimage he'd dreamed of. I can't go with Jimmy; it'd be the ultimate betrayal.'

Suki nuzzled Helen's hand as tears fell down her face.

* * *

When Helen woke the next morning, her heart felt heavy. It took her a moment to realise why.

'Bloody Graceland,' she hissed. She lay still in bed, listening for Jean's dulcet tones singing along to the radio. But there was silence, and that wasn't good. The last time there'd been silence in the morning was when Miriam had poached Jean to work next door. It hadn't lasted long, and Jean had returned of her own accord, relieved to be away from Miriam's criticism and overbearing demands. However, her betrayal had cut Helen deeply. She'd vowed never to take Jean for granted again.

She got out of bed, put on her dressing gown and peered around her bedroom door. Her heart lifted at the sight of Jean arranging rashers of bacon on the grill.

'Morning, Jean,' she called.

Jean didn't reply.

'Morning!' Helen tried again.

There was still no reply.

Helen walked into the kitchen. Suki was lying by the patio doors, looking outside, watching sparrows in the bird bath.

'Jean, are you all right?' she asked.

Jean stopped what she was doing and pushed her glasses up to the bridge of her nose.

'I'm busy, can't you see?' she said curtly.

'Don't you want some music?' Helen offered, walking to the radio.

'Leave it!' Jean snapped. 'I'm all right as I am.'

'What's wrong?' Helen said.

Jean banged the grill pan down. 'You thought I didn't see you last night, but I did! You were spying on me at the Spa, I saw you and Marie, watching me and Bobby.'

Deadly Dancing at the Seaview Hotel

'I was there watching our guests!' Helen bluffed, but she knew Jean would see straight through her. Her shoulders dropped. 'I'm sorry, Jean. You know I'm worried about you. Marie is too. She knows Bobby Tanner and his son, she says they're both villains. Their fight last night in front of everyone was dreadful. I saw them get chucked out. Did you know that Bobby has just come out of prison?'

'Yes, I did,' Jean snapped. 'He says he was innocent, set up.'

'And you believe him?' Helen asked, a little too harshly.

'Yes, I believe him. He's explained things to me and I think he's telling the truth. It's my life, Helen, you've got to let me live it. Speaking of which, I won't be staying on this morning to have coffee as normal, and I haven't brought a cake. I'm off as soon as I've cleaned up after breakfast.'

'No cake?' Helen whispered. Things really were bad.

Jean turned away, and Helen walked back to her bedroom, biting back all the words she wanted to say to protect the woman she loved. The woman who'd shown her nothing but kindness and support from the first day she and Tom had walked into the Seaview. Jean had come with the sale of the hotel, part of its fixtures and fittings, and Helen knew she'd be lost without her. She was her wing-woman, confidante, best friend and surrogate mum. She wanted so much to sit down and tell Jean about Jimmy and Graceland, but she couldn't, not now.

Tears stung Helen's eyes as she showered and dressed, then walked Suki on the beach. She remembered Jodie asking her to tell Jimmy to back off and leave her to make her own decisions. Was she treating Jean the same way? She breathed in the salty air, knowing she had to let her friend make her own decisions and her own mistakes. But at the back of her mind, Jean's inheritance and her lack of experience about what to do with such a large sum loomed. And now she was involved with a man who'd spent time in prison for fraud. A man who'd turned up by coincidence at the very time Jean had revealed the contents of her mum's will. Helen closed her eyes and shuddered.

Chapter 13

Later, back at the Seaview, Helen waited for her guests to come down for breakfast. She heard footsteps on the stairs and looked up to see Bev walking down alone.

'Morning, Bev,' she said. 'You had a visitor last night. He asked me to give you this.'

Bev looked askance at the card Helen handed her.

'I'd prefer it if you could keep this to yourself, Helen,' she said. 'You see, I'm in a spot of bother with a builder, although I never expected him to follow me to Scarborough.'

Helen was taken aback by her frankness. 'Was this the reason you closed your bedroom curtains when you arrived?' she asked.

Bev nodded.

'How did he know you were here?'

'I told him before I left home because I didn't want him to think I was running out on him. But the truth is, Helen . . .' she leaned close and began to whisper, 'I owe him money. Quite a lot of money. He's done work on my home – built a big extension, added a conservatory, installed new windows and landscaped the garden with a patio – but I now find myself financially challenged. It's a temporary blip, I've told him as much, but he clearly doesn't trust me. You see, I'd hoped to have received confirmation by now about Tommy's TV show. I've invested all my savings into getting him this far. Foolishly, I had the work done on my house in anticipation of getting the money from the TV deal. They promised the show would come to us, and I believed them. But as yet they haven't sent the contract. I've never felt so stupid in my life.'

She pulled her phone from her pocket and checked the screen, but it was blank.

'The TV production company said they'd ring with news, one way or the other, while I'm in Scarborough. I need to know if the show is going to Tommy or Rosa, but these people hold all the cards and the power and they're stringing me along.'

'Are they calling Rosa to keep her updated too?' Helen asked.

'No. They'll be dealing with her big-shot agent in London.'

Bev popped her phone back into her bag, then tapped the side of her nose.

'Please, Helen, keep this Mike Skipton business between us. Whatever you do, don't let my brother know that anyone has been asking for me. Tommy isn't aware how deep in debt I've gone to help him achieve his dream of being back on telly. There were countless overnight stays in London to pay for when I was meeting the TV folk.'

'So he doesn't know about your house renovations? Hasn't he seen it? Doesn't he visit you at home?'

Bev narrowed her eyes. 'No, on the rare days off I allow him, he spends his time in the Lake District rather than with me. You must promise not to say a word to him.'

'I won't say anything, I swear,' Helen told her. 'What happens to my guests at the Seaview stays at the Seaview.'

* * *

Deadly Dancing at the Seaview Hotel

Breakfast service was quiet, as Helen was in no mood for chatting with her guests after her run-in with Jean and last night's text message from Jimmy. It felt as if a cloud had landed on her head, and she didn't know how to clear it. Leaving Jean to her clearing-up in the kitchen after breakfast, she and Sally began to clean the stairs, landings and rooms.

'Sally, don't lug the vacuum around in your condition. Let me do it,' she said. She couldn't help but be concerned.

Sally stretched out her back and smiled. 'I'm fine, Helen, really. I'm pregnant, not ill. The minute I can't manage, I'll tell you.'

Helen watched as Sally pulled the vacuum cleaner along the landing. 'In the next couple of months, I'll have to think about who we'll get in to cover for you when you go on maternity leave.'

'I'll ask around at college. There might be someone there who'd like the work,' Sally replied.

'Cheers, Sal.'

They carried on with their work. Sally cleaned Monty's room and Helen headed to Carla's. She knocked on the door to ensure the room was empty before she used her master key. When she entered, she saw the place was awash with clothes. For all Carla's outward elegance and poise, her room was a mess. Jeans and dresses were strewn across the unmade bed, on the floor, over the wardrobe door and flung onto the chair at the dressing table. Helen spotted Carla's beach bag with a dry rolled towel poking from the top, stowed in a corner of the room.

She picked up only those items of clothes she needed to in order to clean the room. She removed dresses and trousers from the floor and hung them over a chair, then moved coats and scarves so she could make the bed. There was a fine line between cleaning a guest's room to make it look presentable and tidying away their personal items, which might make it look like they'd been interfered with. She remembered Monty's neat room from cleaning it the day before. What a contrast between the Curzons, she thought. She wondered if this was the reason they'd asked for separate rooms.

She continued picking up Carla's clothes from the floor: a cocktail dress here, a pair of black stockings there, then a pair of brown slippers with holes in the toes. She stopped and stared. She'd seen those slippers before and knew in an instant they didn't belong to Carla. They were too big, for a start, and that stain on one of them . . . They were the slippers Paul had worn when he came down for breakfast. Puzzled, Helen backed away, as if they might bite. Carla and . . . Paul? How very unlikely, she thought. She tried to rationalise Paul's slippers being underneath Carla's designer dress. Perhaps he had interviewed her for his podcast and forgotten the slippers when he left? She chided herself for being so naive.

'I suppose it takes all sorts,' she muttered.

As she cleaned the window, she noticed Sally watching from the doorway.

'Jean says she hasn't brought in a cake this morning,' Sally said. 'I know she's not up to baking after her mum died, but at least she's been bringing something in from the market. Why has she changed her mind today?'

Helen stopped polishing. The three women had always been close and kept few secrets between them. She thought there was little point starting now.

'Jean and I had a bit of a falling-out,' she explained.

Sally sat down on a chair in the corner of the room. 'Oh no, not again,' she sighed.

Deadly Dancing at the Seaview Hotel

'Don't worry, it's not like last time, when she went to work for Miriam. At least, I hope she won't leave us again. We argued because I saw her and Bobby Tanner last night at the Spa.'

'You *saw* her, what does that mean?'

Helen sank down on the edge of Carla's bed and faced Sally. 'All right, cards-on-the-table time. I spied on her. I wanted to keep my eye on her and Bobby. I'm worried he's after her money. She's grieving for her mum and she's vulnerable, whatever she says. The death of a loved one can take a person to strange places they never thought they'd go to – mentally, I mean. As for him, he's fresh out of prison, serving a sentence for fraud, although he told Jean he was innocent and someone set him up.'

Sally rolled her eyes. 'That's what they all say.'

'Anyway, I've upset her and now she's heading home as soon as she's finished downstairs. That's why there's no cake.'

Sally stood and walked to Helen to give her a hug. Helen accepted it gratefully.

'Both of us will look out for Jean,' Sally said. 'We'll have to be her eyes and ears during this time of grieving when she's blind and deaf to the truth about Bobby. And the sooner we get her back to normal, the sooner we'll have cake again. Gav told me about Frankie fighting with his dad at the Spa. The gossip's all over town. It'll probably be in *The Scarborough Times* this weekend. Oh, speaking of Gav, would it be all right if I left some Gav's Tans VIP opening day vouchers for our guests in each room? He's done publicity like this before for his other businesses and you know what he's like. If something works, he'll repeat it. He likes a routine; he says it makes him feel safe. Anyway, the grand opening's tomorrow and he's offering free spray tans to the first set of customers. It'd be great if those customers were our guests. It'd be fantastic publicity for his new enterprise and for the dance competition.'

'Of course. Put a voucher in each room, on the dressing table, and leave a pile of them downstairs on the table in the hall.'

'Thanks, Helen,' Sally beamed.

Helen finished cleaning Carla's room while Sally was on the landing with the vacuum cleaner. Rosa's room was next.

'All going OK? You feeling all right?' she asked Sally as she passed her.

'Everything's fine, stop worrying about me,' Sally said with a smile.

Helen knocked at Rosa's door, and when there was no reply, she used her master key to enter. The room was tidy and neat. There was a bunch of long-stemmed red roses in a vase on the nightstand next to the bed, with a card. She leaned close to read it. *Roses for my Rosa*, it said, and she wondered who they were from. Frankie Tanner, she supposed.

She felt a headache brewing, and walked around the bed to open the window and let in the warm summer air.

Once all the rooms had been cleaned, she began to lug the vacuum cleaner downstairs to the lounge. But as she passed Bev's room, she could hear raised voices. She felt dismayed. Not another argument between her warring guests! She wondered who Bev was arguing with, but didn't have to wait long to find out. The door to the room was flung open and Rosa stormed out, red in the face. Helen shrank back against the stairwell, pulled a duster from her tabard and busied herself polishing the handrail again.

'You're ruthless and heartless, Rosa de Wolfe!' Bev screamed. 'You know how much Tommy wants that TV show. It means everything to him.'

Deadly Dancing at the Seaview Hotel

And to you, Helen thought, thinking about Bev's house extension that she hadn't yet paid for.

'If the TV show goes to you and not Tommy, I'll make you pay. I swear I'll get my revenge.'

Helen polished the banister furiously. She wondered if she should start whistling or singing, to alert Bev and Rosa she was there.

'I may be ruthless, but at least I'm not twisted with jealousy like you at being unable to dance,' Rosa yelled.

'It wasn't my fault what happened at Blackpool,' Bev growled.

'Let me tell you something, Ballroom Bev.' Rosa took a step forward and leered in Bev's face. 'If the TV show goes to Tommy and not me, I'll go straight to Paul to tell him everything I know about Blackpool. It'll be broadcast to the world on his podcast and your nasty little secret will be revealed.'

Helen twisted a little, trying to hear better, but she knocked the vacuum cleaner, and it clattered down the stairs. Rosa shot her a look, then stormed past, heading upstairs to her room, and Bev slammed her door shut.

The rest of the morning passed without incident, for which Helen gave thanks. The only fly in the ointment was not having Jean to talk to after she'd finished her chores. Sitting at the dining table with Sally wasn't the same. They sat opposite each other in silence, cradling cups of coffee.

'Would you like another digestive?' Helen said, offering Sally a packet of plain, dry biscuits.

Sally shook her head. 'Would you?'

Helen shook her head too. Then she changed her mind, took

one out of the packet, crumbled it in her hand and dropped it on the floor, where it was wolfed down by Suki.

'I miss Jean,' she said.

'Me too,' Sally replied.

They both sighed.

'What are you doing for the rest of the day?' Helen asked.

'I'm off to the hospital for a scan.'

'Nothing wrong, is there?' Helen asked, concerned.

Sally shook her head. 'No, it's just routine. Everything's coming on great with these two,' she said, cradling her stomach. 'After that, I'm helping out at Gav's Tans to get ready for the grand opening tomorrow. Will you come along, Helen? Maybe you could persuade Jean to come too. And it'd be great if the guests could make it. Everyone's talking about them.'

Helen looked at her. 'What do you mean? Who's talking about them, and what are they saying?'

Sally sat up straight in her seat. 'Oh, it's local online chatter, you know, after the fight at the Spa. People are saying that the curse of the dance has followed them to Scarborough. It's piqued everyone's attention.'

Helen thought for a moment.

'I know how hard Gav works. Does he have anyone from the local media coming to cover the opening?'

'Rosie Hyde's coming from *The Scarborough Times* and someone's coming from the radio station,' Sally replied.

'Any podcasters?' Helen asked.

Sally shook her head. 'Not as far as I know.'

'I'll have a word with Paul. He might be able to persuade the dancers to turn up.'

Deadly Dancing at the Seaview Hotel

Sally raised her coffee mug. 'Cheers, Helen, that'd be great.'

Once Sally had left, Helen updated the Seaview accounts and made lists for the cash and carry. Then she went through her email reservations, checking people in and replying to queries.

No, she was sorry, but the Seaview didn't allow pets.

Yes, that was correct, the hotel had indeed won an award for Best Breakfast on the Yorkshire Coast, and she still employed Jean as her chef.

Yes, she could confirm that the sausages at breakfast were locally made.

Yes, it was true that the Seaview now had four stars.

No, they didn't allow stag and hen parties.

She sighed. All this information, and more, was on her website but it never failed to surprise her how many people ignored it.

All done, she took Suki for a walk. The tide was out and the beach almost deserted, so Helen let her off her lead. Once upon a time, when Suki was younger, with more energy, and she'd first come to live at the Seaview after being abandoned at a rescue centre, no further use at winning races, she'd have bounded out of Helen's sight, chasing a breeze on the air. Now she walked sedately at her side. Helen watched her carefully, looking for discomfort in her paw, but saw nothing causing distress.

She walked to a cluster of rocks and sat down. Pulling her phone from her pocket, she reread Jimmy's message. Then she thought again about the relationship advice that both Jean and Marie had given her. Jimmy wouldn't wait for ever. Was it finally time to put her life with Tom behind her and look to the future with Jimmy? Could she really break her vow to her late husband never to go to Graceland without him?

She put her phone away and looked out at the sea. What was the worst that could happen, she mused, if she started a new life with Jimmy? As she gazed across the sands, she saw two figures walking close together at the water's edge. A petite woman with red hair cut in a severe bob and a scruffy man with poor posture. Carla and Paul. Helen had too much on her mind already without getting involved in the tensions and relationships of her guests, but still, she was intrigued.

Chapter 14

When she woke the following morning, Helen was heartened to hear the radio playing in the kitchen. She was even more happy to hear Jean's voice singing along. However, she didn't dare assume that Jean had forgiven her for spying on her at the Spa. She knew she'd upset her and would need to be careful about what she said when it came to Bobby Tanner.

'Morning, Jean!' she said cheerfully when she left her bedroom and walked into the kitchen.

Jean was busy whisking eggs in a porcelain bowl. 'Morning, love,' she replied with an attempt at a smile.

'Everything all right?' Helen asked.

Jean set the bowl on the kitchen top. 'Everything's fine, Helen. No need to pussyfoot around. You and I will always be friends. But please never spy on me again, and never criticise my choice of men.'

'So you're still seeing him, then?' Helen crossed her fingers behind her back, hoping that Jean would tell her no.

'Of course I'm still seeing him.'

She uncrossed her fingers.

'He's a nice man, Helen. You'd like him if you got to know him. Anyway, I thought I'd bake one of my chocolate fudge cakes today.'

Helen felt like giving Jean a hug, but she knew she wouldn't be thanked, so she stayed where she was. Jean and her cake-baking were back! The world had tilted to normal.

'Bobby's going to give me financial advice about my inheritance,' Jean said.

The world was knocked off kilter again.

'Oh Jean, are you sure he's the right person to ask? Sally said Gav knows some financial advisers, so maybe he could give you a recommendation. You've only just met Bobby; surely you're not going to trust him with your windfall?'

Jean picked up the bowl and began furiously whisking the eggs again, putting an end to their conversation. Suki padded across the living room and looked up at Helen.

'All right, Suki, let's go for a walk.'

The dog walked straight to the apartment door.

'Are you coming to the grand opening of Gav's Tans this morning, Jean?' Helen asked as she gathered Suki's collar and lead.

'No, love. Bobby says I have to spend the day with him,' Jean replied.

'Would you jump off a cliff if Bobby said? When did you start to let people push you around?' Helen muttered darkly. If Jean heard her, she didn't respond.

Before she headed outdoors, the local news began on the radio with a report of a power cut affecting businesses along Huntriss Row. Helen paid it no mind and walked outside with the dog. She was saddened to see that the weather had taken a turn for the worse. Gone was the blue sky and sunshine of the previous days. In its place were dark clouds over a grey sea.

Deadly Dancing at the Seaview Hotel

'Looks like a storm's on its way, Suki,' she said as she walked down the cliff path. Suki, as always, said little by way of reply.

When she returned to the Seaview, she spotted Carla letting herself into the hotel, wrapped in the changing robe she'd seen her wearing before. She noticed immediately that the woman's hair was dry. So much for Carla saying she never wore a bathing hat when she went for a swim.

'Couldn't fancy dipping my toes into the North Sea, Suki, never mind my whole body, could you?' she said, but Suki kept her own counsel.

While Helen waited with Sally outside the dining room for the guests to come down to breakfast, she cast her critical landlady's eye over the hallway. The skirting boards and doors looked fine. They weren't too chipped and wouldn't need another coat of paint this year, for which she was grateful. It was always an upheaval having decorators in. She couldn't imagine what Miriam was going through, having her hotel fumigated. She glanced at the wallpaper, which was clean with no peeling edges. The carpet looked fine too. Then something caught her eye: a tiny red bead, lodged between the carpet and the skirting board. It was on the tip of her tongue to chastise Sally for not vacuuming more thoroughly, but then she thought better of it. Sally had more pressing things on her mind, and besides, it was only a bead. She popped it in her tabard pocket.

After breakfast had been served, rooms were cleaned. This time Sally cleaned Carla's room and Helen entered Monty's. His room was again pristine, with the bed made and clothes put away in the wardrobe. Even the drinking glass by his bedside had been rinsed out. He had positioned mirrors on the windowsill, the bedside table and the dressing table, although there was already a full-length mirror attached to the wall, and another above the bathroom sink. Helen paid them no mind. Monty was a dancer, an entertainer, and she expected he wore as much make-up as any of the female dancers. She knew how much Jimmy wore when he performed as Elvis. Besides, Monty, she already knew, was obsessed with his image.

The next room to clean was Paul's. Helen knocked at the door, expecting no reply, assuming that Paul would be out with the dancers, who were being interviewed by local radio that morning. So she got quite a surprise when he opened the door. She got an even bigger surprise when she saw that he was crying.

'Paul, what's wrong?' Then she stepped back, keeping her distance. 'Sorry, I'm not prying. I was trying to come in to clean,' she added quickly.

Paul opened the door wide and indicated for her to enter. He sank onto the bed and Helen stood beside him as he dabbed his eyes with a tissue.

'She's started seeing someone else,' he sobbed.

Helen's brain went into overdrive with an image of Paul's slippers on Carla's bedroom floor. Did he mean Carla? She didn't dare ask. Fortunately, she didn't need to, as Paul began his sorry tale.

'I loved her, Helen. I loved Rosa with all my heart.'

Helen blinked hard. Rosa? Well, this was a surprise.

'There wasn't anything I wouldn't do for her. I was her puppet. I adored her. She was always my favourite podcast guest. I'd had a crush on her for years, but she never cared about me. Just when I dared to get my hopes up that she might feel something for me, it turned out that she'd been using me to reach her fans via my podcast. And last night I discovered that she'd started a new relationship, with Frankie Tanner of all people. The man behind the dance competition. Of course it had to be him; he's got the looks, the money, the power. Oh, why am I so stupid? Why didn't I see the signs?'

He looked imploringly at Helen in much the same way that Suki looked at her when she was hoping for crumbs from the table. Helen was at a loss. She gave Paul a hug, then pulled quickly away from his unpleasant body odour.

'How did you discover she was seeing Frankie?' she asked.

'It happened last night, at the Spa. All she could talk about was him. That's what the fight was about. Bobby doesn't like Rosa, and he lost his temper with Frankie. Oh Helen, I'm churned up. I wish I'd never met her.'

Helen glanced at Paul's feet, which were clad in black socks. One sock had a hole where his big toe poked through. He caught her looking.

'And to cap it all off, now I've lost my slippers. You haven't seen them anywhere, have you?'

Helen kept schtum. Paul began to wail, then banged his fist on the bed.

'I'm hurt, Helen, really hurt. I feel foolish at being taken for a mug. I've wasted my time holding a candle for Rosa when she never cared a jot about me. But I'm angry with her too, so angry that I'm afraid . . . horribly afraid of what I might do when I see her again.'

Chapter 15

'Would you like me to bring you anything?' Helen asked. 'A cup of tea? Coffee? Something from the bar to steady your nerves?'

Paul shook his head and pulled another tissue from his pocket. He wiped his eyes, then blew his nose.

'I miss my slippers,' he said, raising both legs off the end of the bed.

Helen bit her tongue. 'I'm sure they'll turn up,' she said. 'Will you be all right if I leave you now? I really must finish cleaning.'

Paul waved his damp tissue in her direction. 'Go, I'll be fine. I'll try to take my mind off things by working on a podcast about last night's events at the Spa.'

'Will you be podcasting about the fight between Frankie and his dad?' Helen asked.

Paul looked at her, eyes wide. 'Of course. I broadcast everything that goes on when I'm with this troupe of dancers. It's all I know how to do. It's what I've done for years. Even after Blackpool . . .' He paused and wiped his nose again. 'After the glitter-ball smash in Blackpool, I broadcast the events to the world. Mind you, there were certain things I couldn't say, because no one knows which dancer tried to bribe the judge.'

'Is there anyone you suspect?' Helen asked, pushing gently, as Paul seemed in the mood to talk.

Deadly Dancing at the Seaview Hotel

'Well, Rosa . . .' A sob caught in his throat as he said her name. 'She said she knew who it was, and she was about to tell me. I never found out why she didn't. Her revelation might have been podcasting gold, with the potential to send my listener ratings through the roof. And it's all about ratings, in my business, along with clicks for the website. Ratings and clicks bring in pounds and pence. I'm sponsored by advertisers who get their products aired on my website and social media.'

'Ah, I did wonder if there was any money in it,' Helen mused.

'A lot of the dancers are sponsored too, by clothes designers or hair and make-up suppliers. I don't podcast for the money, though,' Paul said, placing his hand on his heart. 'I do it because I love dancing. I love the people who dance. I love the whole dance world, the glitter and glam, spangles and sparkle. I adore it. But since Blackpool, the shine has begun to wear off. I'm sure you must have heard about what happened there. They're calling it the curse of the dance; that's why the competition is being held in Scarborough this year.'

'I'd heard something about that,' Helen said. 'Don't you dance yourself?'

Paul shook his head. 'Good heavens, no. I'm out of shape, always have been. Can't even walk up the stairs in your hotel without getting out of breath. I prefer a more sedentary lifestyle, and podcasting suits me. I can hide behind the microphone, adopt a persona, and no one knows I'm just ordinary.'

'How did you get involved with this troupe of dancers?' she asked, wondering if he'd open up about Carla. His slippers in her room were bugging her.

'Well, I met Ballroom Bev years ago, when she was queen of the quickstep, and we've been friends ever since. She was the one who invited me to come on the road with her and Tommy, and through them I met Carla, Monty and Rosa. When they started touring the country to compete in dance shows, I began tagging along with my microphone to record snippets from their dancing life. I put those sound bites on a podcast, and people seemed to love them. Once I started making money from the ads online, I was able to do this full-time.'

'Where did you work before?'

'I sold fruit at Darlington market,' Paul replied. 'It took a while to build up my listeners, but now they number hundreds of thousands each week. I'm sponsored by advertisers who want to tap into that market and I make money doing what I love. It's been non-stop since I left the market. I'm self-employed now. I've even been thinking about selling merchandise, such as T-shirts with the podcast logo on it.'

'That sounds like a good plan,' Helen said. 'Now, I'd better get on.'

He stood and held the door open for her. 'Thanks for listening, Helen,' he said. 'And if there is anything I can do in return for your kindness, please let me know.'

She was about to walk away, but now she hesitated.

'Actually, there is,' she said. 'My cleaner's husband is opening a new tanning salon today, at noon. I realise it's short notice, but do you think there's any chance you could sway the dancers to come along to the opening? It'd be great publicity for the competition.'

Paul managed a weak smile. 'They already plan to attend, as do I. We saw the vouchers that had been left for us in our rooms. We'll see you there.'

Deadly Dancing at the Seaview Hotel

He closed the door, but before Helen could walk away, she heard him crying again. She paused, wondering if she should go back to give him words of advice or another hug. But the mystery of his slippers being in Carla's room wouldn't leave her mind, and so she left him to it.

After the rooms had been cleaned, Helen and Sally headed downstairs for morning coffee and a catch-up with Jean. Jean handed over thick slices of her soft, moist, dark, gooey, heavenly scented chocolate cake. Helen and Sally smiled at each other. Sally bit into her slice, but then her face fell.

'I'm sorry, Jean, I can't eat this. My pregnancy hormones are doing strange things to my taste buds. It doesn't taste right to me.' She pushed her plate away.

Helen lifted her own slice of cake to her lips. The delicious texture filled her mouth as she chewed, but then suddenly something tasted off, and she too pushed her plate away.

'I'm sorry, Jean, I can't eat it either.'

'What's wrong with it?' Jean snapped.

'Try it,' Helen said.

Jean lifted her slice and took a bite. Helen and Sally watched as she chewed, and saw her grimace as she swallowed.

'Damn and blast! I can't believe it! I forgot to put the sugar in!' she cried. She gathered the plates and walked off to the kitchen. When she returned, she kept her gaze on the table.

'Jean, you're not thinking straight, love. You need time to grieve your mum,' Helen said.

'I'm fine, Helen. I forgot the sugar, that's all. It's not the end of the world.'

'It feels like it is,' Sally muttered.

There was silence at the table for a few moments, then Helen decided it was best to change the subject. She bit her tongue against saying anything about Bobby Tanner, and decided instead to talk about the grand opening of Gav's Tans.

'Gav's so excited!' Sally said.

'Is little Gracie coming along?' Helen asked. 'I haven't seen her in ages.'

Sally shook her head. 'No. It would mean taking her out of school, and I don't want to do that. Her class is doing a project on dinosaurs and it's all she talks about.'

She looked shyly across the table at Helen.

'Did you . . . did you manage to ask any of the dancers if they might like to come along to the opening?'

Helen smiled widely. 'Yes, I spoke to Paul the podcaster this morning and he said everyone is already planning to attend.'

'Perfect! Thanks, Helen,' Sally replied.

'It's going to be great publicity for the dancers and for Gav,' Helen said.

Sally drained her coffee and stood from the table.

'I've got to go and get ready for the grand opening, but I'll use the loo before I go. I'm always needing the loo at the minute.'

'And I'm off too,' Jean announced.

'To meet Bobby?' Helen asked.

Jean held her gaze. 'Yes, to meet Bobby. Do you have a problem with that?'

Helen held up her hands in mock surrender. 'I'm saying no more.'

'Good!' Jean snapped. She thrust her arms into her coat, picked up her handbag and followed Sally out of the door.

Deadly Dancing at the Seaview Hotel

Left alone with Suki, Helen looked at the dog. 'What do you reckon, Suki? Should I trust Jean to know what she's doing?'

Suki said nothing, just cocked her head to one side.

Helen swiped her phone into life and dealt with some enquiries.

Yes, we have en suite rooms.

When the next question came in, she shook her head in disbelief. For heaven's sake, the clue was in the name of the hotel.

Yes, there are sea-view rooms.

Then she sent a quick message to Jimmy.

Hi Jimmy, sorry for my late reply, it's busy here. We need to talk . . . Can we meet? Love, Helen xx

Jimmy's message pinged back immediately.

I'm working today but I'll ring you as soon as I'm free xx

Once she'd finished her admin, Helen put her phone and laptop away, glanced at the clock on the wall and decided to start getting ready to head to Gav's new enterprise. She chose a smart navy trouser suit with a white lacy blouse and comfortable flat navy shoes, then brushed her hair, touched up her make-up and gave herself one last look in the mirror before heading out.

As she walked along Queen Street, she saw a group of people milling around outside the salon. Her heart lifted at the sight. Sally was handing out flyers to passing tourists and shoppers, while Gav bounced around like an excited puppy. He was in his mid thirties, tall and lean, with dark wavy hair that flopped around his pleasant, friendly face. His eyes lit up with excitement at the sight of the dancers, who'd walked from the Seaview. Helen saw Paul with his microphone at the edge of the group, trying to pin down Gav for an interview, and failing. Gav had too much energy to stay still for long. Then she saw Carla. Or at least she saw her red hair, as it was hard to miss, contrasting with her sunshine-yellow dress.

'You look stunning,' she greeted her. 'What a beautiful outfit.'

Carla smiled sweetly. 'It's one of the dresses I'm sponsored to wear. I thought I'd advertise it, you know, in case we get our pictures in the press or on social media today.'

Monty stood beside Carla, looking as handsome as ever. He wore a dark suit with a waistcoat, and a tie in the exact shade of yellow as Carla's dress. He kept turning to admire his reflection in the window of Gav's Tans, slicking his hair behind his ears with his fingers.

'Where are the TV cameras?' he asked, looking around desperately. 'There will be TV cameras, won't there? Make sure they get my best side!'

On the other side of the group stood Bev and Tommy, heads together as always. Bev kept glancing nervously at her phone. Helen walked towards her.

'Still no news on the TV show?'

Bev shot a look at Rosa. 'Nothing yet,' she muttered darkly.

Suddenly Gav was there, bounding up to Helen, kissing her on both cheeks. 'Morning, missus, it's good to see you, and thanks for coming. Ooh! Gav's excited today. Thank you for bringing your dancing guests.'

Helen motioned towards Paul. 'Don't thank me, thank Paul the podcaster. He's the one who convinced everyone to turn out.'

Gav waved at Paul, then turned back to Helen. 'Their pictures are going to look great in *The Scarborough Times*, with such colourful clothes. Rosie Hyde, the journalist from the paper, is here somewhere.'

Deadly Dancing at the Seaview Hotel

Gav glanced around.

'Rosie! Your man Gav's over here!' he yelled.

Helen spotted Rosie in the crowd. She carried an oversized black bag over her shoulder, and wore jeans, trainers and a black denim jacket. Her long brown hair fell around her pale face.

Gav turned to Helen with a cheesy grin. 'Sorry, Helen, I've got to go and sort out the big opening. I think it'll be right up your street.' He gave her a cheeky wink. 'Oh, Gav's in demand this morning! Will you stay for a free spray tan?'

'No, thanks, Gav, I'm not a spray tan sort of girl.' Helen shook her head.

Carla laughed. 'You might not be, but I am.'

'Me too!' Monty added, straightening his tie.

'I want a tan,' Rosa said, stepping forward.

'If they're having free spray tans, I demand Tommy gets one too. It'll look great for the dance competition at the Spa.' Bev nudged her brother forward. 'Tommy, get in the queue for a tan.'

As the dancers lined up outside the salon, Gav clapped his hands to get everyone's attention.

'Ladies and gentlemen, thank you for coming today. I'd like to say a special thank you to my wife, Sally, for all her hard work and support. And I'd also like to thank the Mayor of Scarborough for attending.' He gestured to a man in the crowd, and Helen craned her neck to see him. He was an old friend of Tom's, and she waved.

'I'd also like to thank our special guest, who has agreed to perform at the official opening. Ladies and gentlemen, put your hands together for the one and only, direct from Las Vegas via the A64 . . . Mr Jimmy Brown as Elvis!'

Glenda Young

Helen couldn't believe her eyes as Jimmy stepped out from the crowd, resplendent in his white jumpsuit and dyed black hair. His hips were wiggling and his leg was jiggling as he raised a microphone to his lips. He saw her immediately, and as he began to sing, he made his way to her, as if performing just for her. Helen felt her knees go weak when he winked.

The beat of the music proved too infectious for the dancers, who started to move and sway. Even the mayor was clapping along. Podcaster Paul moved around the crowd, trying to record what was going on. A bus went by, and passengers filmed the scene on their phones. By now, the dancers had arranged themselves into couples. Carla and Monty were jiving, while Tommy and Rosa also gave a sterling performance. If Helen hadn't known about the animosity between them, she'd have thought them the perfect dance team. A crowd gathered around them, clapping and cheering, some trying to join in with the steps of the jive.

The mayor walked towards Helen with his hand outstretched. 'May I have the pleasure of this dance, Mrs Dexter?' he asked.

'Why, yes, of course,' she said, taking his hand.

The memory of the jive steps came back to her easily, a warm reminder of the past. Her feet knew exactly where to go: side, side, back, replace, over and over again.

'When I was a lad, I loved dancing so much they used to call me Boogie-Woogie Billy,' the mayor laughed as he twirled Helen under his arm. 'My whole family loved music. Even the sewing machine was a Singer! Did you know my dad was once crowned Best Pub Pianist in Britain?'

The song ended, and applause filled the air. Gav handed Jimmy a pair of scissors and they both posed for photographs, then Jimmy sliced the ribbon.

'I now declare Gav's Tans open!' he called. He received another round of applause. 'Thankyouverymuch,' he drawled, bowing to the crowd.

As Jimmy began to sing again – an Elvis ballad this time – the dancers trooped inside the salon. Tommy went first, followed by Bev, then Monty, Carla and Rosa. Paul brought up the rear with his microphone, podcasting live from the event.

'I need to record sound from inside the salon,' he said as he walked past Gav sitting at the reception desk.

Gav, assisted by Sally, gave everyone a towel and directed them to the spray tan booths.

'Ladies to the right, gents to the left,' Sally called.

'The booths are easy to operate, but if you need help, shout for your man Gav,' Gav said. 'We're not using the spray tan guns yet as we haven't recruited staff to operate them. It's just the booths for free tans today!'

Helen tried to peer inside but couldn't see anything except Gav waltzing Sally around the salon, joy on both of their faces. Jimmy continued singing, one Elvis song merging into another, and she felt herself relaxing into the day, enjoying the music as thoughts of Graceland, her past with Tom and her future with Jimmy flickered through her mind. Then Paul came to stand beside her, and thrust the microphone into her face.

'How do you feel, Helen, knowing that the dancers helped out at the opening of your friend's new business today?'

'It's wonderful. Thank you for arranging it,' she said.

He smiled at her as he spoke into the mic. 'That was the voice of Mrs Helen Dexter, landlady at the Seaview Hotel,' he said before walking away.

The music finally came to an end. Helen was about to approach Jimmy to arrange to meet him later when Sally ran out of the salon, screaming. Helen caught her before she collapsed to her knees. Her heart plummeted.

'What is it, love? Are your babies all right?' she cried.

Sally's face was ashen. She caught her breath and pointed to the salon.

'In there . . . something's happened.'

Helen held her hand and supported her back inside. Gav was on the phone at reception.

'Ambulance and police. Now. Gav's Tans, Queen Street,' he barked.

She saw Bev holding on to Tommy. Carla and Monty had their arms around each other, tears streaming down their faces, streaking their newly applied fake tans.

'What's happened?' Helen cried.

It was Monty who turned to her.

'It's Rosa . . .' he sobbed. 'She's in there. She's dead, Helen. Rosa's dead.'

Chapter 16

The sound of wailing sirens filled the air as Gav ushered everyone from the salon, pulling on their clothes and stuffing shirts into trousers.

Carla was still crying, and when Monty pulled a linen handkerchief from his top pocket, Helen assumed he would do the decent thing and hand it to his wife. Instead, he used it to dab at the fake tan on his face.

'I must look a state,' he moaned.

Carla turned to him with a face like thunder. 'There's a dead woman in there, have some respect. There are more important things now than how you look.'

Monty had the good grace to look contrite.

Helen hugged Sally to her. 'Come on, let's find you somewhere to sit down. You're in shock. You need to look after yourself.'

A kindly shopkeeper from Mrs Lofthouse's Book Emporium brought out a wooden chair for Sally to sit on. Helen thanked him. Jimmy walked over to them and wrapped his arm around Helen's shoulders.

'Are you all right?'

Helen couldn't speak, so she just shook her head.

Then Gav appeared. Sally stood, and she and Gav held each other tight, sobbing loudly.

Within moments, a police van and an unmarked car had pulled up at the salon. Two uniformed policewomen jumped out of the van and immediately worked to disperse the crowd.

'Everyone back, please,' one of them ordered.

Then the door of the police car opened, and two plain-clothes men stepped out. One was tall with grey hair, and the other was short, with a round, plump face and brown hair. Helen immediately recognised both. The taller of the two men was Detective Sergeant Paul Hutchinson, and the other was his sidekick, Detective Constable David Hall.

'Who's in charge here?' DS Hutchinson demanded.

'Me. Gav,' said Gav. 'And my wife, Sally.'

'Gav, Sally, show me inside,' the DS ordered.

Sally began to shake. 'I can't go back in.'

Helen walked to her and took her in her arms.

'Look after her for me,' Gav pleaded.

'I will,' Helen replied as she tried to soothe Sally.

DS Hutchinson and DC Hall disappeared inside with Gav.

The policewomen were securing an area around the salon with blue and white tape. Rosie Hyde, the go-getting reporter from *The Scarborough Times*, tried asking questions, but the officers were having none of it. Helen peered over Sally's shoulder at Paul. He'd turned off his microphone and was looking forlorn. The dancers' faces and necks and the backs of their hands were a shade more orange than they were before they'd gone into the salon. But when Helen spotted Tommy, he looked ashen.

From a distance came the sound of another siren. When it pierced Queen Street, Helen saw that it was an ambulance. DC Hall left the salon and walked to the driver.

Deadly Dancing at the Seaview Hotel

'It's too late. This is one for the coroner, not the hospital,' he muttered, loud enough for Helen to hear. Nonetheless, the paramedics followed him into the salon.

Sally began sobbing again. Helen pulled her close, and Jimmy shifted uncomfortably in his Elvis suit at her side.

'I wish there was something I could do. I feel useless, especially dressed like this.'

After a few more minutes, the paramedics left the building. Gav approached them and asked them to check Sally over.

'She's pregnant, with twins,' he told them.

They took her to sit inside the ambulance, and Helen watched as they checked her blood pressure. Once they were certain she was fine, they drove off, leaving her in Gav's arms. Then Gav was called back into the salon. The policewomen continued to stand guard. Finally, Helen saw movement at the door.

'They're coming out,' she whispered to Sally, who dried her eyes and turned to look.

DS Hutchinson emerged first, followed by DC Hall.

'It's all right, Gav's coming,' Helen said.

But when they saw him, they realised it wasn't all right at all. He was handcuffed to DC Hall.

'No!' Sally screamed.

Gav turned to her with tears in his eyes. 'It's all right, Sal. Ring my mum, would you? Tell Gracie not to worry. I'll be home in time for tea.'

'I wouldn't bet on it, son,' DC Hall said as he manoeuvred him into the back of the car.

Sally wriggled free from Helen's embrace and ran forward. 'You can't arrest Gav, it's not his fault! He's done nothing wrong!' But she ended up screaming at thin air as the car sped away.

Rosie Hyde approached with her notepad in one hand and her phone in the other. Helen turned on her.

'Shame on you, Rosie. I thought you were decent. Leave her alone, you can see she's in no fit state.'

Rosie handed Helen a card from her bag. 'When she wants to put her side of the story across, get in touch. She's a pretty girl and this is a good story with a strong local angle. I can offer her a double-page feature. I might even sell it to the women's magazines. Could get a Netflix series out of it if we're lucky.'

'Please leave us alone, Rosie,' Helen said, but she took the card anyway and slid it into her handbag.

Rosie began to walk off, but not very far. She stopped in front of Bev and Tommy, firing questions. What had they seen? Who had died? And how? One of the policewomen moved her on, as another police van drove along Queen Street.

'What'll happen now?' Helen asked the officer.

'The premises will be secured and the body taken away. It's an unnatural death, and in such circumstances we arrange for a funeral director working for the coroner to take the body to the mortuary. That's all I can say for now.'

The second policewoman began taking particulars from those who'd been inside the salon with Rosa.

'They're all staying with me at the Seaview Hotel on King's Parade,' Helen explained. 'They're my guests. I'm Helen Dexter.'

'They'll need to accompany us to the station. I'm sure DS Hutchinson will be in touch with you for any background information that you can provide.'

Deadly Dancing at the Seaview Hotel

'You'll need to get in touch with the dead woman's boyfriend to let him know what's happened,' Helen said, her mind spinning over itself. She racked her brains. She felt sure Jean had said something about Bobby living on Paradise Mews. She passed on this information, although she had no idea if Frankie shared a home with his dad.

'We'll check it out. Now, all of you,' the policewoman pointed at the dancers and Sally, 'come with me. We'll need to take you to the station for questioning. The rest of you move along, please.'

'Can I stay with Sally?' Helen pleaded.

'No, but you could make your own way to the station and wait in reception for her.'

'I'll do that,' Helen said immediately.

'I'll come too,' added Jimmy.

The policewoman eyed his white jumpsuit. 'Won't be the first time Elvis has been in the building. We get a lot of stag dos in Scarborough, and some of them dress like you.'

Helen watched as the dancers were loaded into the van. Tommy helped Bev up. Monty climbed in without offering to help Carla. Paul lumbered in after them. Helen kissed Sally on the cheek.

'Don't worry, Sally. Jimmy and I will be at the station, waiting in reception.'

'Will you call my mum for me? She'll need to pick up Gracie from school.'

'Of course I will, love.'

The van drove off, and Helen and Jimmy began the short walk to the police station. As they walked up Eastborough, through the centre of town, Helen became aware of passers-by staring at Jimmy.

'Give us a song, Elvis!' a woman shouted.

'Elvis the Pelvis!' a man called.

'It was all in his knees, not his pelvis,' Helen muttered darkly.

'What?' Jimmy said, head down, oblivious to the comments and remarks.

'I said Elvis should have been called "Elvis the Knees" not "Elvis the Pelvis", although I realise it doesn't rhyme.'

Jimmy looked at her as if she'd gone mad, and so she explained.

'When you're dancing, you need to move your knees in order to move your hips. Watch and learn, Jimmy. Next time you see Elvis dancing on TV, notice how the movement starts at his knees and goes all the way up to his hips.'

'How can you think of Elvis's knees at a time like this?' he said, aghast.

'Sorry. It's a distraction to stop my mind from going over what's just happened.'

More catcalls kept coming, including one that wounded Jimmy – 'You're a rubbish lookalike!' – and so they hurried on.

'Why didn't you tell me you were working at Gav's salon today?' Helen asked him as they walked.

'Because we've hardly been speaking, remember?' Jimmy shot back.

They carried on in silence, turning right at the Rendezvous Café and walking along Northway to reach the large, imposing building that was Scarborough police station.

In reception, they were directed to sit on plastic chairs. Helen took her phone out and rang Sally's mum. Brenda was a taciturn woman, not given to conversation. Helen had had the misfortune of working with her when she'd employed her at the Seaview while Sally went on honeymoon with Gav. She'd taken her on as a favour to Sally, but after suffering Brenda's dour demeanour, it was a favour she wouldn't repeat. The experience had left her so scarred that it hadn't crossed her mind to consider hiring the woman again while Sally was on maternity leave. She'd employ anyone rather than Brenda.

'Brenda, it's Helen from the Seaview. Listen, love, it's nothing to worry about, but Sally's been . . . er . . . well, she's indisposed.'

Jimmy raised his black eyebrows at her.

'Yes, the babies are fine. There's no problem there. She's running late, that's all. She's asked if you could pick up Gracie from school and look after her until later.'

'Tell her the truth,' Jimmy whispered, but Helen put a finger to her lips to stop him from saying more.

'No, like I said, it's nothing to worry about. She's been held up, that's all. I'm sure she'll be in touch very soon . . . Right you are, Brenda, thank you. Bye.'

She ended the call and sank back in her chair.

'I hate telling lies, but there was no way I was going to upset her. If she knew what had happened, she might panic, and she's got Gracie to look after. Besides, it's not my place to tell her. It should come from Sally and Gav.'

She slid her phone into her pocket. A clock on the wall ticked loudly. Thoughts about Rosa ran wild in her mind.

After an hour's wait, Gav and Sally were released. Both looked as shell-shocked as Helen felt.

'What happened?' she asked.

She saw Gav and Sally exchange a nervous glance. Gav shook his head, then laid his arm around Sally's shoulders. He looked from Helen to Jimmy, then back again.

'It looks like respiratory failure,' he said in a flat voice. 'We think Rosa was spray-tanned to death.'

Chapter 17

Helen's jaw dropped in shock. Her blood ran cold. She put a hand across her mouth.

'Oh my word, that's awful.'

Her words came out in a whisper. She felt Jimmy's arm against hers, holding her, steadying her. When she finally regained her composure, she turned to Sally.

'Would you like us to take you back to the Seaview?' she offered, but both Gav and Sally said no.

'I need to pick up Gracie from Mum. Then I want to collapse in front of the telly with a big cup of tea,' Sally told her.

'After we get you checked over by the GP,' Gav said.

Sally rolled her eyes. 'I'm fine, Gav. Didn't the paramedics say so?'

'Are they pressing charges against either of you?' Jimmy asked.

'Not against Sally,' Gav said. 'But they want me to go back to answer more questions. There was talk of having me . . .' He faltered, which was unusual for him. Sally laid her hand on his arm. 'Arrested,' he added.

'No!' Helen cried. 'They can't do that!'

'They can, and they will, if they find enough evidence to prove I was negligent in any way with the installation of the tanning booth. There's health and safety to be considered, to see if the booth was faulty. I'll have to get in touch with the installer, the manufacturer and my insurance company. One thing's for sure, though, Gav's Tans won't be getting any customers.'

'Oh, I'm sure you will, in time,' Jimmy said, trying to gee Gav up. However, Gav's bottom lip began to wobble.

'No, Jimmy. After someone's died like that poor woman . . .' He dropped his gaze to Jimmy's blue suede shoes. 'I'll never open the salon again. I'll work with the police investigation into what went wrong with the machine . . .'

'If that's what caused Rosa's death,' Helen chipped in.

'. . . and then I'll sell the place. I'll gut it, chuck everything away, remove every trace of what happened, then I'll put the building up for sale.'

He slipped his hand into Sally's, and they turned towards the door that led to the street.

'Sally, take as much time off work as you need,' Helen said.

Sally smiled weakly, then the pair of them walked outside.

'Shall we wait for the guests to be released too?' Jimmy asked.

'No, let's go back to the Seaview. You need to get changed out of your Elvis suit. Where are your proper clothes?'

He slapped his hand against his forehead. 'Inside the salon,' he groaned. 'We've got no chance of being allowed in there to collect them. The police have got the place taped off.'

Helen took his hand. 'Don't worry. You can wear my dressing gown when we get back to the Seaview, or you can stay dressed like Elvis for the rest of the night.'

Jimmy smiled mischievously. 'I could wiggle my knees all the way up to my pelvis if you like.'

Helen tried to smile, but the shock of what she'd heard about Rosa had hit her hard.

'I need to stay alert in case the guests return and want me to open the bar. They might need a stiff drink after the police finish with them. And I want to hear the full story of what happened to Rosa. Oh Jimmy, there was talk about a curse on the dance competition after someone was injured last time it was held. It feels like the curse has followed the dancers from the west coast to the east.'

'From Los Angeles to New York?'

'No, from Blackpool to Scarborough.'

She looked at Jimmy and saw his cheeks blush pink, even through his thick Elvis make-up.

When they reached the Seaview, Suki was pacing the floor of the apartment, her teeth chattering. Jimmy stopped dead in the doorway, staring at her.

'What's wrong with your dog? Is she having a seizure?'

Helen immediately clipped Suki's lead to her collar.

'No, she's trying to tell me she needs a walk in the fresh air, if you know what I mean. I'll not be long, Jimmy. I'll just walk her up and down the back lane. And if you want to wear my dressing gown, it's hanging on the back of my bedroom door. Help yourself. Back in a min.'

When she returned with a much calmer Suki, she laughed out loud at the sight of Jimmy in her dressing gown. It wasn't a particularly girlie one, just a plain white waffle robe tied with a belt. But it looked comical on him as it was too tight across his muscled shoulders and too short on his long legs. He tried to close it over his chest and thighs.

'I've left my boxer shorts on, in case the guests come back. You might need me to come upstairs with you to talk to them.'

Deadly Dancing at the Seaview Hotel

Helen was glad to see he'd scrubbed off the Elvis make-up.

'I'll be fine on my own, Jimmy. It's best if you stay down here, looking like that.'

'Are you sure? Seems a big job for you to cope with. They'll be upset at the death of their friend.'

'I'll cope, Jimmy. Don't push me.'

He held up a hand. 'Sorry, Helen. I'm being overprotective with you, aren't I? Just like Jodie accused me of being with her.' He leaned back on the sofa. 'Consider this me butting out and not interfering.'

'Perfect,' Helen said, and she leaned over and kissed him on the lips.

As they kissed, Jimmy gently pulled Helen down to the sofa, where she snuggled at his side.

'Did you click on the link I sent you?' he asked.

'How can you think of Graceland at a time like this?' she cried.

He shrugged. 'For the same reason you were thinking of Elvis's knees. It's a distraction to take my mind off what's been a horrible day.'

Helen sighed. 'Graceland, eh?' she murmured. 'I don't know, Jimmy. It seems too big, too important. Why don't we go away for a weekend somewhere in England instead? Northumberland's nice.'

'Too rural,' Jimmy said.

'What about London?'

'Too many people. I lived there, remember. I have no wish to go back.'

Helen stood and walked around the kitchen, picking up tea towels and bundling them into the washing machine.

'Scotland?'

'Too cold.'

'Wales?'

'Too hilly.'

'Dublin's nice.'

'Too many stag parties,' Jimmy complained.

Three blue tabards hung on pegs by the door, and Helen decided to chuck them in the wash too.

'How about a weekend in Brighton?'

'I'd prefer to stay in Scarborough,' Jimmy replied.

She delved into the pocket of each tabard before placing them in the washing machine. Sally had a terrible habit of leaving tissues in her pockets. She didn't find tissues, but she did find the red bead that she'd picked up from the carpet upstairs. It was too pretty to throw out, too sparkly, so she put it in the fruit bowl next to three oranges, then switched on the machine.

'How about Norfolk?' she said as she made her way back to Jimmy.

He thought for a moment, then dismissed that too, along with five more British resorts she suggested.

'Then let's go abroad, but somewhere closer to home, like Spain or Portugal,' she said.

Jimmy sighed. 'No, Helen. Those are the places I work. I know every Elvis tribute bar in every European country. Please let me take you to Graceland. It's something I've always wanted to do, and I can't think of anything better than going with you. It'll give us time to be alone together. No Jean, Sally, Seaview or Suki.'

The dog gave a strange guttural cry, and Helen had to stroke her head to calm her. All the while, she struggled with her reply. She didn't want to say a flat-out no to Jimmy because it would sound as if she was denying any chance of a future with him. But if she said yes, she'd be reneging on her silver wedding anniversary promise to Tom. She hadn't the courage to tell him the real reason she couldn't go.

'I need more time to think,' she said at last, still hoping he might change his mind about Graceland. To help him on his way, she tried singing the praises of Bamburgh Castle and the beautiful wild beaches of Northumberland and Lindisfarne. Nothing did any good.

Jimmy leaned forward and pulled his phone from a secret pocket that he'd sewn into his white trouser suit, which was now hanging over a chair at Helen's dining table.

'Hand me your phone, Helen,' he said.

She didn't move. 'Why?'

He turned to her and looked deep into her eyes. 'Trust me,' he said.

Helen hesitated a moment before passing her phone over. With his phone in one hand and hers in the other, Jimmy connected them via Bluetooth. Within seconds, a beating red heart emoji appeared on Helen's screen.

'What is it?' she asked.

'Press it and see.'

She pressed the red heart, and a countdown appeared. She turned to Jimmy, puzzled.

'What have you done?'

'I've booked the holiday.'

'That's presumptuous of you!' she cried, affronted.

But Jimmy wasn't deterred.

'When the countdown runs out, we'll be sitting in the VIP lounge at Leeds Bradford airport waiting for a plane to Amsterdam. From there, we'll be flying first class to Atlanta, Georgia, where I've booked to spend the night in an airport hotel.'

Helen raised her eyebrows.

'How can you afford it?' she asked.

Jimmy looked at her. 'There's a lot you don't know about me, and one day I hope you will. Anyway, the next morning, we'll be flying first class to Memphis International Airport. There we'll be met by Graceland's free Elvis-themed shuttle bus, which will take us to a suite at the Guest House at Graceland on Elvis Presley Boulevard.'

'Jimmy . . .' Helen was astounded and couldn't seem to form her words. 'You've just assumed I'm willing to go. How dare you!'

'I had to do it this way, don't you see? If we'd talked about it reasonably, you would have put the Seaview first. You'd have denied yourself a break, as always.'

'But why . . . when . . . how can you afford this?'

'I've been saving up for this trip for most of my life,' he replied seriously. He gently caressed her hand. 'Now it's up to you. There are two seats on each plane, two tickets to Graceland. With Jean's help, I've even sorted out our visas. She knew where your passport was. Plus, Jean and Sally have promised to look after Suki. Jodie's going to call at my house while I'm away to water my plants. The offer's there, Helen. It'll be a holiday of a lifetime. What do you say?'

Helen was saved from answering when the CCTV monitor in the kitchen burst into life.

'It's the guests, they're back. I've got to go and see them.'

Deadly Dancing at the Seaview Hotel

She flew off the sofa, leaving Jimmy closing her dressing gown over his muscled legs. Suki sat guard, watching him closely.

When she reached the hall, she ushered the guests into the bar. They looked done in, emotionally drained, as shell-shocked as Gav and Sally had done. Paul's eyes were red from crying. The dancers' faces were tinged an odd shade of teak after their spray tan. All except for Tommy.

The five of them sat around a table, and Helen brought a bottle of brandy and six glasses. She needed a stiff drink herself. She poured a measure into each glass, then proposed a toast.

'To Rosa,' she said.

'To Rosa,' the others chorused as they each took a sip.

'I know you must all be in shock, but if anyone feels the need to talk about what's happened, I'm a very good listener,' she said, looking around.

'All right, I'll go first,' Bev said.

Chapter 18

'We all walked into the salon, and the chap who runs the place gave us each a towel,' Bev said. Her hands shook as she took a sip of brandy then set the glass down. 'I followed Rosa and Carla into the ladies' area, where there were separate booths. They were like a shower cubicle, about the same size.'

'So no one sprayed the tan on you?' Helen asked.

Carla shook her head, and her red bob swung. 'No. That was an option Sally said would become available after they'd recruited staff. Inside the booth, we simply pressed a button and the spray tan came out.'

'What was it like in the salon?' Helen asked.

'Plush,' Tommy said.

'Everything was brand new. It was beautiful,' Carla agreed.

'Very well appointed, good lighting, with lots of mirrors,' Monty added.

'I tried recording sound inside for my live podcast, but I obviously couldn't get into the ladies' area,' Paul said. His eyes were still red and puffy, and he kept dabbing at them. Bev patted his arm and carried on.

'As dancers, we're used to having fake tan applied. You need stage make-up under harsh lights. If you're not tanned, you look ghostly. So we knew what we were doing.' She took another sip from her glass, her hand still shaking, and her voice wavered as she continued. 'Then we . . .'

'Would you like me to carry on, Bev?' asked Carla.

Bev nodded. 'Thanks.'

Carla bit her lip, paused for a moment then began to speak. 'When the spray tan hits your body, it's cold at first and you need to get used to it. You turn around, lift your arms up, let the tan coat your arms and your chest and your face. Everything was going smoothly. I finished my session, the spray tan stopped automatically after a few minutes . . .' she reached for Monty's hand across the tabletop, 'but for poor Rosa, it didn't. Bev and I stepped out of our booths and were getting dressed. Rosa wasn't there. We grew concerned, because she was still in the booth.'

'I was worried she was overdoing her tan,' Bev chipped in.

Carla squeezed Monty's hand. 'And I was worried she'd fainted. Anyway, we called for Sally, because we couldn't open the booth door. She came running in, then went back to reception to tell Gav.'

Carla took a deep breath.

'I'm sorry, Helen, talking about this is awful.'

'Don't push yourself. If you don't want to say more, I'll understand,' Helen said.

But Carla shook her head. 'No, I want to get it out. I must. It was Gav who found Rosa's body. She was slumped inside the booth and the spray tan was still going. The police told us at the station that it seems likely she died from respiratory failure, breathing problems caused when the spray wouldn't stop.'

Tears began to roll down Carla's cheeks and Monty laid his arm around her shoulders. Paul began crying again too.

'What an awful way to die,' Carla said.

Bev took another sip of brandy.

'And that's as much as we can tell you,' Monty said. 'As for us chaps, we didn't know anything about it until we heard a commotion in the reception area while we were getting dressed. That was when Sally told us what had happened. I went immediately to my wife to comfort her after the shock.'

'And I went to my sister,' Tommy said.

Helen glanced at Tommy, wondering again why he didn't look as tanned as the others. Then she looked at Paul.

'You came out of the salon before Rosa's body was found, didn't you? You interviewed me for the podcast.'

'Yes, that's right,' he said with a catch in his voice.

They all sat in silence for a few moments.

'Does anyone know Rosa's family? Will the police let them know what's happened?'

'Rosa's dad is her only living relative, but they were never close. He lives in Australia, but I've passed on his details to the police so they can tell him what's happened.' Paul's face clouded over. 'Of course there's her boyfriend, he'll need to be told the tragic news.'

'The police know about Frankie Tanner,' Helen told him.

Someone's phone began to ring, disturbing the sombre atmosphere. It was Bev who bent down and picked up her handbag. She glanced at the phone screen, then at Tommy.

'Sorry, everyone, I must take this call. It's from the TV company,' she said.

She walked out of the lounge, then Helen heard the Seaview's front door open and close. From the lounge window she watched as Bev walked across the road to the bench on the clifftop, where she sat and spoke into her phone. It prompted her to remember the last time she'd seen Bev there, sitting next to Monty. They'd talked about Blackpool, about wanting Rosa silenced because she knew something that they wanted kept quiet. She'd also heard Rosa and Bev arguing about Bev keeping a nasty secret about Blackpool. Were these two things connected?

She cast a sidelong glance at Monty, wondering what really went on behind his polished smile. She knew she should speak to DS Hutchinson and tell him everything she knew about her guests in relation to Rosa, but not now, not yet. She was in a state of shock over what had happened and was very concerned for Sally and Gav. Gav had found a dead body, lost his new business and was now part of a health and safety investigation into Rosa's death. And pregnant Sally didn't need the stress.

When Bev returned to the room, Tommy's eyes darted to her. 'Well?' he said.

But Bev shook her head. 'There's still no decision, sorry, Tommy.'

'Did you tell them that Rosa's dead, that there's only one horse in the race now?'

'Tommy! Have some respect!' Carla barked.

Monty narrowed his eyes. Paul burst into tears again.

'Be more considerate, little brother,' Bev said quietly.

Tommy sank back in his seat, contrite. 'I'm sorry, so sorry. I'm not in my right mind. I don't know what I'm saying. Rosa's death has destroyed me. Oh, you all know we didn't get along, but we'd been dancing toe-to-toe and cheek-to-cheek, and it doesn't seem real that she's gone. I think I'll go upstairs for a nap. The only way I can cope is to sleep.'

When Tommy had left, Paul stood. 'I'm going to my room too. I need to be alone.'

'I understand. Let me know if you need anything,' said Helen.

'Darling? Do you need to go and lie down?' Monty asked Carla.

Carla nodded, and her red bob jiggled.

'Then excuse us, please,' Monty said as he helped her to stand and escorted her from the room.

Helen was left alone with Bev. Bev pushed her glass towards her, and Helen refilled it.

'What must you think of me, Helen?' she asked suddenly.

Helen thought it an odd question.

'In what way?' she said.

'Well, there I was running outside just now to take a phone call when really I should be mourning Rosa. The truth is, Rosa and I never got along. I can't be two-faced and sit here and say I'm grieving her loss when I'm not. Of course I'm shocked by what's happened, but that's as far as it goes.'

'I'm not judging you, Bev,' Helen said sternly.

Bev touched her hand lightly. 'I'm sorry, I think the brandy has gone to my head. I should go up to my room too and have a nap, then Tommy and I can discuss what to do next. With Rosa gone, he has no dancing partner.'

Or a rival for his TV show, Helen thought.

'Will the dance competition still go ahead?' she asked.

Bev shrugged. 'It depends on Frankie and Bobby Tanner. They're the men behind it. If they cancel, I'm sure people will understand. However, there are hundreds of dancers in Scarborough who've been practising for months for this competition. If it's cancelled, there's going to be a lot of disappointed people.'

'Do you know Frankie and Bobby?'

'No, but I knew that Rosa had started a relationship with

Deadly Dancing at the Seaview Hotel

Frankie and was stringing Paul along. Poor lad, he doted on her, but Rosa was ruthless. Heartless and selfish. Poor Paul, he's distraught.'

'Do you think he loved her?' Helen asked, fishing for more.

'Paul falls heavily when he falls in love. It's all or nothing with him. I think he truly believed that Rosa loved him as much as he loved her. That's why it hit him so hard when he found out she'd started seeing Frankie Tanner.'

'Has Paul had relationships with other dancers?' Helen asked, wondering if Bev would reveal anything that would make sense of the slippers in Carla's room. However, Bev didn't reply. She'd sat up straight in her seat and was staring out of the window.

'Oh no,' she said, curling her body away from Helen, then she got down on all fours and began to crawl out of the lounge. 'Make him go away,' she whispered.

Helen peered out of the window and saw that Mike Skipton's builder's van had pulled up outside the Seaview.

Chapter 19

'Get up off the floor! I'm not going to lie to Mike if he asks if you're here,' Helen said firmly. 'Sort it out now and make sure he doesn't come back. This is unacceptable behaviour from one of my guests!' Her face flushed red. It'd been doing that a lot since she'd turned fifty. But this time, the flush was caused by anger at Bev. The last thing she wanted or needed was a guest's personal problems following them to Scarborough and landing at her door.

The doorbell rang. Bev glared up at Helen. Then she stood and brushed at the knees of her trousers before pushing her shoulders back and marching to the door. Helen waited out of sight in the lounge, where she could hear every word.

'Mrs Cassidy, I've come for my money,' Mike said. His voice was flat, but it contained a slight hint of menace.

'Mike, dear—' Bev began.

'Don't you *Mike, dear* me, Bev. I've waited long enough. Now, either you give me the money I'm owed, or I go back to your house and undo the work I've done. I'll start by smashing the windows in your smart new conservatory. Then I'll remove the boiler I've installed. Then I'll—'

'Stop!' Bev snarled. 'I'll get your money for you.'

'I've heard that before,' Mike said.

Deadly Dancing at the Seaview Hotel

Helen peered out of the window and saw him turn away to walk down the path.

'Wait!' Bev called. 'You will get your money. Something's happened and . . . well, I've come into funds. I can pay off some of the debt right now.'

This stopped him in his tracks. He walked back to the door as Bev whipped her phone from her trouser pocket.

'What's your bank account number?' she asked.

Mike reeled off a long number. Bev punched it into her phone.

'And your sort code?'

He gave a shorter number.

'Would five thousand pounds be sufficient for now?' she said. 'Is that enough to stop you smashing windows and breaking into my house to take back what you've installed?'

'It'll do,' Mike replied.

Bev held her phone out to him. 'Turn on your Bluetooth,' she said.

Mike put his phone next to hers, as if the two devices were air-kissing, then there was a loud ping. Helen peered around the curtain in the lounge. She saw him check his screen and smile.

'That's now in my account. But I want the rest, and I'll be back.'

'I'll have the money soon,' Bev said in a quaking voice. 'I promise.'

When Helen heard the front door close, she busied herself behind the bar, straightening bottles that were straight, tidying cloths that were tidy. She caught Tom watching her from the wall.

'Sorry, Tom. I know I shouldn't eavesdrop on our guests, but it's been a stressful day.'

Bev's orange curls appeared around the door of the lounge.

Glenda Young

'Please, Helen, don't tell Tommy that Mike was here. I'm going up to my room. I need a lie-down.'

'Give me a shout if you want anything,' Helen replied.

She waited until she heard Bev's footsteps disappear, then sank into a chair in the bay window. Ahead of her the sea gently rolled in on the North Bay beach. To her right was Scarborough Castle, standing high on the clifftop under the clouds. To her left was the Sea Life Centre, crazy golf and the swanky five-star apartment block at the Sands. In the distance she could see Peasholm Park. She thought about Bev and Mike the builder. Bev said she hadn't the money to pay Mike the last time he came looking for her. Why now, suddenly, just hours after Rosa's death, did she have access to five thousand pounds? Was her phone call earlier really from the TV production company, as she had told everyone? Or had it something to do with money mysteriously turning up in her bank account, something connected to Rosa's death?

She pushed her bobbed hair behind her ears, then stood up and stretched her arms in the air. The shock of Rosa's death and the odd behaviour of her guests was making her stressed and tense. Her shoulders ached, and she rolled them back and down, like she was instructed to at her yoga class at the bowls centre each week. She turned away from the window and was readying herself to return downstairs to Jimmy when the doorbell rang again.

'Oh no, what now?' she cried. Bracing herself, she forced a professional smile to her face and checked her appearance in the mirror in the hall. Satisfied that she looked presentable, she opened the door and was stunned to see Miriam. She was even more surprised to see Miriam's suitcases.

'Ah, Helen dear. I've had a spot of bother in Bridlington. And I

Deadly Dancing at the Seaview Hotel

can't move back into my beloved hotel until my, er, little problem has gone. So you see, you find me in something of a dilemma.'

Miriam pushed her way into the Seaview, leaving her luggage on the step.

'Be a darling and bring in my cases. Be careful with them, they're genuine Louis Vuitton.'

Helen was dumbstruck. She looked from the cases to Miriam, who was swanning along the hall, heading into the lounge. She knew she couldn't leave the cases on the doorstep, so she lugged them inside, being less than careful with them, and banged them against the wall before storming into the lounge.

Miriam had taken up residence in a chair in the window. She looked for all the world as if she owned the place. Helen put her hands on her hips and glared at her.

'What do you think you're doing?' she snapped.

The older woman's defiant stance wavered a little and her bottom lip trembled.

'I didn't think you'd let me in if I asked, so I knew I'd have to barge in,' she said.

Helen crossed her arms. 'What's going on? I thought you'd gone to stay with your sister while the Vista del Mar was fumigated.'

Miriam tapped her fingers against the tabletop. 'My sister and I had . . . well, let's call it a difficult conversation. The upshot of it was that I decided to leave.'

'She threw you out, didn't she?'

'We came to an understanding,' she said quickly. 'Anyway, here I am, finding myself with no fixed abode at the current time.'

She turned her face to meet Helen's death stare.

'That look does you no favours,' she said coolly.

Helen sat down opposite her.

'Be honest. Why are you here? There are thousands of places to stay in Scarborough. Surely you can find somewhere until you move back into the Vista del Mar.'

'I *have* found somewhere,' Miriam said, looking around the lounge. 'It's a bit shabby for my taste, but beggars can't be choosers. I need to stay as close as possible to my beloved hotel until the little problem is solved.'

Helen looked at her, incredulous. 'Are you saying you want to stay *here*?'

'Just for a night or two, until the all-clear is declared at the Vista del Mar. I'll pay you, obviously, although not the going rate. We both know how much the mark-up is.'

Helen stood and pointed at the lounge door. 'No. You're not staying here. I've got guests in and there are things going on that you don't know about. I think you should leave.'

Miriam didn't move.

'Out!' Helen demanded.

'Helen, dear . . .' Miriam pleaded. Helen saw tears brimming in her eyes and her heart began to thaw. She walked back to her and sat down.

'What's happened?' she said gently. 'Tell me the truth this time.'

Miriam swallowed hard, then looked out of the window. 'You're right, my sister threw me out.' She turned to look at Helen. 'I know I'm an acquired taste.'

Helen gave a wry smile. 'Well, at least you acknowledge it,' she said. 'But do you really have nowhere else to stay? I've got a hotel full of guests.'

Deadly Dancing at the Seaview Hotel

Miriam patted her knee. 'Now we both know that's not true. You've got one room empty.'

'How on earth do you know that?' Helen demanded.

Miriam shrugged. 'I bumped into the delightful Tommy Two Shoes in a patisserie in Bridlington while I was there. He said he was taking time out from rehearsals. I recognised him from when he used to be on TV as a boy. He's got a terrible sweet tooth, you know. He bought two peach melbas and stuffed them both in his mouth at the same time.' She grimaced. 'Anyway, he told me that the dancers have exclusively booked your hotel but that there's one room going spare. I dare say it won't be up to the standards I'm used to next door at the Vista del Mar, but it'll have to do.'

Despite Miriam's patronising insults, which Helen was used to by now, there was something vulnerable about the woman that touched her heart. She'd never seen her like this before.

'All right, you can stay.'

Miriam clasped her hands together. 'Perfect!'

Helen waited for *thank you*, but it didn't come.

'Now, if you'd be so kind as to help with my cases, I'll settle in. I need to make a few phone calls to the pest control company to see how they're getting on. They should be almost done by now, but I'm not going back in until I know every last bug has been zapped.'

'I haven't seen any pest control vans outside since you left,' Helen replied.

'Of course not, dear. I told them to park at the back. I didn't want them at the front, in view of passing tourists. I don't want anyone to know what's going on. The only reason I told you is because you caught me running out of the hotel screaming.'

'You said you were practising scales,' Helen said.

'I'd just been bitten by bedbugs,' Miriam confided in a low voice. She looked around the room and down at the carpet. 'They haven't come in here from next door, have they? The walls that separate our hotels are very old, with many cracks.'

'Bedbugs don't crawl through walls, Miriam. They travel on people. I hope you haven't brought them in with you.'

'Don't be so crude!' Miriam snapped.

She stood and walked to the bar, ran her hand along the bar top then inspected her fingertips.

'Is Sally still cleaning for you?'

Helen forced a smile. 'Yes, she is, and she does a wonderful job.'

Miriam rubbed her fingertips together, wiping away imaginary dust.

'Well, if you're happy with her work, I suppose that's what counts. Seems to me that now she's pregnant with the twins, her mind's no longer on her work. Now, which room am I in?'

Helen seethed with anger as she walked to the hallway. She opened the key box, took out a key and handed it to Miriam.

'You're in Room 10, on the top floor,' she said, and the woman disappeared upstairs.

She was about to pick up Miriam's suitcases when the doorbell rang again.

'No!' she cried. 'For heaven's sake, what now?'

She pulled the door open, red in the face, to find DS Hutchinson and DC Hall standing there.

'Nice suitcases,' DC Hall commented as he stepped inside. 'They look like the Louis Vuitton knock-offs that are doing the rounds in town.'

Deadly Dancing at the Seaview Hotel

Helen walked into the lounge. She felt tired, defeated, done in. She thought of Jimmy downstairs in her dressing gown. He'd be wondering what she was up to and what was keeping her so long.

'Sit down, please,' she said, indicating a table away from the window. She glanced outside, glad to see that the detectives had arrived in an unmarked car. Just as Miriam didn't want pest control vans outside her hotel, Helen preferred not to have police cars outside hers.

'We've come to talk about what happened at the tanning salon,' DS Hutchinson said.

DC Hall was looking around the lounge. 'Is Jean at work today baking her famous cakes?' he asked, patting his ample stomach.

Helen looked at him, aghast. How could he think about cakes at a time like this?

'No, she's not here right now, and as for her cakes, well . . .' She remembered the awful taste of the chocolate cake that morning, when Jean had forgotten to put in sugar. 'I could rustle up a plate of biscuits with coffee while we chat.'

'That'd be great,' DC Hall said, licking his lips.

She stood to leave, but as she did so, a van drew up outside the Seaview. Her blood ran cold. It had the words *Forensic Unit* written on the side. She gasped out loud.

'Forensics? What's going on?' she asked the detectives.

'Ah, Mrs Dexter,' DS Hutchinson said, clearing his throat. 'I was hoping to explain what was going on before our colleagues arrived. I'm afraid the team will need access to Ms de Wolfe's room to remove her personal belongings.'

Helen gathered herself. She took a deep breath and tried to rationalise what was happening.

'I suppose that in a case of unnatural death, there would be questions, of course.'

But DS Hutchinson shook his head. 'I'm afraid we're no longer investigating an unnatural death, Mrs Dexter. We're investigating a murder.'

Chapter 20

'Murder?' Helen squeaked.

'I'm afraid your friend Gav, the owner of the salon, will be taken in for questioning, again. He's currently our main suspect,' DC Hall said.

Helen sank into her chair, shaking her head. She couldn't think straight.

'No . . .' she gasped. 'Not Gav. He wouldn't hurt a hair on anyone's head. He hasn't anything to do with this, I refuse to believe it.'

The doorbell rang again and DC Hall went to answer it, bringing two forensics officers into the lounge. Both were dressed in white suits.

'Mrs Dexter, the forensics team will need access to Ms de Wolfe's room,' he said.

Helen's legs were shaking as she forced herself to stand. She had to put her hand on the bar to steady herself before she left the lounge.

'I'll fetch the master key,' she said.

'And after that, we've got some questions to ask you about your guests,' added DS Hutchinson.

Slowly, carefully, Helen walked downstairs, gripping the handrail for support. She was in shock at what she'd learned. When she reached the bottom of the stairs, she pushed the door open and almost fell into her apartment. Suki rushed to her, wanting attention, followed by Jimmy in her dressing gown.

'Hey, you've been ages, what's going on?' he said.

'It's the police, Jimmy. They're upstairs. They want forensics to search Rosa's room.'

'Why?' he asked, concerned.

She could hardly get the words out, it seemed so unreal.

'They say she was murdered.'

As she fell into Jimmy's arms, she heard him gasp in shock, but she held her nerve. She wouldn't cry. She had to be strong. Two detectives and a forensics team were waiting upstairs. She had to answer their questions, then get them out of the Seaview as quick as she could. It'd do her business no good to have a forensics van outside the hotel . . . again. It wasn't the first time one of her guests had died in mysterious circumstances. She sent a silent wish that it would be the last.

'Why is it always *my* guests?' she cried. 'Why me? Why the Seaview? Oh my word, the curse of the dance has come true.'

She pulled away from Jimmy and walked to the safe box where she kept the master key.

'Let me come upstairs with you,' he said.

Despite the turmoil she felt, the sight of Jimmy's chest and thighs peeking out of her dressing gown made her smile.

'It's best if you stay down here. I'm not sure the detectives are ready to see Elvis in his dressing gown. You know they're both big fans of yours, and you'll distract them from their work. I want them gone as soon as possible. Stay here, Jimmy, I won't be long.'

As she said this, she crossed her fingers and hoped she was right.

Deadly Dancing at the Seaview Hotel

'Is there anything I can do to help?' he asked.

She nodded at the kettle. 'You could make coffee and put biscuits on a plate for the detectives. DC Hall has got a sweet tooth and it's always best to keep on his good side. I'll pop down in a few minutes to collect everything.'

Jimmy jumped to attention and started pulling mugs from the cupboard. Helen walked to the door with Suki at her side.

'Not now, Suki,' she said, and the dog slunk away to lie under the dining table, keeping a watchful eye on Jimmy.

Back upstairs, Helen asked the forensics officers to follow her to the room where Rosa had stayed. She unlocked the door and let them in.

'Thank you, Mrs Dexter,' one of them said politely, then they blocked the doorway so she couldn't enter. She hoped that none of her other guests would leave their rooms and see the white-suited officers. It might upset them too much when they were already feeling fragile.

'I'll leave you to it,' she said as she walked away. She paused on the landing to give herself a moment and looked around at the doors to the other rooms, behind which were Rosa's dance colleagues. Her mind began to churn. Murder? Had one of them killed Rosa? They all had reasons to hate her. Whatever happened next, she had to do what she could to ensure Gav's good name was cleared. She knew she had to prove his innocence . . . but how?

She returned to the lounge to find DS Hutchinson and DC Hall sitting side by side at a table by the bar.

'Would you like something stronger than coffee?' she asked.

'No, we're working, Mrs Dexter. But another time,' DS Hutchinson said.

'Please, call me Helen. I feel as if we know each other by now,' she said wearily. 'I'll go and fetch the coffee and biscuits.'

As she walked into the hallway to head downstairs, she heard the dumbwaiter rumble into life. She turned, surprised, as she'd never shown Jimmy how it worked. However, she was grateful for his quick thinking because she didn't think her trembling legs and shaking hands would have coped with carrying the coffee. She opened the dumbwaiter hatch and carefully removed the tray with three mugs and a plate. Jimmy had even added a small jug of milk and a sugar bowl with spoons. This attention to detail made her smile.

Slowly she walked into the lounge and laid the tray on the table. DC Hall eyed the biscuits and reached out to take one.

'It's a shame Jean's not here. I always enjoy her cake,' he said.

Helen began to grow annoyed. How could cake be top of his agenda when there was murder to discuss?

'Jean usually only works mornings,' she said, glaring at him.

He snapped his biscuit in half and dunked it in his coffee, then slurped the biscuit into his mouth. 'We'd like to speak to her,' he said.

Helen steeled herself and told herself to keep calm. The man was unbelievable.

'If you're after her recipe for coffee and walnut cake, I'm afraid it's a Seaview secret.'

He lifted his mug and took a long drink.

'It's not her recipe we're after. We want to warn her about the company she keeps.'

Helen's heart missed a beat. 'What company?' she said, although she had a bad feeling she already knew. A pair of Cuban-heeled shoes tap-danced through her mind.

Deadly Dancing at the Seaview Hotel

DS Hutchinson leaned forward with a steely glint in his eye. 'Helen . . . what do you know about Bobby Tanner?'

She took her time replying. She didn't want to get Jean into trouble. However, she was very concerned. And so she began to tell the detectives what she'd learned.

'I know he's one of the financial backers of the dance competition at the Spa. I also heard that he'd recently been released from prison, where he served two years for fraud.'

DS Hutchinson tapped the tabletop with a black biro. 'We'd ask you to let Jean know that Bobby Tanner is a person of interest to us. We've been watching him since he was released from jail. We know he's become friendly with her, but we don't yet know why.'

Helen sat up straight, all ears.

'Tell her to be vigilant. He's a charmer, old Bobby,' DC Hall added. 'Aye, he can charm the birds from the trees.'

'And the money from the ladies,' DS Hutchinson added with a warning look at Helen. 'Bobby Tanner is very bad news.'

Chapter 21

Helen heard a woman's cry. With a sinking heart she realised it was Miriam.

'Helen, dear. Where are my cases?'

She looked from DS Hutchinson to DC Hall. 'I'm sorry, would you excuse me a moment. I've got a rather difficult guest.'

Walking out of the lounge, she found Miriam puffing and panting her way downstairs.

'Honestly, the service here is terrible,' Miriam moaned. 'Hand me my small suitcase and you bring the large one.'

Together they made their way up to the top floor.

'Shocking service,' Miriam repeated when they reached her room.

Helen was too flabbergasted to reply. She left Miriam to it and walked back down to the lounge.

'Everything all right with your guest?' DC Hall said.

'No, but it will be once she moves out,' Helen muttered. She turned her full attention to the men.

'What do you know about Bobby Tanner's son?' DC Hutchinson asked.

'Frankie?' Helen replied. 'Not much. I know he went to school with Gav. Frankie was jealous of Gav's business success. He also had a fling with Gav's wife, Sally.'

Deadly Dancing at the Seaview Hotel

'Sally had an affair with Frankie Tanner?' DC Hall asked.

Helen shook her head. 'No, that's not what I meant. Sally would never cheat on Gav, they're soulmates and devoted to each other. She went out with Frankie long before she met Gav. However, she dumped him when he started losing his temper. She was terrified he might hit her and so she ended the relationship. Frankie was also involved in putting money into the dance competition at the Spa with his dad, and . . . oh!'

She stopped and tapped her hand against her forehead.

'He was outside the Seaview the other day. It was before I knew who he was, so I didn't recognise him. But now that I've seen him, I know it was him. He was filming the hotel. I asked what he was up to, but he walked away saying something into his phone like "She's here. I've found her." Then he got into a 4x4 and sped off. I wondered if he meant Jean, you know. She was in the lounge at the time, near the window. Frankie would have seen her if he was looking in. I was worried that his dad had targeted her and that Frankie was confirming where she worked.' Helen's mind was spinning.

The detectives gave each other a knowing look, which unsettled her.

'What are you not telling me?' she demanded.

'I'm afraid you're right, Helen. We suspect Frankie was keeping tabs on her for his dad. Bobby Tanner has form for preying on vulnerable women. He usually ropes in his son to join his nasty schemes.'

DS Hutchinson took a notepad from his jacket pocket and began to make notes.

'We could have gone straight to Jean to tell her about Tanner, but we know how close you two are, and we thought she'd take more notice if the warning came from you. Tell us more about her.'

Helen raised her mug of coffee, but her hand was still shaking and she put it back down.

'Well, her mum's just died and she's not thinking straight. On the day of the funeral, she discovered she'd come into money from her mum's will, then suddenly Bobby turned up. But what I don't understand is what this has to do with Rosa's . . .' She floundered, unable to bring herself to say the word *murder*. 'With Rosa,' she said at last.

'We're still trying to figure out if there is a connection,' DS Hutchinson said. 'One of my men has already spoken to Frankie and he's admitted what you've told us about being jealous of Gav. He said it was his lifelong ambition to get one up on him. Putting money into a prestigious event like the dance competition at the Spa was his way of doing this. He wanted his name up in lights all over town, but when that didn't happen, he went off the rails. He's been drinking, arguing with his dad, fighting at the Spa.'

'I was there, I saw their fight,' Helen said. She kept quiet about hiding behind the banner and being taken to task by two beefy bouncers.

'Which of your guests seems most affected by Ms de Wolfe's death?' DC Hall asked, checking his notes. That was an easy one for Helen to answer.

'Paul Knight. He was obsessed with her.'

'Were they involved in a relationship?'

She shook her head. 'No, they weren't having a relationship. From what I understand, Paul was besotted with Rosa, but she wouldn't have anything to do with him. He's the group's podcaster,' she added.

DS Hutchinson's brow furrowed. 'Podcaster? Tell me more.'

'He broadcasts about ballroom dancing. He follows the dancers when they go on tour.'

'Like a groupie,' DC Hall said.

'Like a podcaster,' Helen replied sternly. 'I think he loved Rosa, but she didn't feel the same way about him. On the night of the fight, he discovered she had started seeing Frankie Tanner and he was heartbroken. Now that Rosa's dead, the poor lad doesn't know what to do with himself. But he did say something odd.'

The detectives leaned forward.

'He said he was so upset over what Rosa had done, so angry, that he was afraid of what he'd do to her the next time he saw her. Oh. You don't think he killed her, do you?'

DC Hall made a note, but no one answered her question.

'Anyway, back to Frankie Tanner,' DS Hutchinson cut in. 'As I said, he went off the rails after his plans to have his name up in lights in Scarborough flickered out. He was livid. He'd been desperate to prove to Gav that he could be successful, but it didn't happen the way he wanted. He'd imagined his name plastered all over Scarborough, on billboards, in the paper, on hoardings along the seafront. All he got instead was a mention in the show programme. It's a two-page coloured leaflet. Hardly the promotion he had dreamed of.'

'Could Frankie be behind the murder? Could he have tried to sabotage Gav's grand opening out of jealousy and it all went horribly wrong?' Helen asked.

'We've already questioned him and his dad. However, Frankie's as clean as a whistle in the murder investigation, as is Bobby. They both have alibis: they were drinking in Scholar's Bar at the time of Rosa's death and we've got CCTV coverage to confirm it. Anyway, please tell Jean to keep her eye on her purse when Bobby's about.'

'It's not her purse I'm worried about, it's her bank account,' said Helen.

The sound of footsteps on the stairs reached the lounge.

'We're finished upstairs,' one of the white suits called from the hallway. Helen could see that the forensics officers were carrying what looked like plastic bin liners. She assumed they were filled with Rosa's belongings. 'You can go into the room to clean or whatever you need to.'

Helen breathed a sigh of relief as she watched their van disappear along the street, hoping that Miriam hadn't spotted it from her window. The thought of Miriam made her stomach turn. How was she going to cope with looking after her snobby neighbour in the middle of a police investigation? Why on earth had she let the woman railroad her into taking her in? Chiding herself for not having a stronger backbone, she balled her hands into fists.

'Helen?' DS Hutchinson said.

She uncurled her hands and snapped her concentration back. DS Hutchinson opened a new page in his notepad. DC Hall stood and walked out of the lounge, closing the door behind him.

'My colleague will wait in the hall to ensure none of your guests come in. We need privacy here. Tell us about Rosa's fellow dancers. Would you say there was anyone she'd rubbed up the wrong way? Anyone she didn't get along with. Anyone, Helen, who might want her dead?'

Deadly Dancing at the Seaview Hotel

Helen closed her eyes and felt the room swim. She wondered where to start.

'Come on, Helen,' DS Hutchinson urged. 'You know your guests better than anyone. You see them with your trained, expert landlady's eye. They think they're not being watched, but they are.'

'I don't spy on my guests, Detective, and I never will,' Helen said, affronted.

DS Hutchinson tutted out loud. 'That's not what I mean and you know it,' he said. 'A hotel landlady knows things, sees things, understands what's not being said over a breakfast of scrambled eggs.'

Helen thought of all the things she already knew about the two detectives, everything from what their body language revealed to DC Hall's insatiable appetite for Jean's cakes.

'Point taken,' she said. 'I'll tell you all I can if it helps you catch the killer and bring this awful episode to an end. All I want is a quiet life, Gav's name cleared and no more upset for Sally, especially in her condition.'

DS Hutchinson nodded. 'I believe you already know that Ms de Wolfe was spray-tanned to death.'

'Yes, so I heard.'

'I can confirm it was a deliberate act,' the detective continued.

Helen steeled herself to hear more.

'The mechanism in the booth Rosa used had been tampered with. When the button was pressed to operate the spray, it kept coming and wouldn't stop. There'll be a full health and safety investigation, and that's why Gav is top of our list to speak to. But there was something else, which is why this is now a murder investigation rather than an unnatural death caused by a faulty machine.

The door to the booth had been deliberately jammed shut. Rosa would have tried to leave, to get away from the spray. It must have filled her nostrils and mouth, her lungs – there was no way to avoid it. It kept spraying until she couldn't breathe.'

'Stop!' Helen cried. She took a moment to pull herself together. 'I appreciate your trust in me, really. But there's only so much information I can take. I don't need the grisly details.'

'Sorry, Helen, I apologise,' he replied. He picked up the plate of biscuits and offered it to her. She shook her head and he took one himself.

'Tell me about this podcaster . . .' he checked his notes, 'Paul Knight. Do you think he's capable of murder? He's certainly got a motive. A crime of passion. A man left broken-hearted after being spurned by a beautiful woman. Plus, news of a dead body would pull in a lot of listeners to his podcast.'

Helen glanced nervously at the lounge door and DS Hutchinson caught her looking.

'It's all right, Helen. DC Hall will alert us if anyone comes. Don't worry, what we say in here won't be overheard.'

He glanced up at the ceiling.

'How much sound from down here travels to the room above?'

'Hardly any. We had this room soundproofed when we used to hold Elvis parties on Saturday nights, when Tom was still alive.' She glanced at the photo on the wall behind the bar.

'You must miss him,' DS Hutchinson said.

She choked back a lump in her throat. 'Every day,' she said.

She glanced at the lounge door again, then leaned forward. What she said next came out in a whisper, for she was almost too scared to admit the truth.

Deadly Dancing at the Seaview Hotel

'To be honest, Detective, all my guests have motives for wanting to see the end of Rosa de Wolfe.'

DS Hutchinson picked up his pen and looked her straight in the eye.

'Then you must tell me all you know.'

Chapter 22

After speaking to Helen, DS Hutchinson and DC Hall asked to talk to each of her guests in turn. This meant that she had to knock on their doors to wake them from their afternoon naps.

After the police left, she joined the guests in the lounge. Paul was in tears. Bev and Tommy huddled close together, faces drawn. Carla sat alone in silence while Monty captured his sad expression on his camera from as many different angles as he could. Helen couldn't look at him; she felt her stomach turn.

'If you don't feel up to going out for dinner tonight, you'd be welcome to bring takeaways into the lounge,' she offered. 'It's not something I usually allow, but under the circumstances . . . well . . .' Her voice faltered.

However, they decided to head into town, saying a breath of fresh air might do them good.

Once they had left and dusk settled, Helen turned on a light in the bar. It gave a welcome glow for any passers-by who might be looking in, drawing tourists like a moth to a flame. The noticeboard outside outlined the tariff, displayed pictures of the rooms and details of the website. And above all of that, so that no one could miss it even if they tried, was a certificate announcing Jean's award-winning full English breakfast, voted Best on the Yorkshire Coast.

Deadly Dancing at the Seaview Hotel

Happy that the Seaview looked welcoming from the outside, and was secure within, she finally made her way downstairs, carrying the tray with the empty mugs and plate. She felt more than ready for a cup of tea and something to eat. Her rumbling stomach reminded her that she'd eaten little that day. She hoped Jimmy might offer to cook; even something simple like beans on toast would suffice. But when she opened her apartment door, she found him asleep on the sofa. Suki lay on the floor beside him, and she was snoring too.

Helen walked into the kitchen, trying to be quiet so as not to wake either of them, but Jimmy stirred when she clicked on the kettle.

'Sorry, I lost track of time. You were upstairs for ages,' he said, sitting up on the sofa, pulling Helen's dressing gown together. Alerted by his voice, Suki stood too, then stretched and padded across the floor to Helen.

'The strangest thing happened with your dog, Helen,' Jimmy said, still readjusting the dressing gown. 'She kept giving me her paw as if she was shaking my hand.'

Helen got down on her knees and lifted Suki's front paws in turn.

'She's been doing that a lot lately. I think there must be some irritation, although I can't see anything. I'll ring the vet later for advice.'

She made a fuss of Suki, who seemed happy with the attention before she walked away to lie under the table.

'Would you like to stay for dinner, Jimmy?'

He walked into the kitchen and wrapped his arms around her. 'I'd like to stay for ever,' he said, nuzzling into her neck.

Helen let the warmth of his body seep into hers, enjoying the scent of his lemon spice aftershave. 'It feels odd hugging my dressing gown,' she laughed.

'It feels good being here, though,' Jimmy murmured softly in her ear.

Her stomach rumbled again.

'Then stay tonight.'

'Are you sure?' he asked.

'I'm positive. I don't want to be on my own after such a distressing day.'

He pulled away and tightened the dressing gown cord.

'Can I help you cook dinner?' he asked.

This was music to Helen's ears.

'I'm exhausted. How does beans on toast sound? It's all I've got the energy to make.'

'Then let me do it,' Jimmy offered, looking around the kitchen. 'Right, where do you keep the beans?'

Helen pulled a tin from the cupboard and handed it to him.

'Where's the bread?'

She took bread from the bread bin.

'Pans?'

'Shall I make it instead?' she offered.

'No, I'll do it. You sit down and I'll bring you a drink. A glass of red wine?'

'That'd be perfect, thanks.'

Helen sat at the dining table, sipping her wine and watching as Jimmy went from cupboard to drawer, taking out plates, knives and forks. She liked how it made her feel, watching him figuring things out in her domain. But she still wasn't sure that she wanted him living there with her full-time.

Deadly Dancing at the Seaview Hotel

'What did the police say?' he asked.

'They want me to keep a close eye on my guests. They think one of them might have killed Rosa.'

Jimmy stopped what he was doing and stood stock still with the tin of beans in his hand.

'Go on,' he said.

'That's it. I've told them all I've learned so far about the guests. Any of them could have done Rosa in; they all have motives.'

Jimmy poured the beans into a pan, popped bread into the toaster then came to sit next to her. He gently held her hand.

'How so?'

Helen began counting on her left hand, starting with her thumb.

'Firstly, there's Paul the podcaster who DS Hutchinson reckons might have committed a crime of passion because Rosa spurned his advances.'

She pointed her index finger at Jimmy.

'Secondly, there's Bev, the small woman with orange hair. She's an odd one. She admitted to me that she's in debt to her eyeballs – she owes thousands to a builder – yet suddenly and mysteriously she was able to pay him a huge sum today, just hours after Rosa's death. Plus, she'd sell her own granny to get her brother his TV show, which Rosa was also up for. With Rosa gone, it looks like Tommy Two Shoes might be a shoo-in for the show.'

She wiggled her middle finger.

'Thirdly, Tommy. With Rosa gone, he has no rival for the TV show. So he could have got rid of her to clear the way to go after his lifelong dream.'

She raised her ring finger.

'Then there's Carla, who I can't make head nor tail of. She was supposed to dance a tango with Monty to open the competition, but Rosa pulled strings with Frankie Tanner, one of the backers, to have it changed at the last minute. So Carla might have been feeling more than a bit peeved to have been shunted out of the spotlight.'

'Peeved enough to kill her? Come on, Helen, you're letting your imagination run away with you,' Jimmy said.

'Oh, and I found a pair of Paul's slippers in Carla's room,' Helen added.

He raised his eyebrows at this revelation.

'Mind you, I've found a lot worse than that in guests' rooms before.'

Finally she lifted her little finger.

'And lastly, there's Carla's husband Monty, who fancies himself something rotten. He's always taking selfies and looking in mirrors.'

'That doesn't make him a killer,' Jimmy said, before moving away to give the beans a stir. 'Do you mind if I have a beer, Helen? There are some in the fridge.'

'Help yourself,' she said. 'No, being vain doesn't make Monty a killer. But I overheard him and Bev talking outside when they first arrived. He said something about Rosa knowing the truth about what happened in Blackpool and that she had to be stopped before she told Paul the podcaster. Remember I mentioned the curse of the dance, when a glitter ball fell on the dance floor in Blackpool and missed hitting a judge who someone had tried to bribe? It was Bev who was injured when the glitter ball fell, and she hasn't danced since.'

'Who do you think tried to bribe the judge?' he asked as he buttered toast.

Helen shrugged. 'I have no idea and no way of finding out. Meanwhile, sweet, innocent, lovely Gav remains suspect number one with the police for a murder I know in my heart he didn't commit.'

'I think you're right about that,' Jimmy said.

He brought two plates to the table and set one in front of Helen.

'What if it was Rosa, the dead woman, who tried to bribe the judge?' he said.

Helen frowned.

'Hear me out,' Jimmy pleaded. 'Maybe Ballroom Bev discovered what Rosa had done, and had been secretly seething ever since because she cut her dancing career short. See, there's another motive for Bev to have killed her.'

Helen mulled this over. 'But why did she wait until *now* to kill Rosa?' she said. 'The group has been together many times since Blackpool. Why wait until Scarborough?'

The question hung in the air as they tucked into their food. Suki came to stand at Helen's chair.

'No. Down, Suki,' she ordered, and the dog slunk to the floor. 'She's getting into some bad habits, coming to the table for food. She doesn't normally do that.'

'Guilty as charged,' Jimmy muttered. 'Sorry, Helen, I fed her a packet of crisps earlier. I also found a slice of chocolate fudge cake in the cupboard, which I was going to eat with a cuppa, but it tasted awful. Even Suki wouldn't touch it.'

Helen took a sip of wine. 'Jean forgot to put sugar in it, and it sounds like she forgot to throw it all in the bin. She's not thinking straight, which is something else the police wanted to talk to me about. Jean's met this man called Bobby Tanner. He's just been released from jail, where he was in for fraud. He also wears Cuban heels.'

'That's hardly a crime,' Jimmy said.

She ignored him and carried on. 'At the same time, by complete coincidence, Jean's come into money from her mum's will. Suddenly Bobby's on her like a rash and he's all she can talk about. I don't know what to do. The police gave me information to pass on to her. They say she needs to be careful where Bobby's concerned. He's got form for diddling money out of vulnerable women.'

Jimmy waved his fork in the air. 'Jean's as tough as old boots. She grew up in Hull. She's nobody's fool. I don't think you need worry. She's got her head screwed on tight.'

'Normally I'd agree with you. But she's still mourning, and grief does strange things. She was holding herself together as well as could be expected after her mum died, but the funeral knocked her for six. See, I'd normally sit on a morning with Jean and Sally, and we'd enjoy our coffee and cake after finishing work, putting the world to rights. But not any more. Jean's distracted. She's not herself. Don't you see how someone like Bobby could take advantage of that?'

They finished their meal in silence, then Jimmy cleared the table and began to load up the dishwasher.

'Leave that, Jimmy. Come and sit next to me,' Helen said.

He did as he was bid, struggling with the dressing gown cord, which wouldn't stay closed around him. Helen snuggled into his side on the sofa.

Deadly Dancing at the Seaview Hotel

'I need something to take my mind off what happened today. We could open the laptop and have a look at the Graceland website, start planning our holiday,' Jimmy suggested cautiously.

Helen turned her gaze away and bit her lip. 'No, Jimmy, let's leave it for now, please.'

He nuzzled into her neck, and she felt her defences weaken.

'OK . . . then what do you say to an early night instead?' he asked.

'I'd say that might work,' she replied. She sat up and looked into his brown eyes. 'Promise me one thing.'

'I'd promise you anything.'

A mischievous smile played around her lips. 'Please never wear my dressing gown again, it really doesn't suit you,' she said.

Jimmy gently ran his finger along her arm, sending a shiver right through her. 'I could always bring spare clothes to keep here, in case I end up again with nothing to wear but my Elvis suit.'

Helen let his words hang between them for longer, she realised, than Jimmy might have liked. She wasn't sure how to reply. His remark sounded ominously like the first of many steps they'd make that might end up with him moving in. She still wasn't certain about that and it needed more thought. A lot more.

'I'll think about it,' she said, then she tugged on the dressing gown cord, pulled Jimmy to her, and gave him a great big kiss.

Chapter 23

The next morning, Helen left Jimmy snoozing in bed while she donned her hoodie, jeans and boots to take Suki to the beach. Jean had already arrived and was humming along to the radio as Helen walked into the kitchen.

'Morning, Helen,' she said cheerily.

Helen was taken aback. The stocky woman with the short blonde hair looked like Jean and sounded like Jean, but something wasn't right. It took her a second to realise what it was.

'Where are your glasses?'

Jean turned to her and squinted. 'I thought I'd try going without them to see how I get on,' she said, as if it was the most natural thing in the world.

'I've never seen you without your specs,' Helen said, trying to get used to the sight of Jean's face without her trademark glasses. 'Can you see what you're doing?'

Jean squinted again, then opened her eyes wide. 'I can see well enough,' she replied firmly. 'Now, why don't you take Suki out for her W.A.L.K. and I'll crack on with breakfast.'

'Jean, I tried to ring you last night to tell you what's happened to Rosa, but there was no reply from your phone. Did you watch the TV news? Do you know what happened?'

Jean's face clouded over. 'That poor girl. Yes, I saw the news.

Deadly Dancing at the Seaview Hotel

I was going to call you back, but I was with Bobby and he doesn't like me ringing my friends.'

Helen balled her fists to stop herself from exploding. Bobby Tanner was the worst.

'The reporter said Rosa died in suspicious circumstances at Gav's tanning salon,' Jean went on.

'I'm afraid it's worse than that. The police came here last night and told me she was murdered.'

Jean staggered backwards with a hand on her heart. 'Oh my word. No. Not another of our guests murdered!'

'She didn't die here, Jean. The Seaview is in no way connected and we must always remember that. None of our guests have ever died inside the hotel.'

'It's tragic,' Jean cried.

Helen went to her, but Jean brushed her away. 'I'm fine, lass. Let me be. Take your dog out and leave me to work.'

'Oh, Jimmy's here, by the way,' Helen said.

Jean beamed a smile. 'Well, that's wonderful news. I'll cook him a bacon sandwich and make a pot of tea.'

Helen narrowed her eyes. 'When were you going to tell me that he'd asked you and Sally if you'd look after this place, and Suki, if he took me away on holiday?'

Jean shrugged. 'It was supposed to be a surprise. I hope you've said yes.'

'I haven't said anything yet,' Helen said carefully. 'I'm still mulling it over. You know how I feel about Graceland. It was the place . . .'

'. . . where you and Tom were going to celebrate your silver wedding anniversary. Yes, yes, I know all of that. The question is, does Jimmy?'

Helen snapped Suki's lead to her collar, ignoring Jean's question as it was too difficult to answer. She watched as Jean picked up a box of mushrooms, bringing it right to her face, squinting at the use-by date on the side.

'These have plenty of life left in them; another three hours at least,' she smirked.

Helen stood by her side, trying to get used to Jean's blank face.

'Why have you decided not to wear your glasses? Are you thinking about getting contact lenses instead?'

Jean turned away and began to chop mushrooms. 'Bobby says I look better without them,' she said.

Helen felt her shoulders tense. 'So you and Bobby are an item now, are you?' she said, noticing the anger coming out in her voice.

Jean slammed the knife on the chopping board. 'Yes, we are. And I'm happy, Helen. Please, can we leave it at that! And just in case you're wondering, I won't be staying for coffee and cake today. I'm going out for the day, to York.'

'With Bobby?'

'With Bobby!' she said firmly. She pushed her finger against the bridge of her nose. 'Damn! I keep forgetting I'm not wearing the blasted things. Yes. I'm going out with Bobby. I'm treating him to lunch at Bettys tea rooms. He says he's always wanted to go there, and last night he persuaded me to take him. I'm going to pay for the train fares.'

There was something about Jean's tone of voice that Helen didn't like.

'And what about you, Jean? Do you want to go to York?' she said.

'Well . . .' Jean began, but then she faltered.

Deadly Dancing at the Seaview Hotel

Helen looked at her carefully. 'Is Bobby making you do things you don't want to do?' she asked gently. When Jean didn't respond, Helen continued slowly. 'Is he coercing you into doing things you feel uncomfortable with?'

Still Jean didn't reply, which was unusual. Helen wanted more than anything to reach out to her friend and hug her. There was silence between them while she tried to figure out the kindest way to tell her to be careful and warn her about Bobby again. However, it seemed that each time she tried, Jean became defensive and wouldn't hear a word said against him. Helen decided this was no time to be subtle.

'The police were here last night, asking questions about Rosa. They told me something about Bobby. Something they've asked me to pass on to you.'

Jean blinked hard and squinted.

'They say you need to be careful. Bobby's got form for preying on vulnerable women and taking their cash.'

Jean held up her hand. 'I won't hear another word. As for being vulnerable. Me?' She prodded herself in the chest. 'This is Jean you're talking to. I know what I'm doing. If you don't like Bobby, that's your problem, not mine.'

'But the police said—'

Jean held up her other hand. 'Please leave me to my work.'

Suki had begun chattering her teeth and was standing by the door, looking at the handle. Helen knew when she was beat, so she left Jean to make breakfast and headed out for a walk.

The day was overcast but warm, with a slight breeze. She walked along King's Parade then down the cliff path to the North Bay beach, where the tide was in. There was a slim stretch of sand where dog walkers strolled. Out on the waves were surfers in wetsuits, and Helen spotted a group of women, sea swimmers, to one side of the bay. She walked on, feeling hurt and angry after her run-in with Jean. They were running in a lot since Bobby Tanner had turned up.

With each step she took along the damp sand, she tried to process what was going on. There was a dead guest, a strange troupe of dancers, Jean acting weird, Jimmy hinting about moving in, and to top it all off, Miriam. As the waves pushed and pulled at the shore, Helen concentrated on timing her breathing to match. And in, two, three, four . . . she felt her shoulders start to fall and her mind relax. And out, two, three, four . . . then Miriam's face, the police, Jean's inheritance, Gav and the salon, Rosa, Jimmy in his Elvis suit, the beating heart of the Graceland countdown on her phone popped into her mind and her shoulders tensed again. All the while, Suki stayed at her side, not chasing or running. Helen watched the dog closely, looking for a limp or a weakness that might explain her lifting her paw, but saw nothing of concern.

'You're clingy today, Suki. Is it because Jimmy is in our flat?'

Suki kept her own counsel as they continued along the beach.

A slim, petite woman wearing a black swimsuit walked out of the sea, waving at Helen. As she neared, Helen saw a shock of red hair and knew immediately who it was. She waved back as Carla headed to a pile of clothes and bags on the sand and pulled on her changing robe.

'Carla, good morning. Did you enjoy your swim?' she asked.

Carla sat on the sand, took a large towel from her beach bag and began to dry her feet.

'It was exhilarating, Helen. You should try it.'

Deadly Dancing at the Seaview Hotel

'No, thanks. While I was brought up by the sea and I love it, there's no way I want to immerse myself in cold water.'

Carla smiled and shrugged. 'Each to their own.'

'How are you this morning?' Helen asked. 'I mean, after what happened yesterday. You must be in shock.'

Carla's face clouded over. 'We're all in shock and nothing seems real.'

'I understand,' Helen said.

Carla stood and put on a pair of flip-flops, then picked up her beach bag and stuffed her wet towel inside. She looked at Suki.

'What a gorgeous dog. A greyhound, yes?'

'A very special greyhound,' Helen replied. 'She came from a rescue centre. Her name's Suki.'

Carla made a fuss of Suki, stroking her head, and Suki lapped up the attention.

'I'm heading back to the Seaview now, to get ready for your cook's amazing breakfast. Would you like to walk with me, darling?' Carla said.

Helen decided that she would, as Paul's slippers flashed through her mind.

The two women fell into step as they began to climb the cliff path. Suki walked between them, turning her head from Helen to Carla as they spoke.

'The Seaview is a beautiful hotel, Helen. It's balm to my soul after what happened to Rosa. When the police spoke to us yesterday, they explained that they're treating her death as suspicious. They've asked us to stay on in Scarborough while the investigation is ongoing, but we hadn't planned to leave. We're going to stay to dance at the Spa.'

Helen was surprised to hear this. 'Do you mean that the dance competition will still go ahead?'

'We'll dance through our grief. That's the magic of what we do. We remain impassive, professional. We plaster on a smile and dance through the pain. You'd never know the reality of what goes on behind a dancer's smile. We're too focused to give up and go home. There are hundreds of dancers in Scarborough this week dancing for their lives. Therefore, we'll dance too. It's what we train for all year.'

'I admire your grit,' Helen said.

Carla gave a wry smile. 'Plus, there's the little matter of Bobby Tanner insisting that we won't get paid if we don't dance. And if we don't get paid, we can't pay you for our stay at the Seaview. Also, our travel expenses won't be covered.'

Helen let this sink in, noting Bobby Tanner's involvement again.

'You know, Helen, there's something restful about you. You're very calm,' Carla said.

Helen felt herself blush. 'Thank you, I think.'

'Just as your hotel is a salve to our souls, having you as landlady is a steadying force. We appreciate the comfort and peace at the Seaview.'

'Thank you,' Helen said again.

'Anyway, as a group we're going to dance a tribute to Rosa at the competition,' Carla said, changing the subject. 'It'll be the opening dance; an exhibition show dance. We spoke about it last night over dinner. Monty will choreograph a routine that will involve us all.'

'Who will Tommy dance with now that Rosa's gone?' Helen asked.

'Bev's stepped up to the mark,' Carla replied without hesitation.

Deadly Dancing at the Seaview Hotel

Helen couldn't believe her ears. 'But she swore never to dance again after what happened in Blackpool!'

Carla's eyes shone. 'I know, isn't it wonderful! It's going to give the event a real edge. There'll be press from all over the world turning up to see her take to the floor. It should be a crowd-pleaser: Ballroom Bev and Tommy Two Shoes dancing together again.'

'Did they often dance together in the past?' Helen asked.

'They danced together all the time, until Bev's accident in Blackpool. Then Rosa came along and swept Tommy off his feet. She tried to woo him romantically, but he's too focused on his career. Besides, he has a boyfriend, who lives in the Lake District, though I understand they don't see each other often as Bev keeps Tommy on the road. Anyway, once Bev was out of action after her accident, Tommy and Rosa became a dancing partnership.'

Helen glanced at Carla, wondering how much she dared ask.

'Will Paul be podcasting from the event?' she asked, ushering his name into the conversation to see where it went and if slippers might be mentioned.

'I expect so, he's always there. We can't turn around without him shoving his microphone in our faces.'

'You don't sound happy about that,' Helen noted.

'Oh, it gets tiresome, that's all. Anyway, I don't want to talk about Paul or his podcast, darling. I hope he treats Rosa's death with respect and doesn't broadcast any gory details to his listeners.'

'I'm sure the police will have had a word with him about the legalities of what he can publicly reveal at this stage,' Helen said.

They reached King's Parade, and the Seaview was ahead. Helen had only a few minutes more with Carla before she left her at the front door. She had to act quickly. She loved Gav and Sally as if they were family, and would do anything to help Gav prove his innocence. And if, as DS Hutchinson had hinted the previous night, there was the possibility that one of her guests was involved in Rosa's murder, she had to do what she could to get to the bottom of the matter – and fast. News of Rosa's death would reach *The Scarborough Times* that day, and then spread beyond, to the regional and national press. Social media would escalate it, clickbait it, and there was every chance that her beloved Seaview would be mentioned. She had to nip this in the bud for her sake, for the Seaview and especially for Gav and Sally. And so she decided to press Carla for more.

Chapter 24

'Carla, would you have five minutes spare to chat with me?' Helen said, indicating the clifftop bench.

'Of course, it's such a beautiful view,' Carla said as her gaze swept to the ruins of Scarborough Castle.

They sat on the bench and Carla placed her beach bag on the ground. Helen gave a little cough, then began.

'Carla, I need to ask you something.'

Carla scraped her wet hair back from her face. 'Go on,' she said.

'As a hotel landlady, I see things. I notice things in my guests' rooms, and whatever it is, it's my guests' own business. I also hear things I shouldn't, but I never listen deliberately.' Helen crossed her fingers against the little white lie. The walls at the Seaview were old and sound carried too well. 'But we're in strange times after Rosa's murder, when anything out of the ordinary needs to be addressed.'

She turned to Carla and looked her straight in her eyes.

'When I cleaned your room this week, I saw something that shouldn't have been there.'

Carla's face drained of colour. She put a hand to her cheek.

'I found a pair of men's slippers. And later that morning, Paul told me he had lost his slippers. Now, I may have it wrong, but . . .'

Carla sighed heavily. 'No, you have it right.'

'Oh my word,' Helen said. 'I'm sorry. I didn't mean to pry.'

Carla waved her hand dismissively. 'No need to apologise. Paul and I . . . well, this is strictly *entre nous*. Our little secret. Paul and I had a one-night stand.'

Helen rocked back in her seat. 'You and Paul? But what about your husband?' She clamped her mouth shut, worried she'd gone too far.

Carla turned away and looked out at the sea. When she began speaking, her voice was frail and low.

'Monty has his lovers and I have mine. It's no secret we have an open marriage. But we have one cast-iron rule that both of us abide by. And that rule is that we don't sleep with anyone else in the immediate group we're working with. So you see, I broke that rule when I slept with Paul, and that's why Monty must never know.'

'But Paul loved Rosa, didn't he?' Helen said, trying to make sense of it.

'Yes, he did. He was obsessed with her. After the night at the Spa when he found out she had started seeing Frankie Tanner, he came to my room. He was lost, Helen, crying and upset, and I didn't know what to do. So I gave him a hug and he hugged me back. We ended up kissing, and the next thing I knew, he was kicking off his slippers to stay the night.'

Helen felt ashamed of herself for pushing the conversation. It really was none of her business. Her desperation to help Gav was leading her into strange ways.

'Please don't tell my husband, darling. I beg you,' Carla said.

Helen patted her hand. 'Your secret is safe with me. Come on, let's go back to the hotel. Breakfast will be ready soon.'

Deadly Dancing at the Seaview Hotel

When they reached the Seaview, Helen bade farewell to Carla then walked with Suki around to the back. When she entered the kitchen, she was stunned to see Sally working with Jean.

'Sally, what are you doing here? How are you? Did you get checked over by your GP?'

Sally waved her hand dismissively. 'The doc says everything's tickety-boo, there's no need to worry.'

'But you should be at home with Gav. How is he? Have the police taken him in again?'

Suki went to lie under the dining table.

'He's been at the police station all night with his solicitor. He's at home now, but he's tired and run-down. Poor Gav. Murder? It's too awful to think about. He's grabbing a nap, then heading to the salon to work with the forensics people, who are looking at the spray tan mechanism and the booth that Rosa used.'

Helen hugged her tight. 'If you're sure you're fine to work, that's great, but if you need to go home or to the salon to support Gav, please do.'

She nodded at Jean.

'What do you think of Jean without her glasses?'

'I've already told her it's strange seeing her without them,' Sally said, then she turned to Helen and added in a low voice, 'I think you should make her wear them. It might be because she can't see well, but she's forgotten to cook the eggs.'

'Don't talk about me as if I'm not here,' Jean snapped. 'I haven't forgotten the eggs, I was going to do them next.'

But when Helen looked at her, she saw that she seemed flustered, looking around the kitchen as if it was unfamiliar territory, not somewhere she'd worked for most of her life.

Jean leapt into action, breaking eggs into a bowl, whisking and adding milk.

'Please, Jean, wear your glasses at work,' Helen said.

Jean blinked hard, twice, but she didn't reply.

When Helen and Sally went upstairs to serve breakfast, Miriam was sitting at a table in the corner of the dining room.

'Morning, Miriam, did you sleep well?' Helen asked.

Miriam sniffed. 'Not as well as I would have done at the Vista del Mar. Now, Helen dear, I've heard from the . . .' she stopped and silently mouthed the next two words, '*pest control* people that they'll be finished today. Everything's sorted, so I can move back home after breakfast.'

Helen and Sally shared a smile of relief. Helen went into the hallway, out of Miriam's line of sight, and punched the air with glee.

The other guests began to make their way downstairs. Monty was first, looking as fresh as a daisy, his skin almost translucent and his eyes bright. Helen had to stop herself from swooning.

'Morning, Monty, how are you today?'

'Bereft, Helen. But the show must go on. I'm channelling my grief into choreographing a tribute to Rosa for us to dance at the opening of the competition.'

Next down was Bev, closely followed by Tommy.

'I hear you're going to be dancing together again,' Helen said.

Tommy took his sister's hand and twirled her under his arm. Bev bowed theatrically.

'We can't wait!' Tommy beamed, his white teeth gleaming.

Helen looked up when she heard more footsteps on the stairs. It was Carla and Paul. She noticed that Paul's feet had been reunited with the slippers.

'Morning!' she said cheerfully. She watched as they entered the dining room. Paul went one way and Carla the other, sitting as far apart from each other as they could.

'Good morning, darling,' Carla greeted her husband, but she still didn't sit at the same table as him. Meanwhile, Monty was taking a selfie.

'Morning, darling, you look great today,' he said, not taking his gaze from his phone.

Now that all the guests were seated, Helen introduced Miriam.

'This is an ... er ... a friend of mine who is joining us for breakfast today. It's just a one-off. She won't be any bother.' She glared at Miriam. 'Will you?'

Miriam smiled sweetly.

Helen and Sally sprang into action, carrying in plates of bacon and sausages, hash browns and toast, hot tea and coffee, marmalade and jam.

'Where are the eggs?' Sally asked.

Helen heard the dumbwaiter rumble. 'Jean's sending them up now,' she said.

They both stood by the hatch, waiting for the food. But when Helen opened it, there was just a glass bowl containing uncooked egg and milk. She stared at the wet, soggy mess, then headed into the dining room to apologise for the lack of eggs.

Miriam was working the room, walking from table to table. When Helen realised what she was up to, she was incredulous at first ... and then she was livid! The blasted woman was handing out her own business cards.

'It's the Vista del Mar, next door. Next time you're in Scarborough, do consider staying there. I earned my four stars before Helen. They'll give four stars to anyone these days. And of course, my hotel is a lot more refined than this one. I cater for a much higher class of guest, you see.'

Helen stormed across and took Miriam by the arm. She gritted her teeth. 'Sally, could you finish serving breakfast while I have a little word with our neighbour?'

She marched Miriam into the lounge and slammed the door shut.

'What the hell do you think you're doing?'

Miriam's mouth opened, then closed.

'I've got enough on my plate without you trying to steal my guests. Now listen to me, Miriam.'

The older woman's bottom lip began to tremble, but Helen's dander was up, and she wouldn't be stopped.

'Go back into the dining room, sit down and eat your breakfast. And behave yourself, or I'll chuck you out right now.'

She walked to the lounge door and pulled it open. But Miriam stayed where she was.

'You're in no position to speak to me that way, Helen dear. Last night I saw a forensics van outside the Seaview. I peeked around my door and watched you let officers into the dead woman's room. I then watched the news on TV and put two and two together. Another one of your guests has been murdered.'

Helen bristled. 'Yes, I'm afraid so. But it's got nothing to do with you, Miriam, so I'd be grateful if you'd keep your nose out of my business.'

'Oh, but it is my business,' Miriam said smugly. 'The news

Deadly Dancing at the Seaview Hotel

report mentioned the curse of the dance after what happened in Blackpool with the glitter ball.'

'And?' Helen said, getting infuriated now.

A little smile flickered across Miriam's face. 'Well, dear. I know all about Blackpool. I know who tried to bribe the judge.'

Chapter 25

Helen ushered Miriam away from the lounge door. She wanted her as far away from her guests as possible so they couldn't hear a word. She put her hands on the woman's shoulders and, none too gently, encouraged her to sit in a chair facing the window. Then she leaned in.

'What do mean, you know all about Blackpool? How?'

'I heard about it on the podcast, dear.'

'Paul's podcast?'

'Paul who, dear?'

Helen had to try hard to steady her temper. Miriam was really trying her patience.

'Paul Knight, of the *Dancing Knight & Daye* podcast,' she said through gritted teeth. 'He's one of my guests; he's in the dining room now. He podcasts everything about the dancers.'

'Paul Knight?' Miriam said, gazing out of the window. 'No, dear. That's not the podcast I listen to. The one I enjoy is a members' only podcast. It's called *Dancing Dayes*. You must subscribe; it's private and very exclusive. The woman who runs it decides who she lets listen to it. She sends us an encrypted link each week. It goes live each Sunday morning. I love to listen with a cup of Earl Grey with a squeeze of lemon after my cleaner has left.'

Helen felt her head going around in a circle.

Deadly Dancing at the Seaview Hotel

'*Dancing Dayes*? As in Dayes spelled with . . .'

'An *e*, yes, dear.' Miriam nodded.

Helen thought this too much of a coincidence.

'Does she ever mention Paul Knight?' she asked. This was getting complicated, and she didn't like it.

'Oh yes, she was married to him, dear, and she never has a good word to say about him. Sadie Daye, that's her name. She used to podcast with him before she set up on her own. He got to keep their original podcast name in the divorce.'

'Does Sadie ever say why they split up?'

'It was because of the dead woman, Rosa de Wolfe. Paul was having . . .' Miriam lowered her voice, 'an extramarital relationship with her, and Sadie found out.'

Helen bristled, surprised to find herself wanting to protect Paul.

'I don't think it was an affair. From what I understand, Paul was obsessed with Rosa; he had a crush on her, nothing more.'

Miriam waved her hand. 'Anyway, Sadie mentioned the curse of the dance last week in her podcast.'

'I didn't know you were a dancing fan,' Helen said.

Miriam sat up straight, then held her arms in a waltz frame Helen recognised from watching *Strictly Come Dancing*.

'I'm a huge dance fan, dear. I used to dance when I was a young woman; I've even won trophies. It's why my posture is so good and why I don't slouch.' She shot a pointed look at Helen. Helen stopped slouching and pushed her shoulders back.

'And what did Sadie Daye say about Blackpool?'

There was a knock at the door and Sally poked her head into the lounge. 'Sorry, Helen, I need you.'

'Can't it wait, Sally? I'm discussing something important with Miriam.'

Sally shook her head. 'No, it can't.'

Helen excused herself from Miriam and walked into the hall, where Sally looked unusually flustered.

'It's Jean, she's had a bad turn,' she said.

Helen's heart flipped and she rushed down to her apartment. Jean was sitting on the sofa, crying her eyes out. Next to her, with his dressing-gowned arm around her shoulders, was Jimmy.

Helen walked to Jean and knelt in front of her. 'What's happened?' she said, taking her friend's hands. When Jean didn't pull away, she knew things were serious.

'I need to go home, Helen. I'm not feeling great.'

'Are you unwell? Is that it?'

'No, love. Not physically, anyway. It's Mum's passing, you know, and her funeral the other day set me off again. I don't think I've dealt with her death very well. I can't believe she's gone. I've tried to cope, love. I've done my best. But I forgot to put sugar in the cake, I've messed up the eggs, and heaven only knows what other mistakes I'll make.'

She turned her tear-stained eyes to Helen.

'Could I have the day off tomorrow, please?'

'Of course you can, Jean. Take as much time as you need, and don't worry about the Seaview. Jimmy can help us do breakfasts.'

Jimmy gulped. 'Can I?'

Helen shot him a look, and he nodded.

'I can!' he said decisively. 'Let me run you home in Helen's car, Jean.'

'Not wearing my dressing gown you won't!' Helen said. 'You'll

Deadly Dancing at the Seaview Hotel

get arrested if a copper pulls you over. Put my old anorak on over the top and wrap a bath towel around your waist to hide your legs.'

'OK. And after I've dropped Jean off, I'll go home to get dressed, then bring your car back and . . .' he paused, 'maybe a suitcase of clothes to keep here?'

Helen's face fell. 'Now's not the time to discuss this, Jimmy,' she said firmly, nodding at Jean.

While Jimmy was getting ready, Helen sat next to Jean on the sofa. It was on the tip of her tongue to repeat the police's warning about Bobby, but she knew she couldn't nag her into submission, and now was certainly not the right time. So she kept quiet, the words burning on her tongue.

After a moment, she reached out a tentative arm for a hug, and was amazed when Jean accepted it.

'My word, you must be feeling bad,' she said, to which Jean raised a weak smile.

'I'll be back to my normal self soon.'

'Please wear your glasses when you come back,' Helen said.

'But Bobby said . . .'

Helen's stomach twisted at the sound of Bobby's name.

'Don't make me pull out the employer card, Jean, but I will if I must. When you're working, you need to see what you're doing. You're cutting with knives; you're working with a hot oven. You need to be sure that food's cooked. No glasses, no work. Got it?' She spoke gently but firmly, knowing it was the best way to handle her stubborn friend.

'Got it,' Jean replied.

As Jean and Jimmy left, Sally walked in.

'All OK upstairs?' Helen asked.

'Everyone's finished eating, and they've gone up to their rooms. Monty told me they're going to the Spa for rehearsals today. He's called Gav's Cabs to take them.'

Helen looked around the kitchen, which had been left in disarray after Jean's disastrous breakfast. 'I'll clear up in here,' she said.

'I'll send the dirty dishes down in the dumbwaiter.' Sally headed back upstairs.

Before Helen began to load the dishwasher, she swiped her phone into life and searched for the *Dancing Dayes* podcast. A picture of an attractive blonde woman with a forced smile popped onto her screen. She scrolled down the list of available episodes, and her heart almost leapt out of her chest when she saw one called 'Curse of the Dance'. She clicked the link and waited. A login form with a payment demand appeared. She sighed, wondering if she was willing to go through the palaver of signing up when she could simply ask Miriam what she'd heard. But that would mean spending time with her difficult neighbour, something she didn't want to do.

She sat down and tapped in her details, and received a message to say her application was pending. A few moments later, another message said her application had been successful and payment had been taken. She was now a member of Sadie Daye's exclusive dancing podcast. She pressed play and tuned in. She hoped she might learn something that would shed light on her guests, on who was most desperate to get rid of Rosa or who would benefit from her death. However, she was to be disappointed. Sadie Daye's podcast gave nothing away. It simply repeated what Helen had read online or seen on TV about the curse of the dance and the move of the competition to Scarborough. She tutted out loud as the woman's high-pitched voice encouraged the listener to tune in again to another of her insider podcasts.

'Insider, my backside,' she muttered.

Then Sadie's voice deepened a little and slowed as she explained that she had bonus content available to those willing to pay more through her subscription site. Helen felt conflicted. If she wanted to listen to the exclusive content, she had to pay more. So much more that she was shocked.

'I'm not paying that!' she cried. There was only one thing for it. She'd have to gird her loins and speak to Miriam.

Chapter 26

As Helen made her decision, Sally walked into the kitchen.

'Sally? Could you hold the fort for a few moments? I need to pop upstairs to see Miriam.'

She took the stairs two at a time. Finally, panting and out of breath, she reached the room at the top where Miriam had spent the night. She knocked at the door, and Miriam opened it straight away.

'Helen, my dear. What on earth do you want?'

Helen barged into the room without waiting to be asked.

'Is this how you treat all of your guests?' Miriam tutted. 'My word, Helen. You really need to go to landlady charm school.'

Helen decided not to waste time on a sarcastic retort. Her friend Gav was being investigated for a murder he hadn't committed, and she had to help prove his innocence.

'This subscription thing on Sadie Daye's podcast. Have you paid extra to join it?'

'Helen, dear. Can't you leave me in peace? I need to pack and go home. And let me tell you, the first thing I'll do is take a long, hot shower, to wash the smell of your dingy boarding house away.'

'Miriam!' Helen snapped.

Miriam almost jumped out of her skin. Knowing she'd got her attention this time, Helen began again, more gently. She didn't want to scare the woman away. Not yet, anyway, until she'd learned all that she could.

'Miriam, please have a seat, I need to speak to you.'

Miriam perched on the edge of her bed, her eyes darting about nervously.

'I'm sorry for shouting at you,' Helen said, 'but I need to know what the bonus content said about the curse of the dance.'

'Then sign up to the subscription site and pay,' Miriam said dismissively.

'It's ridiculously expensive! I've already paid to listen to the standard content, and that was far more than I expected to spend. There's no way I can afford to pay more, not at Sadie Daye's prices,' Helen said.

Miriam narrowed her eyes at her. 'So you thought you'd burst in here, demanding that I tell you what I heard. You want me to share content with you for free. Content that I can afford to pay for, but you can't. Is that right?'

There was silence between them for a few moments before Miriam spoke again.

'Look, Helen. You've hardly been a model landlady while I've been staying here. You interrupted my breakfast and now you're barging into my room. Heaven only knows how you get so much repeat business when you treat your guests so badly . . .'

'I do not treat my guests badly,' Helen hissed.

'. . . but if you can forget the little matter of the bill for my overnight stay, then in return, maybe I could find my way to telling you what I heard on the podcast.'

'Consider it done,' Helen said without hesitation. She put her finger to her lips and nodded at the door. 'My guests are still in their rooms until Gav's Cabs arrive to take them to the Spa. Speak quietly; the walls have ears.'

'There's no need to remind me of that, Helen dear. I can hear everything through our adjoining wall in the hall downstairs when I'm in the Vista del Mar.'

'Carry on,' Helen said, undeterred.

'Well, dear, there's an episode called "Glitter Ball Glory". It begins innocently enough, with tales of glitter balls from all over the world. Sadie Daye details a disco ball as high as a three-storey house, and one so small it fits in a matchbox.'

'That's a load of balls,' Helen said with a smirk.

Miriam wasn't amused. 'Don't be childish, dear. It really doesn't suit. Now then, in the bonus content available on Sadie's site, she talks about a smashed glitter ball in Blackpool.'

Helen's heart gave a one-two. Now she was getting somewhere. She clasped her hands in her lap and listened intently.

After Miriam had finished, Helen walked downstairs to her apartment, where Sally was cleaning the kitchen.

'My word, Helen, are you all right? You look as if you've seen a ghost.'

'Sit down, Sally. I need to tell you something.'

Sally sat opposite Helen at the dining table.

'What is it? Is Jean all right?'

'Yes, she's fine. Or at least she will be. Jimmy drove her home; he'll be coming back later.' *Without his suitcase*, Helen thought.

'I've been speaking to Miriam upstairs. She pays to listen to a podcast about ballroom and Latin American dancing, and it mentioned my guests.'

Deadly Dancing at the Seaview Hotel

'You don't normally pry into our guests' lives, Helen. That's something you instilled in me from day one.'

'This is different. It's a podcast. It's public knowledge. Or at least it is for those who can afford to pay for it, and Miriam does.'

'I didn't know she liked dancing,' Sally said.

'She's full of secrets, that one,' Helen replied. 'She told me she won trophies for dancing when she was a young woman, and she still likes to keep tabs on the dancing world.'

'What did she say that's upset you so much? You look strange.'

Helen bit her lip and raised her eyes to the ceiling. 'She heard on the podcast that one of our guests tried to bribe a judge in Blackpool, and when the judge . . .'

'. . . wouldn't budge, yes, we've been through this already,' Sally said impatiently.

'Indeed, so our guest arranged for him to come to a sticky end and planned for a glitter ball to fall on him. If it had hit him, it might have killed him.'

Sally shook her head. 'No, I don't think it would have. I remember years ago when a glitter ball fell on the soul singer Henry Marvel. He had to go to hospital, but he was all right.'

'What's Henry Marvel got to do with my guests?' Helen said.

'Sorry, Helen, I'm just saying. It knocked him out when it fell from the ceiling. A wire holding it in place snapped when he was rehearsing with his band in Tenby.'

'Did it land on his head?' Helen asked.

Sally searched on her phone. 'No, it says it clipped his face and landed on his shoulder, then shattered into pieces when it hit the floor. He went on to perform the same night, so he must have been all right.'

Helen thought about this for a moment.

'But if the glitter ball in Blackpool had landed directly on the judge's head, it could have done more serious injury. As it was, Bev was injured when she fell back in shock and hit herself on a table.'

Sally reached for Helen's hand across the tabletop. 'We know this already, Helen, so why do you look so shocked after speaking to Miriam?'

'Because I now know who tried to bribe the judge!' she said, eyes blazing.

Sally leaned forward. 'Who was it? Ooh, I bet it was Tommy Two Shoes. He seems far too good to be true.'

Helen shook her head. 'No, it wasn't Tommy.'

Sally's face clouded over. 'Well, it couldn't have been Bev. She would have stood well away from the judge so as not to be injured if she knew the glitter ball was on its way down. So was it the woman with the bobbed red hair?'

Helen shook her head again. 'No, it wasn't Carla . . . It was her husband, Monty Curzon.'

'No! But he's a dish!' Sally cried.

'Dishy or not, Monty's a devil in disguise. Sadie Daye revealed on the podcast that she saw him unsuccessfully trying to bribe the judge at Blackpool. She reckons the glitter ball falling was Monty getting revenge on the judge for failing to place him and Carla higher in the competition. The Magnificent Curzons aren't so magnificent after all. At least, Monty isn't, which makes me wonder if Carla knew what he'd done.'

Helen thought about Carla and Monty's separate bedrooms and, it seemed, separate lives.

'Or maybe Carla didn't know,' she muttered darkly.

Deadly Dancing at the Seaview Hotel

She felt a rush of heat building up in her neck, reaching her face, cheeks and forehead then spreading into her shoulders.

'Hold on, Sally. I'm having one of my Caribbean moments.'

She fanned herself with both hands. Sally brought her a glass of cool water and Helen drank it gratefully, waiting for her hot flush to dissipate. When it finally did, she and Sally shared a look.

'Anyway, where was I?' Helen pointed at her phone. 'Both Bev and Rosa knew the truth about what Monty did in Blackpool. I heard Bev talking to Monty on a bench on the clifftop and saying that Rosa had to be silenced. But what I don't get is why she's protecting him. If he was behind the glitter ball smash, then he was the one responsible for her injuries when she fell back in shock. I don't understand, Sally, it's so confusing.'

Sally's face clouded over. 'So this story about Monty in Blackpool is on the podcast that Miriam listened to?' she said.

'Yes, but it's hidden behind layers of admin and bureaucracy. You have to apply to Sadie Daye to listen, and believe me, it's not cheap. It's like a secret club. And that's just for first-level access to generic information that's available online, like the news about the curse of the dance. But even at the basic level, which I paid for, Sadie chooses who she'll let listen in . . . and who she keeps out. Then for bonus content, such as the full glitter ball story, she forces you to jump through more financial hoops. It's extortionate. I couldn't justify paying such a large sum. However, Miriam does pay extra. So all I have is Miriam's word that Monty is the one who bribed the judge and loosened the glitter ball. Now, as you know, I'm not a Miriam fan.'

Sally rolled her eyes. 'Me neither. She's snobby and offhand and thinks she's above us.'

Helen nodded her head in agreement. 'Yes, she's all of those things, but I don't think she's a liar. Mind you, she did tell a little white lie the other day when she ran out of her hotel screaming. She said she was practising scales, but I know now that she was protecting herself about the news about the bedbugs. She would have been in shock at finding them. I'd have been the same. No, Miriam is generally honest to a fault. However, we have no way of knowing if Sadie Daye is telling the truth.'

After Sally left for the day, Helen received a phone call from Jimmy. He asked if he could keep her car a while longer, as Jodie had called him to ask if he could help transport furniture from the hostel for someone moving out to live in a flat. Helen agreed immediately, as her car was much bigger than Jimmy's. She told him to keep it as long as he needed; she wasn't going to need it that day. She was happy to hear that he and Jodie were back on good terms.

Then he told her that he'd dropped Jean at home, seen her safely inside and made her a cup of tea. When Jean had assured him that she'd be perfectly all right on her own, he'd left. But, he added, as he'd walked back to the car, he'd seen a man in Cuban heels loitering at the end of Jean's street.

Chapter 27

Cuban heels could only mean one thing – Bobby Tanner. Helen felt sick on hearing Jimmy's news, but there was little she could do about it. She'd done her best to warn Jean. She'd have another try when Jean felt strong enough to return to work and was wearing her glasses, putting sugar in her cake mix and cooking eggs at breakfast again.

'What do you think, Suki?' she asked.

The dog lifted her paw in response.

'Not again,' Helen sighed.

She checked Suki's deep pad. There was nothing inside, and it wasn't red or inflamed. However, clearly something was bothering her. Helen rang the vet to ask if she should bring Suki in, but the receptionist wasn't too concerned.

'It might be a corn,' she said.

'But I can't see or feel anything,' Helen said, inspecting Suki's paw with both hands while she nestled her phone under her chin.

'Is the dog in distress?' the receptionist asked.

Helen looked into Suki's steel-grey eyes.

'No, she's as happy as ever. She's not crying and doesn't seem to be in pain. She's not limping either.'

'Is she eating well?'

'As much as always.'

'Then just keep your eye on it, and if you see inflammation, bring her in. Until then, I wouldn't worry too much. It's probably attention-seeking.'

Reassured, Helen hung up the phone and made a fuss of Suki, stroking her.

'Would you like to go out?' she asked.

Suki cocked her head to one side.

'For a walk?'

At the sound of the magic word, the dog walked straight to the door and waited patiently while Helen fastened her lead to her collar. Within minutes they were walking along King's Parade to the beach. However, when Helen saw the tide was in again, she decided to change her route.

'How about a longer walk today?' she asked. She knew that Suki, like most greyhounds, didn't enjoy long walks. Twenty minutes twice a day usually sufficed, but Helen felt like she needed to get a breath of fresh air, as she had a lot on her mind. If Suki began to flag, she'd sit on a bench and enjoy the view of the sea while the dog had a rest.

She headed in the direction of the castle, past her friend Marie's teashop, Tom's Teas. She waved at Marie, who was serving morning coffee and cheese scones. Marie waved back and smiled.

Helen walked on, up and over the top of the hill, past the castle, meandering along the path. Ahead of her the sea sparkled in Scarborough's South Bay. She saw the working harbour with its fishing boats. She saw lobster pots piled on the waterside. She saw ice cream parlours, fish and chip shops, donkeys on the beach and amusement arcades. There was more life on the South Bay, more noise and traffic. The contrast between the bays was one of the joys

Deadly Dancing at the Seaview Hotel

of Scarborough, one of the many things Helen loved. She sometimes wondered if she and Marie were the Scarborough bays in human form. Marie would be the South Bay; brassy and bold, confident and colourful. Whereas Helen would be the North Bay; prim and proper, quiet and calm. The thought of this made her smile. Ahead of her was the Grand Hotel, a Scarborough landmark, an icon and beautiful to look at from the outside. Inside, its faded grandeur still attracted coachloads of tourists to stay there each year.

'Are you doing all right, girl?' she asked Suki, who wasn't yet protesting at being walked for longer than normal.

Helen carried on, along Foreshore Road, and came to the Bay View café. There were tables and chairs outside in the sunshine, and she decided to stop for a while. She ordered a cappuccino, and Suki lay in the shade at her feet, drinking from a bowl of water the waitress set down. As Helen sipped her coffee, she watched donkeys walking on the beach, carrying children on their backs. She saw deckchair attendants, candyfloss sellers and whelk stalls. Beyond it all was the golden sand and blue sea of the beautiful sweeping bay.

'Ready to walk on, Suki?' she asked as she stood.

She walked along the prom, past amusement arcades with their bright lights and music, past Zoltan the fortune-teller in his glass box, promising to reveal the destiny of passers-by in exchange for a pound in the slot. She walked past the Victorian Central Tramway that travelled uphill from the beach to town. Finally she arrived at the Spa, one of the many jewels in Scarborough's crown. The grand Victorian building now staged family entertainment, comedy nights, conferences and wedding fairs. It stood proudly by the beach, providing unrivalled views across the bay. Views that lifted Helen's heart. It was picture-postcard perfect.

As she had Suki with her, she knew she couldn't enter the Spa. Only assistance and guide dogs were allowed inside, and Suki was neither of those. Instead, she walked around the impressive, historic sun court, where an organist played and tourists sat on striped deckchairs, feet tapping to the music. Outside the entrance to the Ocean Room, she caught sight of a tall, slim man. She recognised him straight away. It was Monty, but he didn't look his usual self, and his phone was nowhere in sight. Helen realised it was the first time she'd seen him without it. She walked up to him.

'Hello, Monty, nice to see you.'

'Yes, it is. How wonderful,' he said, smiling.

'What are you doing here? Shouldn't you be inside, rehearsing?'

'I needed some time away from the music, to think,' he said. He backed away from Suki. 'Do you normally walk your dog here?'

'Not usually. But just like you, I needed time to think too. I decided to take a long walk.' She examined his face. 'I have a lot on my mind.'

'We all do, it's a difficult time.'

'Have the police been in touch with you again?' she asked.

Monty nodded. 'Yes, to repeat their request that we stay in Scarborough while they carry out their enquiries. None of us have the heart to leave anyway, it wouldn't be right. Plus, if we see the dance competition through, it'll help us to heal after the shock of what happened to Rosa.'

'And how are your rehearsals coming on?'

His face fell. 'Not great, to be honest. We're having to dig deep into ourselves to get over the loss of our friend.'

Deadly Dancing at the Seaview Hotel

Helen turned her back to the wall, standing shoulder to shoulder with Monty. She decided to speak to him without eye contact, thinking it'd be easier to ask the questions she needed to know the answers to in order to help Gav. They both gazed at the sea.

'Yes, it's a terrible business about Rosa,' she said softly. When Monty didn't stir, she carried on. 'Monty, have you heard of the podcaster Sadie Daye?'

He turned to her quickly. 'Yes, she's Paul's ex-wife. Why do you ask?'

Helen took her time and chose her words carefully.

'I listened to her podcast this morning,' she said. It was a little white lie, but she figured that Monty would never know that it was Miriam who'd listened and told Helen what she'd heard.

'Oh,' Monty said, despondent, as he turned back to face the sea.

'I heard about the curse of the dance and the Blackpool glitter ball.'

She felt him stiffen at her side.

'What about it?' he said, looking straight ahead. Helen squared her shoulders and carried on. She'd said too much now not to get it all out.

'You were mentioned in the podcast, Monty, and what I heard wasn't good. Is it true you tried to bribe a judge?'

There, she'd said it. The words were out. Monty hung his head, and Helen peered at him from the corner of her eye. He looked genuinely upset, and she felt a twinge of guilt. She felt even more guilty knowing that he had nowhere to run. He couldn't escape, as she had positioned herself in front of the door that led to the Ocean Room. However, she'd come this far, and she was determined not to leave without discovering the truth.

'Did Rosa know? You see, I overheard you telling Bev that Rosa had to be silenced before she told Paul about this for his podcast.'

'Are you accusing me of Rosa's murder, Mrs Dexter?' Monty said darkly.

There was menace in his voice that Helen didn't like. She forced a little laugh, which came out more high-pitched than expected and made her feel embarrassed. She made herself carry on.

'It's a difficult time, Monty. Forgive me, my imagination has run away with me. I've got the police asking questions, and forensics have been to the Seaview. It's been tough on me and my staff. Plus, Gav who runs the tanning salon is my good friend, and he's currently the only suspect. I refuse to see him charged for a crime I know he didn't commit. And once the Seaview is mentioned in the news, business will fall, we'll start to get cancellations . . .'

She carried on, hoping to catch Monty off guard.

'Were you responsible for the glitter-ball smash? Was it your revenge on the judge?'

This time, Monty turned to her with fury on his face, his eyes shooting daggers.

'The smashed glitter ball was nothing to do with me!' he snarled. 'Now, if you'll excuse me, I need to get back to my colleagues and my wife.'

He stepped in front of Helen, but if he'd been expecting her to move away from the door so he could disappear inside, he was disappointed.

'Ah yes, your wife. The Magnificent Mrs Curzon,' she said with a smile. 'Does Carla know that you and Bev talk together about what happened in Blackpool?'

Monty drew in a lungful of air and puffed out his chest. 'My wife and I have an understanding,' he said. The words tripped easily off his tongue, in a smooth, practised way. Helen guessed it wasn't the first time he'd said them. 'Carla has her lovers and I have mine. It's no secret that we have an open marriage. But we have a cast-iron rule. It's one that both of us abide by.'

'A rule?' Helen asked innocently, feeling she knew what was coming. She'd heard these exact words before, from Carla.

'Yes, the rule is that we don't sleep with anyone else in the immediate group of dancers that we're working with. So you see, I broke our golden rule when I slept with Bev in Blackpool, and that's why Carla must never know. Besides which, Bev and I were over a very long time ago. However, it's really none of your business,' he added formally. 'Now, if you'll excuse me, I need to get back to choreograph the routine. Paul is podcasting live from our rehearsals. I'm sure that if you want to keep tabs on us all, you could tune in to his podcast.'

Helen stood to one side, fully aware of the sarcasm in his voice. How she hated being so suspicious, but she also hated the Seaview being mentioned in a murder inquiry, and her friend Gav being implicated. Then a thought struck her, and an idea popped into her head.

Chapter 28

Helen ruminated on her idea as she walked Suki on the golden sands. Families were playing frisbee, and children were running in and out of the waves. She needed to be somewhere quiet, so she continued along the beach, away from the Spa. The sand turned to shingle, and she watched Suki to see if her paw acted up. However, the greyhound seemed fine.

She reached a narrow strip of shingle where tiny pebbles and sea glass washed up. She couldn't resist looking down as she walked, hoping to find a piece of glass smoothed and tumbled by the sea. A tiny fragment of royal blue, wet with seawater and sparkling in the sun, caught her eye. She bent down, picked it up and dropped it into her pocket. When she reached the end of the shingle, she flopped down onto dry stones, and Suki lay beside her. It was quiet there and she was alone. The only sound was the gentle push and pull of the waves.

She took her phone from her handbag and swiped it into life, then opened the *Dancing Knight & Daye* podcast. The episode she wanted to listen to was near the top of the list, dated the previous day when Paul was podcasting from the salon, and was titled 'Live Podcast'. Perfect, this was just as she'd hoped. She clicked the link, turned the sound up and tuned in. But the link didn't open. There was no podcast to listen to. She wondered if Paul had deleted it after what had happened to Rosa.

Instead, she clicked on the link to listen to Paul's current livestream from the Ocean Room at the Spa. It sounded fun and brought a smile to her lips. She could hear the music for a samba and her feet moved in time to the beat. She absent-mindedly stroked Suki's ears, thinking about her guests inside the Ocean Room. She thought again about what Monty had told her about his relationship with Bev, although it seemed to be in the past now. Was that what they'd wanted kept secret from Rosa?

'Why do people get themselves tangled up this like, Suki?' she said. She thought of both Carla and Monty taking lovers, then lying to each other about not sleeping with people in the troupe they were currently working with.

'Each to their own. Who knows what goes on behind closed doors?' she said, letting Suki's ears ripple through her fingers. She tried to think of Carla with Paul, but had to admit she found it hard to see what someone so glamorous and well turned out saw in someone like Paul, who wasn't. Then she thought about Monty and Bev. Again, the image was hard to digest. Bev was a lot older than Monty.

'It takes all sorts to make the world go around,' she muttered.

She stood and brushed down her jeans, then began to head slowly home. The easiest way to walk between Scarborough's beautiful bays was around the headland, following the sea. But this was also the longest route. The shortest route was over the hill by the castle or through town centre streets. She knew Suki would be tired after all the walking that day and so opted for the shorter route. Even then, it took an hour to get home, and involved two ten-minute rests, sitting on benches on the clifftop.

When she eventually reached King's Parade, she walked past the Seaview towards the corner. As she passed the lounge window, she saw Paul sitting alone and made a snap decision. At the back of the hotel, she quickly unleashed Suki and let her into her apartment, noting that Jimmy hadn't yet returned, then ran upstairs. She paused at the top before opening the door to the hallway. She didn't want to appear out of breath and desperate, although that was exactly what she was. She took a deep breath, then walked slowly into the lounge.

'Oh, hello, Paul,' she said casually. 'I had no idea you were here. I've just come to do a quick stock-check. You don't mind if I make a little noise while I count the bottles, do you?' Not waiting for a reply, she slid behind the bar. She glanced at Tom's photo on the wall and wondered what he'd have told her to do. Then she turned to Paul.

'Fancy a drink? It's on the house.'

Paul didn't reply; he just kept gazing out of the window. Helen yawned theatrically, stretching her arms above her head.

'I know I could do with one. Sure you won't join me?'

He finally turned to her and smiled. 'Could I have a glass of red wine, please?'

She opened a bottle of Rioja and poured two large glasses. Taking them over to Paul, she indicated the seat next to him.

'Mind if I sit down?' She didn't wait for a reply.

Paul lifted his glass by the stem and raised it aloft. 'To my Rosa,' he said.

Helen followed suit, then sipped her drink, watching Paul carefully.

Deadly Dancing at the Seaview Hotel

'You must be devastated,' she said softly.

Paul nodded slowly. 'It's good that I've got my podcast to concentrate on; it helps stop me over-thinking. I've been podcasting live this morning from rehearsals. Now I'm planning a special episode as a tribute to Rosa. I'll live-stream from the competition when the troupe dance to Monty's specially choreographed piece. I'll be able to describe the dance to my listeners in time to the music.'

Helen noticed that when Paul talked about his podcast, his face lit up and his eyes sparkled. She sipped her wine again and looked out of the window.

'It's a beautiful view, isn't it? I never tire of looking at it,' she said. Paul began to murmur in agreement, then Helen went in for the kill. 'Do you podcast live often?'

He looked at her then, synapses firing, a smile on his face and a gleam in his eye, and she knew she'd got his attention. He began talking about microphones, editing software, social media sites he posted to, sound levels, quality, consistency, the right choice of jingle. He explained about uploading files, revenue streams and contacts he'd made in the industry who now regarded him as an expert on the subject of dance. With the overload of information, Helen's mind began to wander; she felt too bogged down in detail, which wasn't what she wanted.

'I see,' she said when he finished speaking. She didn't see at all, but she nodded thoughtfully, for effect, and was pleased that Paul seemed happy she'd taken such an interest. She suspected the dancers didn't ask him about his podcasting as much as he might like.

'And on the day . . .' She paused, forming her words as gently as possible. Paul might be unshaven, unwashed, wearing dirty clothes and awful brown slippers, but he *was* grieving. 'On the day at the tanning salon, you were podcasting live then, right?'

'Yes, I was. I interviewed you, remember? I still have the original file on my laptop so you can listen to it whenever you like.'

Helen didn't want to admit that she'd already tried to listen to it earlier on the beach, and so she chose her words carefully.

'Is that podcast still available?'

Paul managed a weak smile. 'No. The police asked me to send them the sound file, which I did. I think they're hoping to hear something that might help them catch the killer. They also demanded that I take the podcast offline, but I'd already done that, out of respect to Rosa. I still have the original file on my laptop, though; it's a recording of the live podcast.'

He choked back a tear, turned his face away from Helen and picked up his drink. He sipped it, then turned back to her.

'I could explain again how podcasting works, if you're unfamiliar with it. I know some people of your age aren't really au fait with technology.'

Helen lifted her glass and took another drink. *Her age?* She was only fifty. Feeling a hot flush starting at the back of her neck, she picked up a beer mat and wafted her face. She thought for a moment. She'd never played dumb before, but there was a first time for everything, and, well, there was a murder to solve. So if Paul thought she was too old to understand podcasting, she decided to use this to her advantage.

'Oh, people my age haven't a clue, Paul,' she said, still fanning her face with the mat. 'Why don't you tell me all about it.'

Paul's eyes lit up again. 'I could show you if you'd like? I mean, upstairs in the room I'm using as a studio. The editing software I've got can replay it all, and it'll include details you don't get when you listen online.'

'Such as the time you started and ended a live podcast?' Helen asked innocently.

'Timing? Yes, of course, it's all there in the file. I can talk you through the recording of the live podcast on the day when . . .' He swallowed hard. 'Well, the day we were at the tanning salon.'

'Are you sure you feel up to it? I don't want to upset you by listening to something you recorded that day.'

But Paul had already pushed his chair back and was carrying his glass to the lounge door. 'Come on, Helen, I'd love to show you how it works.'

And so Helen followed him up to the room that he was using as his studio. She sat on the edge of the bed as he played the podcast she'd tried to listen to earlier on the beach. She played dumb and asked questions she already knew the answers to. And all the while, she kept her eye on the recording time in the editing software. The time he had started recording that day had been captured, as had the time his live podcast ended. She concentrated hard. And then she heard Sally's voice, a scream. Followed by silence. And she knew, without a doubt, that as Paul had been podcasting live from outside the salon at the time Rosa was murdered, it was unlikely he could have killed her.

She stood, thanked him profusely for showing someone of her advanced age – and here she fluttered her hands at her heart for added irony that she felt was lost on him – how podcasting worked. Then she walked out of the room, mentally ticking him off her list of suspects for Rosa's death.

Chapter 29

When she returned to her apartment, her mobile rang with a call diverted from the Seaview's landline.

'Good afternoon, Seaview Hotel,' she said politely.

'Helen, it's DS Hutchinson. How are things?' he asked.

Helen sank onto the sofa and rolled her eyes at Suki.

'If you're asking me how I am, I'm not good,' she replied honestly. 'I could be harbouring a murderer at the Seaview, unless you're ringing to tell me you've caught the culprit.'

'I wish that was the reason for my call, but sadly it's not. I'm calling to ask you to continue to keep your eyes and ears on your guests. They already know they're not allowed to leave Scarborough, and from what I understand, they have plans to dance at the competition. So that gives us time to continue our investigation at the salon. Forensics are all over it. How *are* your guests, by the way?'

'Tell me how Gav is first,' she said.

'He's still on our list of suspects, Helen. That's all I'm allowed to share.'

Helen's shoulders dropped. It wasn't what she'd hoped to hear.

'Now, your guests,' DS Hutchinson said.

Helen thought for a moment.

'Well, I've just had a long conversation about podcasting with one of them,' she said.

Deadly Dancing at the Seaview Hotel

'Podcasting? There's no need to be flippant, Helen,' he snapped. 'This is a murder inquiry.'

'Flippant? Me? You should know me well enough by now to know I'm anything but,' she said firmly. 'The conversation I had was with Paul Knight. He was podcasting live from outside the salon at the time Rosa was murdered. The timer on his editing software proves it.'

'I see,' DS Hutchinson said. 'Good work, Helen. I'll send DC Hall over to question him again. Anything more you can tell us? What about . . .'

Helen heard the rustling of paper and guessed the detective was consulting his notes.

'What about Mr and Mrs Curzon – Monty and Carla. Plus Bev Cassidy and her brother, Mr Two Shoes?'

Helen stifled a smile. 'His name's Tommy and he's a lovely guy. Look, DS Hutchinson, I'm a seaside hotel landlady, not a detective. You can't expect me to interrogate my guests. I've got the Seaview to run, and to add to my woes, my grieving chef has forgotten how to cook. Plus, my cleaner has more on her mind than vacuuming floors. She's trying to support Gav as much as she can. She's also pregnant with twins, caring for her child, looking after her mum and going through her exams at college. These people are my friends and I want to help them.'

There was more on Helen's mind that she kept quiet about. For a start, there was the ticking app, the beating heart emoji on her phone, counting down the days to the holiday to Graceland, a trip she still wasn't sure she could make with Jimmy. Not in the year of her silver wedding anniversary. Plus, Jimmy kept bringing up the possibility of moving into the Seaview, something she wasn't sure about. There wasn't the space, for a start. He'd need a spare room just to hang up his Elvis outfits. Then there was Miriam's bedbug infestation. The Vista del Mar was separated from the Seaview by a wall built over a hundred years ago. Was it possible that bedbugs *could* pass through walls? She made a mental note to google it. And there was her best friend, Marie, who she'd neglected recently. Oh, for a night out, gossiping and laughing over pizza and wine. Finally there was Suki's paw, which was still a concern.

'Helen? Are you still there?'

'Yes, I'm here. But I'm telling you now, as much as I want the murder inquiry to end and my life to go back to normal, I'm not spying on my guests. It's something I'd never do.'

'Don't think of it as spying,' he said. 'Think of it as doing your duty for the police. You're the eyes and ears of the force.'

'Don't you have police dogs for that?' she said. 'Next you'll be feeding me doggy treats, patting me on the head and telling me I'm a good girl.'

'There's no need to be sarcastic,' DS Hutchinson said.

'Oh, I wasn't. You'll know if I was,' Helen said sarcastically.

'Helen, listen, we'd really appreciate it if you could keep an eye on your guests. That's all I ask. Think you can do it?'

She sighed. 'I'll do what I can.'

'Good girl,' DS Hutchinson said, and rang off.

Helen threw her phone down. She closed her eyes, pressed her head back against the sofa and tried to calm her racing heart by breathing deeply, one, two, three. There was a noise at the unlocked door and Jimmy walked in. She wondered if she should cut a key for him. He looked handsome, she thought, dressed in a white

T-shirt and black jeans. She was relieved to see he'd arrived without a suitcase.

'I've brought your car back, and your anorak and towel,' he said.

'Cheers, Jimmy.'

He sat down on the sofa and reached for Suki to stroke her, but Suki backed away.

'She's still not sure about me, is she?' Jimmy said, sounding hurt.

'There's only one way to win Suki round. You've got to get on her good side and feed her. She'll be putty in your hands after you give her a tin of sardines from the cupboard. If you open that and put them in her bowl, she'll love you for ever.'

Jimmy turned to her. 'You look done in.'

Helen gave a wry smile. 'Yup, the murder of one of my guests is proving hard to deal with.'

He looked at her with concern. 'Would you rather I went home? I could call Gav's Cabs. Or as it's so nice outside, I could fancy the walk.'

Helen stuffed her hands in the pockets of her hoodie; she hadn't taken it off since she'd come in. Her fingers found the tiny piece of blue sea glass she'd found on the beach. She pulled it out and turned it over.

'Pretty, isn't it?' she said. She held it up against the light streaming in through the patio doors. 'Mind you, it's not as pretty as it looked on the beach, when it was wet with seawater and glistening in the sun. I might take it back next time I'm down there and return it to the sea.'

She stood and walked into the kitchen, dropping the sea glass into the fruit bowl next to the tiny red bead that she'd found in the hallway. She liked how the red and the blue looked together.

'I wish I was crafty; I could make something nice,' she said, admiring the sea glass and the bead.

Jimmy walked across to her. He was looking sheepish, she thought. 'What is it?'

He laid his hands on the kitchen worktop, then looked into her eyes.

'I was wondering, you know . . . about what we talked about.'

Helen had an awful feeling she knew where this was going. She braced herself.

'Do you mean about you moving in?'

A smile broke out on Jimmy's face. 'Actually, no, that's not what I wanted to speak to you about . . . not right now, anyway. But sometime, I hope.'

'Yes, sometime,' she said, holding his gaze.

He looked crestfallen. 'But not yet?'

Helen shook her head. 'No, not yet,' she said firmly. 'So what was it you wanted to say?'

Jimmy pulled his phone from his jeans pocket and slid it onto the worktop in front of her. In the middle of the screen was the beating heart emoji.

'I was wondering, Helen, have you made a decision about whether to come with me?'

There was silence in the kitchen while Helen tried to form her reply. She heard Jean's voice urging her to tell Jimmy the truth.

'I can't . . .' she stuttered.

Tell him about your promise. Tell him that you swore you'd never go to Graceland without Tom. Tell him, Helen. Tell him.

Deadly Dancing at the Seaview Hotel

'Why?' Jimmy asked, the air knocked out of him.

Helen's mind ran riot with Jean's words.

Tell him, Helen, tell him.

'I can't tell you!' she cried, then she ran to the sofa and sat with her head in her hands.

Jimmy sat next to her and put his arm around her. Tears streamed down her face and her shoulders heaved. She pulled a tissue from her pocket and wiped her eyes. She hated him seeing her like this.

'I'm sorry, I didn't mean to pressure you,' he said. 'I've been insensitive. I shouldn't have booked it without speaking to you first. I assumed you'd want to be with me as much as I want to be with you.'

Helen rested her hand on his knee and tried to pull herself together.

'I *do* want to be with you. I want to go on holiday.'

Tell him.

'But I can't go to Graceland.'

Tell him.

'Because . . . because I . . .' She turned to face him and looked deep into his brown eyes. 'Because I swore I'd never go to Graceland with anyone but Tom.'

Jimmy's shoulders sank. 'Oh. I see,' he said.

'No, Jimmy, you don't. Please, let me explain.'

Look, Jean! I'm telling him the truth.

She told him everything, about her upcoming silver wedding anniversary, the pilgrimage that Tom had always wanted to make, the promise that she'd never visit Graceland with anyone else. It all came tumbling out. Afterwards, Jimmy held her in his arms.

'I understand,' he said, but she could tell how much she'd hurt him. She felt dreadful and hated seeing him upset. But she also felt relieved that her secret was finally out.

'I'm sorry, Jimmy. But you see, there's no way I can go to Graceland.'

He slowly removed his arm from around Helen's shoulders and stood. His face was crumpled and his eyes were red.

'I'll, er . . . well, I think I'll walk home. I might call at the Stumble Inn for a pint on the way. And I'll, er . . . I'll be in touch, Helen. If you need me, just ring.'

Helen stood too, feeling awkward. Her beautiful, wonderful Jimmy was standing in front of her with a hole in his heart, because of her. She'd wounded him and she knew it. She choked back a lump in her throat and stepped forward, hoping to take his hand, to stop him from leaving, but he stepped back, shook his head, then turned and walked away.

Chapter 30

Helen felt bereft. She wanted to race after him and hug him, but she had to let him go. She couldn't bring herself to say the words he wanted to hear. She couldn't go to Graceland.

She turned to Suki. 'Oh, don't look at me like that,' she tutted.

Suki didn't reply, because, well, she was a greyhound and also because the Seaview's doorbell rang at that moment. It chimed downstairs in Helen's apartment as well as upstairs in the hall. She checked the CCTV monitor on her kitchen workbench, and it showed a delivery man at the front door. Leaving Suki behind, she walked upstairs and signed for a parcel of her new tabards, which included the larger ones for Sally and Jean. She was about to close the door when Tommy Two Shoes sauntered up the path. She beamed a smile at him. Despite getting a free spray tan on the day of Rosa's death, he still looked pale and wan.

'Good afternoon, Tommy. How are you?'

He cast his gaze to the floor. 'I'm not good, Helen, truth be told. I'm feeling sick to the stomach about what happened to Rosa. Whilst at the Spa today I tried to dance away the demons and kick away the curse, but my heart's not in it. I've left the others to it, with Monty in charge of getting the show dance right.' He headed to the stairs.

Helen suddenly had an idea. Well, it'd worked with Paul just now, so why not try it again?

'Tommy, would you like a drink from the bar? It's on the house.'

'I could really do with going to my room, Helen. I'm worn out,' he said.

She knew she'd have to try harder.

'I'll throw in a packet of cheese and onion,' she said with what she hoped was a tempting smile.

Tommy paused with his hand on the post at the bottom of the stairs.

'All right then. I could do with a sit-down and a chat. Make it a packet of salt and vinegar, and I'll have a rum and Coke.'

Helen put her parcel down, then searched behind the bar for a bottle of rum she felt sure she had but couldn't remember where. Finally, she found it, poured a measure into a glass and took it to Tommy with a small bottle of Coke. She poured herself a glass of red wine and sat next to him. She remembered how she'd manipulated Paul into revealing where he was at the time of Rosa's death. Could she do the same with Tommy? She sat up straight in her seat, looked at Tommy from the corner of her eye, then nodded at the window.

'Lovely view, isn't it? I never tire of looking at it.'

But Tommy didn't glance up.

'I don't really enjoy the sea, Helen. My parents died in a boating accident when Bev and I were kids. It was Bev who took care of me, she brought me up. She does everything for me. She manages my dancing career. She looks after my accounts and my diary. She even works out my diet sheets because I've got such a sweet tooth and I'm always putting weight on, no matter how much I dance. I owe her my life.'

Deadly Dancing at the Seaview Hotel

Helen's well-meaning plans to get the truth out of Tommy had taken an unexpected, sad turn. She felt tears well up in her eyes.

'I'm very sorry, I had no idea.'

'It's all right,' Tommy said, beaming his ultra-white smile. When he smiled, his face lit up and Helen recognised the star he'd once been, little Tommy Two Shoes dancing on Saturday TV. 'You know, when we dance at Blackpool or here in Scarborough, or any seaside town in the country, it's hard on me and Bev. It's a constant reminder of how Mum and Dad died. They were such wonderful dancers, they danced in Europe and won trophies. I can only hope to be half as good as them.'

Helen eyed him. 'Is there any news on the TV show, after what happened . . .?' she asked cautiously.

He shook his head. 'No,' he said firmly.

He picked up his rum and Coke and downed half of it in one gulp. Helen looked on in astonishment.

'I've made a decision, Helen. As I walked back from the Spa, I decided that if I don't get my show, I'm giving up dancing for ever.'

'That's quite a change. Are you sure?'

He turned to her and smiled weakly. 'No, but what else can I do? I'm fed up with flogging myself as a jack of all trades in village halls and community centres. Even the celebrity cruises become dull once you've worked on a few. I really can't face any more. You know, I've resigned myself to thinking that my TV dream won't happen, although Bev tells me to keep believing. As you know, Rosa and I were rivals for the show, but even with Rosa gone, the TV production company haven't made a decision. Besides, if I was given the show, there are people out there who'd point their finger at me. They'd say I didn't deserve it after Rosa died. Some of them might even blame me for what happened to her.'

Helen looked askance at him. 'Surely you don't mean people would assume you murdered her?' she asked. Which was exactly what she wanted to know. She picked up her glass, took a sip, all the while keeping her gaze on Tommy over the rim.

'There's a lot of jealousy out there in the dancing world,' he said quietly, then he turned his head away. 'I can't help thinking I'd be better off giving up this life. There's too much heartbreak involved.'

'What would you do instead?' she asked.

'I'd bake,' he said without hesitation. His eyes lit up. His smile brightened the room, and he sat up straight, becoming animated in a way Helen had never seen before. 'I'd buy a cottage in the Lake District, set up a professional kitchen and bake cakes, bread and pies. Baking is a passion of mine.'

Helen loved finding out snippets like these about her guests, discovering their secret talents.

'The cook here at the Seaview – I mean the chef, Jean – loves to bake. Her cakes are wonderful . . . or at least they used to be.'

Tommy thought for a moment.

'I bought the most delicious peach melba in town,' he said, but then his face fell. 'Actually, I bought it on the day Rosa died, from a café close to the tanning salon.' Helen heard a tenderness in his voice. He picked up his rum and Coke again. 'I'll think of her each time I eat one.'

Helen thought about peach melbas, with their pastel orange icing, fruit and cream in the middle, all enclosed in a pastry case.

'It was a small café called Bonnet's on Huntriss Row,' Tommy continued. 'What a gorgeous place it was. Old-fashioned and quite delightful, with exquisite hand-made chocolates for sale.'

Helen knew Bonnet's coffee shop well. It was where she often met Marie for lunch. Their quiches and salads were sublime, and Tommy was right about the hand-made chocolates, they were delicious. She also knew that on the day Rosa died, Bonnet's had suffered an electrical outage, as had all the cafés and shops on Huntriss Row. The businesses had been closed until noon. Local social media had been abuzz for hours.

'What time did you go to Bonnet's to buy your peach melba?' she asked.

Tommy's face blushed pink, and again Helen wondered why he wasn't as tanned as the others.

'Oh Helen, promise you won't tell Bev?'

Helen held up her right hand and crossed her fingers. 'I give you my seaside landlady pledge.'

'I didn't know there was such a thing,' he said.

'There is now,' she replied quickly. 'What time did you buy the cake?'

Tommy faltered. 'Time?' he said nervously.

Helen went in for the kill. 'I saw you troop into the tanning salon with the others.'

'And I trooped straight out again. That's why I didn't get the full tan,' he replied, pointing at his face.

Helen recalled that quite a crowd had built up around Jimmy when he was singing, and people had been dancing in the street. She knew this could have obstructed her view of Tommy leaving the salon. It wasn't as if she was keeping tabs on her guests at the time. She'd been somewhat distracted by Jimmy in his tight white

Elvis suit. There was something about the way it hugged his thighs that she particularly liked. She snapped her attention back to Tommy, who was still talking.

'Bev will kill me if she finds out I wasn't at the tanning salon for the full session. Firstly, I shouldn't be eating cakes, and if she finds out I nipped to Bonnet's for a peach melba, I'll be put back on my diet. She likes to keep my body lean for dancing. She says nobody likes to watch a flabby fandango or a tubby tango. And secondly, she wanted me to have a full spray tan – she always says I'm too pale. She manages everything about me, you see, even my image. So after I bought the cake at Bonnet's, I ate it en route back to the salon, then I went inside for my spray tan. Gav showed me how to use the booth. But I suffer from claustrophobia, Helen, so I never went in. I was too scared. He was with me all the time, trying to reassure me. The next thing I knew, I heard a woman scream, there was a kerfuffle and then Rosa's body was found.'

Helen let this sink in.

'So tragic,' she said, eyeing Tommy carefully, trying to gauge his mood, wondering how best to change the conversation. 'Mind you, the staff at Bonnet's are great, aren't they?'

She winced at her own tactlessness. Sometimes she could kick herself. But still, now she'd started, she might as well carry on.

'Can you remember who served you there?'

Tommy's brow furrowed. If he was thrown by Helen's odd question, he was too polite to say.

'A young woman; she was pretty, with long dark hair. She was very polite and spoke with a local accent. The shop had just reopened after suffering a power cut that day.'

Helen recognised Tommy's description of the waitress who

regularly served her and Marie. In fact, the woman had impressed Marie so much with her excellent customer service and polite manner that Marie had tried to poach her to work in Tom's Teas. However, the girl had turned down her offer, saying she was happy where she was.

She quickly tried to work out what time Tommy had left to go to Bonnet's and what time he might have returned to the tanning salon. It was all a blur. But if he was telling the truth – and Helen hoped with all her heart that he was – she knew it wouldn't be hard to check out his story. All she had to do was ask the waitress at Bonnet's.

She pushed away her glass of red wine. 'I need to get back to work,' she said.

'Thanks for the chat, Helen.'

'No, thank *you*,' she replied. 'It's been illuminating.'

Downstairs, the first thing she did was pick up her phone to call Bonnet's coffee shop. She asked to speak to the waitress, and after exchanging small talk, Helen said she was calling on behalf of one of her guests who'd visited the previous day, after the electricity had been restored to Huntriss Row and the shop had reopened.

'You might not remember him, but he thinks he left his wallet behind.'

'Wallet? No, there's nothing in lost property. I can see the box from here, we keep it under the counter. I'm sorry, Helen. What's your guest's name? If a wallet turns up, I'll look inside to check for details and call you straight away.'

'He's called Tommy Cassidy, but you might know him better as Tommy Two Shoes. He once had a show on children's TV.'

Glenda Young

'Tommy Two Shoes!' the waitress screamed. Helen had to hold her phone away from her ear while she waited for the girl to calm down. 'Yes, it was him. He was here in the café. Oh, we were starstruck. He came in when the shop reopened after the electricity came back on. He bought a peach melba!'

Helen thanked the waitress, then ended the call.

Chapter 31

The following morning, Helen lay in bed as the sun streamed in through her bedroom window. She hadn't slept well again, waking often with night sweats. It was another symptom of the menopause that she was struggling with, and she made a note to speak to her GP. She'd also speak to Marie to see how she was coping with her own flushes and sweats. She would have asked Jean about her past experience, too, if they'd been on better terms. Tired and with a headache, she yawned, then flung the duvet back over her head. She couldn't bear to face the day. She'd upset Jimmy over Graceland, upset Jean over Bobby, and as for her guests, she felt sure she would upset them too in her bid to find out the truth.

She remembered that Jean had asked to have the day off, but then she heard a noise from the living room. She forced herself out of bed, padded in her bare feet to her bedroom door and slowly pulled it open, assuming that Sally had come to work early. But when she peeked into the kitchen, she was confused to see Jean. She was relieved to see she was wearing her specs, but the radio wasn't on, and Jean wasn't singing as usual, so maybe things weren't quite back to normal.

'Morning, Jean,' she called. 'I thought you were taking the day off?'

Jean was in the middle of putting tin foil under the grill. She swung around with the grill pan in her hand.

'Morning, love. I changed my mind. I need to be busy.' She turned back to her work.

Helen took that as her cue to leave her alone. She showered and changed into her hoodie and jeans and pulled on her walking boots. Within minutes she was walking Suki along King's Parade and down the cliff path. The day was calm and warm, but cloudy. As she walked along the beach, her phone rang in her pocket. When she saw DS Hutchinson's name on her screen, she answered straight away.

'Good morning, how are you?' she said.

'Any news?' he barked.

'Blimey, do you need refresher training on your customer care skills?' she teased.

'Helen, please, I've been working all night. I'm under pressure to find Ms de Wolfe's killer as soon as I can. I've no time for small talk. So tell me, is there any news?'

Helen walked down to the edge of the sea. Suki stood by her, unmoving, and she gently tugged the lead.

'Come on, dog,' she said as she began to walk on.

'What's that?' DS Hutchinson barked.

'Nothing, I wasn't talking to you.'

'Helen, this is important. Tell me if you've learned anything about your guests since we last spoke. Anything at all. Anything that might help the investigation.'

And so Helen told the detective about Tommy Two Shoes and his secret visit to Bonnet's to buy a peach melba. In return, DS Hutchinson told her that DC Hall had now reviewed the podcast file, and confirmed her theory that Paul was no longer a suspect as he was outside the salon at the time of Rosa's death, with many witnesses who had seen him, or spoken to him when he was interviewing them on his live stream. Helen's heart lifted at this news. She liked Paul a lot.

'Now then, have you spoken to Jean about Bobby Tanner?' the DS demanded.

Helen sighed. 'I've tried, but she won't listen. Why don't you speak to her yourself?' she said tartly.

'We haven't enough staff,' he said, and rang off.

Helen slid her phone into her pocket. She was starting to feel angry at being treated like a skivvy by the police. She wondered if she had the nerve to invoice them for the rum and Coke, red wine and crisps she'd used to coax information from her guests. Then she decided against it; they'd simply tell her to get lost. She shook her head to get rid of DS Hutchinson's voice rattling inside it.

Back at the Seaview, she was pleased to see that Sally had arrived and was helping Jean lay rashers of bacon and sausages on the grill.

'Would you two like a bacon sandwich and a mug of tea before you start work?' Jean asked.

'That'd be great, thanks,' Helen replied.

'Smashing,' Sally agreed.

'How are things, Jean?' Helen asked.

Jean pushed her glasses up to the bridge of her nose. 'Fine. Just fine,' she said, not sounding fine at all.

'And how are things with Bobby?' Helen ventured.

Jean wagged a finger. 'None of your business. Let's leave it at that. If you can't be happy for me, then say nothing. I don't want to fall out with you, Helen.'

Helen forced herself to walk away, scared she would blow her top. She couldn't understand why Jean was choosing to ignore the police's warning.

'How's Gav?' she asked Sally, changing the subject.

Tears sprang to Sally's eyes and her bottom lip began to tremble. 'He's really suffering, Helen. The health and safety inspector had bad news about the tanning booth where Rosa died.'

She stopped what she was doing and put down a rasher of bacon.

'He said the booth had been tampered with, and of course, it was only me and Gav who had access to the salon. We're the only key holders. It's not looking good. And just when it seems as if things can't get worse, they do. You'll never guess what's happened now.'

Both Helen and Jean turned to her. 'What?' they said in unison.

'Frankie Tanner's made an offer to buy the salon when the investigation's done. It's an insult of an offer. Gav would rather leave the place to rot than sell it to Frankie.'

'Why does Frankie want to buy it?' Helen said, confused.

'Because he's always wanted everything that Gav's got,' Sally sighed. 'Do you remember when I first met Gav, when he came here to install the CCTV cameras?'

'Oh, he was a cheeky little button back then,' Jean chuckled.

'Yes, I remember. Go on, Sally,' Helen said.

'Well, Frankie found out that me and Gav had started seeing each other, and he got in touch with me online. He was trying to get me away from Gav, thinking I'd be daft enough to go out with him again after how badly he treated me the first time. He started sending me offers of nights out in fancy restaurants, the high life, weekends in Harrogate.'

'Now that's posh,' Jean noted as Sally carried on.

'I didn't tell Gav at the time because I didn't want to upset him.

Deadly Dancing at the Seaview Hotel

I knew the two of them had feuded for years. Frankie's jealous of Gav; he always has been, but he's nowhere near as talented or as business-savvy as Gav. When Gav first started Gav's Cabs, Frankie tried to set up a rival business, Maxi's Taxis, but it fell flat. He could only find one driver to work for him and he didn't treat him well, so the man left and now works for Gav. Frankie's a nasty piece of work.' She looked at Jean. 'He comes from bad stock, I'm afraid.'

Jean turned around with a knife in her hand and menace and hurt in her eyes.

'Leave his dad out of this. What Frankie gets up to has nothing to do with Bobby.'

'That's not strictly true, Jean,' Helen said. 'Bobby invested money with Frankie in the dance competition at the Spa. They're the ones who brought the competition to Scarborough after what happened in Blackpool—' She froze.

'Helen? What is it?' Sally said.

'It's the curse of the dance,' Helen breathed. 'It's starting to make sense. Horrible, awful sense.'

Jean and Sally were looking at her like she'd gone mad.

'Can you two manage without me for a bit? I need to head upstairs to have a word with one of our guests.'

Jean held out a plate, on which was a brown bun with crispy bacon inside. 'What about your breakfast?' she cried as Helen flung open a cupboard and pulled out the biggest screwdriver she could find.

Upstairs, she knocked politely and waited. The door opened, and Monty stood before her, looking as gorgeous as ever. How did he do that so early in the morning? she wondered. Was it good genes, make-up or both? She pulled herself together and gripped the screwdriver.

'Ah, Monty. There's a slight problem with your shower and I need to get into your bathroom to fix it. Right now,' she said.

'A problem? But it seemed fine when I showered and shaved,' he said, alarmed.

Helen walked into the room with the screwdriver aloft, showing she meant business. As she marched confidently to the bathroom, Monty perched on the edge of his bed, angling his phone in front of his face, smiling broadly and pouting. She rattled the screwdriver around the shower cubicle, trying to make it sound as if she was doing something.

'Just trying to fix the loose widget. Won't be a min!' she called.

'Fine, take your time. I'm busy uploading pictures to my fans,' Monty called back.

Helen peeked around the bathroom door and saw him smiling, winking and laughing into his phone. She wondered if Marie was looking at the pictures. She walked out of the bathroom, waving the screwdriver.

'Well, I think I've fixed it,' she said, trying to sound authoritative.

'How wonderful you are,' Monty said, not taking his gaze off his phone.

Helen stood in front of him, waiting for him to notice she was there. It took a few moments and a little cough from her to break his preoccupation with himself.

'Sorry, Helen, did you want something?' he asked impatiently, looking up at her.

'Yes, there is something,' she said. She pointed the screwdriver at him. 'I want the whole truth about what happened in Blackpool, and I want it now.'

Chapter 32

Monty leaned away from the screwdriver.

'Would you mind not waggling that thing in my face?'

Helen lowered it slightly. Monty took one last glance at his phone.

'Ciao, bellas!' he cooed, then laid the device down. He sighed impatiently.

'What happened in Blackpool stays in Blackpool,' he said dismissively.

'No it doesn't, not when what happened there brought the curse of the dance to Scarborough, to the Seaview.' Helen tapped her forehead. 'And it's causing me sleepless nights after one of my guests was killed.'

Monty laid his hand on his heart. 'I am so very sorry,' he said. He turned his face to her, and she saw his bottom lip wobble.

In that moment, she sensed a vulnerability in him that she hadn't seen before. She relaxed her grip on the screwdriver.

'Now, I may be wide of the mark, Monty, but after we spoke last time, there are thoughts that won't leave me alone.' She sat in a chair opposite his bed and faced him.

'For instance?' he asked, and Helen thought he looked genuinely puzzled. However, she held her nerve and tried not to be distracted by his lovely dreamy eyes. She sat up straight in her chair.

'I want to know the truth about why you bribed that judge in Blackpool,' she said.

Monty went pale and his left knee began to bob up and down. The light suddenly left his eyes and his shoulders slumped. For the first time, his posture was less than perfect. Helen knew she'd hit him hard, for if she'd learned one thing over her years as landlady of the Seaview, it was that the body language of her guests never lied.

'I wish I'd never told Sadie Daye,' he hissed.

'You told her?' Helen cried. 'Why?'

'Because we were lovers at the time,' Monty said, as if that explained everything.

Helen stood and began pacing the room.

'Hang on a minute.' She shot a look at him. 'You and Sadie were lovers?'

'Yes, after her marriage to Paul began to fall apart, when he became obsessed with Rosa.'

Helen paced from the window to the bed, trying to get a grip on who'd been having a fling with who, when and why.

'So let me get this straight. Sadie Daye was married to Paul Knight.'

'Correct,' Monty said.

'But they divorced after Sadie discovered Paul was infatuated with Rosa.'

'Also correct,' Monty said.

Helen turned to him. 'Then Sadie went on to have a relationship with you.'

'It was hardly a relationship, Helen. I comforted her, that's all.'

Undeterred, Helen carried on.

Deadly Dancing at the Seaview Hotel

'Then you had a fling with Bev in Blackpool. Oh my word, I feel dizzy.'

She kept quiet about discovering Paul's slippers in Carla's room. She knew that Carla and Monty were lying to each other about not taking lovers from the group they were currently working with. They were both breaking their own golden rule. She sat down and gripped the screwdriver, trying to focus.

'Let's get off the relationship roundabout,' she said. 'I want to know all about the judge in Blackpool.'

'Oh Helen, must we talk about it? I'm starving, and breakfast will be ready soon.'

Helen looked at her watch. 'We've got another ten minutes. Now listen, and listen good.'

Monty rolled his eyes, which infuriated her. She determined to power on and get the truth out of him. She gripped the screwdriver so tightly that it dug into the palm of her hand.

At last he nodded thoughtfully, then glanced out of the window. When he turned his gaze back to Helen, he was subdued.

'Helen, if you heard it from Sadie's lips on her podcast, then you've heard the truth. I'm not proud of what I did. The judge I tried to bribe reported me. I was fined and banned for six months. I've paid my dues. I did charity work and voluntary work during those months, working with everyone from children to pensioners to teach them how to dance. I taught community groups free of charge, everything from the botafogo in Blackpool to the corta jaca in Cleethorpes.'

'The bota . . . corta what?' Helen said, confused.

'They're samba dance moves,' Monty said impatiently. 'Teaching free of charge was the only thing I could do to make amends. If you don't believe me, I'll give you my phone, and you can go through my contacts, ring all the community groups, village halls, scout huts, Women's Institutes and afternoon tea clubs. Ask them how many times I turned up during the six months when I wasn't allowed to compete in the dance world.'

He held his phone out to Helen, who was tempted to take it, but there was something in Monty's eyes, his face, the way his body slumped that suggested he was telling the truth.

'I don't need to see your phone,' she said.

'Trying to bribe a judge was the most stupid thing I've done in my life. I'll never do it again. Now, is that all you wanted to ask, or was there something else?'

The glitter ball flashed through Helen's mind. She had five minutes left before she was due downstairs. If she didn't find out the truth, she'd never forgive herself. She took a deep breath and dived in.

'What do you know about the smashed glitter ball in Blackpool? Sadie Daye claimed it was loosened by the same person who bribed the judge. And you've admitted that person was you.'

Monty shook his head vehemently. 'I had nothing to do with the glitter ball. I swear on . . .' He looked desperately around the room, then picked up his phone. 'I swear on my Instagram account that I had nothing to do with the glitter ball in Blackpool. Do you really think I'd have done that? I'm not a monster, Helen. I'm just a very stupid, yet rather good-looking man, who tried to bribe a judge. Bev was injured when the glitter ball smashed, it ended her career. I'd never do that to another dancer. Never. In fact, after she announced she was giving up dancing, I pulled strings with my showbiz contacts to help her when she became focused on getting Tommy back on TV. Bev is now a very good friend.'

Deadly Dancing at the Seaview Hotel

'And what about Rosa, was she a good friend too?'

He pressed his hands onto the duvet. 'No. We never got along, but she was a wonderful dancer. That's why I offered to choreograph the tribute dance.'

Helen narrowed her eyes. 'Rosa's death has worked to your advantage in that way,' she said cautiously. 'It's meant you've stepped up from dancer to choreographer to show the world what you can do. It's put you in the spotlight.'

Monty leapt to his feet. 'Now look here! If you're suggesting I had anything to do with Rosa's death, you need to think long and hard. I have an excellent lawyer, and I warn you, Mrs Dexter, that he'll sue you for slander if you say more.'

His use of Helen's formal title and surname wasn't lost on her.

'I'm not accusing you of anything,' she said, keeping her gaze on his face.

He sank back onto the bed.

'Yes, all right, I hated Rosa, I was jealous of her talent, but I didn't want her dead. It was the judge I wanted in my pocket, and that backfired badly.'

Helen looked at her watch. Two more minutes before breakfast. She knew Sally would be waiting at the dining room door.

'What about this so-called curse of the dance?' she asked quickly.

'Pfft! It's a load of nonsense. It's just a headline dreamed up by the people at the top to sell tickets.'

Helen raised her eyebrows. 'The people at the top . . . do you mean Frankie and Bobby Tanner?'

Monty tutted. 'Yes. Those two. They sent out a press release titled "Curse of the Dance", knowing it would drum up publicity. You know what journalists are like. Half of them don't write their own stuff any more; they cut and paste it onto websites to fill content boxes. The curse of the dance is a gimmick to hide the real reason the show moved from Blackpool to Scarborough.'

'And the real reason is . . .?' she asked, leaning forward. She had one minute left. She waited with bated breath.

'For Frankie Tanner to get his name up in lights in his home town of Scarborough, of course. He's a scoundrel. We all had to move to Yorkshire for this year's competition because of Frankie's ego. Oh, don't get me wrong, Scarborough's got its charms, but I really miss Blackpool. There's a hotel landlady called Anna on the Golden Mile who warms my sausage to perfection each morning.'

Helen shuddered at the thought. Monty stood and towered over her.

'Look, Helen, I didn't murder Rosa, I'm not that kind of man.'

She looked into his eyes, and he didn't waver.

'No, I don't think you are,' she said. 'I think you've been stupid trying to bribe the judge. And I think you're using Rosa's death to your advantage to put the spotlight on yourself. You're selfish and self-obsessed.'

A playful smile reached Monty's lips. 'Why, thank you.'

Helen tutted. 'It wasn't a compliment. There are many things I think you are, but I don't believe you're a murderer. Now, if you'll excuse me, I need to go downstairs to serve breakfast.'

Monty lifted his phone and angled it to his face. He moved to stand beside her.

'Could I take a selfie with you?' he asked.

She ducked out of range of the camera.

'No, you may not.'

Deadly Dancing at the Seaview Hotel

She stormed to the door, ready to head downstairs, but before she left the room, she heard something that turned her stomach.

'Keep my sausage warm for me, Helen,' Monty cooed.

Downstairs in the hall, Helen joined Sally at the dining room door. She noticed that Sally was wearing her new tabard, which fitted a lot better over her baby bump.

'Is the new tabard all right for you, Sal?' she asked.

'It's smashing,' Sally replied.

'Look, Sally. Can you deal with Monty when he comes down? I can't face him. And if he says anything crude to you, anything about a warm sausage, let me know and I'll have a stern word with him.'

Sally looked at her as if she'd gone mad. 'Are you all right, Helen? You look a bit flustered.'

Helen straightened her tabard and pushed her bobbed hair behind her ears.

'Sally, did Rosie Hyde ever call you for an interview for *The Scarborough Times*?'

'No, but even if she had, there's no way I'd speak to a journalist after what happened to Gav. You're not thinking of calling her, are you?'

'Yes, I am. But don't worry. I won't be talking about you and Gav. I want to check that she's not giving the Seaview too many mentions in anything she writes about Rosa's death. It'll do business no good if word gets out that Rosa was a guest here, although I suspect it's already too late. And there's something else I want to speak to her about.'

'What?' Sally asked.

'I want to find out more about the curse of the dance.'

Chapter 33

After breakfast had been served, and Monty had been skilfully avoided by both Helen and Sally, they went downstairs. Helen was heartened when she walked into the kitchen to smell a citrus tang in the air. And her heart lifted even further when she saw a lemon drizzle cake cooling on a wire rack. Jean was bustling around the kitchen, cleaning, wiping, putting things straight. It felt as if a little bit of normality had returned. Even her glasses were on straight. Suki lay under the dining table, waiting for crumbs.

'Sit yourselves down, girls,' Jean said as she brought a tray to the table. 'I thought it best to have our coffee and cake early today, before you clean the rooms, because I've got an appointment in town and I need to dash off.'

'An appointment with Bobby?' Helen asked gently.

Jean shot daggers at her and so Helen zipped up. On the tray was the cafetière, three blue mugs and three plates. Jean sat down too, and Helen and Sally exchanged a smile.

'I'll get the cake,' Helen said.

Jean tutted. 'Oh dearie me, the cake. I'd forget my head if it was loose.'

Helen brought the lemon drizzle to the table. She cut three slices and placed them on plates.

'How are you, Jean?' Sally asked.

Deadly Dancing at the Seaview Hotel

'I'm still not myself, but I'll be back to normal in my own time. The grieving process takes a while. I've just got to go with the flow. Some days I'm better than others.'

'Grieving is never easy,' Helen agreed. 'Look what it did to me. When Tom died, I was in a right state. I didn't know whether to sell the hotel and move on or stay and run the place on my own.'

She reached her left hand to Jean and her right hand to Sally.

'When I made the decision to stay and run the Seaview without Tom, I couldn't have done it without you two.'

She picked up the cafetière and poured coffee into mugs, then lifted her slice of lemon drizzle cake.

'This smells divine, Jean. Ooh, it's still warm.'

'I hope you remembered to put sugar in it,' Sally said. She'd meant it as a joke, but Jean shot her a look.

She picked at her cake and popped a tiny piece in her mouth, then pulled a face.

'I'm sorry, Jean. I can't eat it. My pregnancy hormones and tastebuds are telling me not to. It tastes odd to me.'

Helen bit into her own slice and chewed, then immediately picked up her coffee mug to wash the taste away. She glanced at the kitchen counter, where a plastic tub of salt stood next to the tray where the cake had been cooling.

'Jean . . .' she said carefully. 'I don't think you did put sugar in, love.'

'Of course I put sugar in!' Jean retorted.

Helen knew she had to keep calm.

'No, Jean. I think you've put salt in instead.'

'Rubbish! Are you saying I don't know what I'm doing after all these years? I've made more lemon drizzle cakes than you've had hot dinners. It's perfectly all right, there's nothing wrong with it!'

Jean picked up her slice of cake and took a large bite. She chewed and swallowed. Then, in silence, she stood, collected up the plates and scooped the cake into the bin. At the table, Helen put a finger to her lips, warning Sally not to say a word.

'Right, I'll be off,' Jean said, marching to the coat pegs by the door.

'Jean, wait,' Helen said. She followed her across the room. 'Look, love, it was a mistake anyone could make.'

'I'm not just anyone, Helen,' Jean said. 'I never make mistakes. There must be something wrong with me.'

'Jean, there's nothing wrong with you. You're suffering the loss of your mum. You're not allowing yourself time to grieve. Please stay. We can talk.'

Jean thrust her arms into her coat and picked up her handbag.

'No, we can't. I'm meeting Bobby in town.'

Helen tried again, gently holding Jean by her arm to stop her from leaving.

'Jean, we care for you. We don't want to see you get hurt. Please reconsider about Bobby. When even the police are warning you not to get involved, don't you think you should listen to them, even if you won't listen to me?'

'It's my life, Helen. Let me do what I want. I'm a grown woman and I know my own mind.'

Jean stormed out. Helen walked back to the dining table and sat next to Sally.

'Oh Sally, what are we going to do?'

'We could follow her to town,' Sally suggested.

Deadly Dancing at the Seaview Hotel

Helen thought about this for a while.

'When Marie and I followed her to the Spa, she was furious when she found out. If she knows we're spying on her again, it might tip her over the edge. She could walk out, go and work somewhere else, and we might lose her for ever. I think we've got to let her go and trust she'll be back to her old self soon.'

Sally drained her coffee.

'I'm not happy about this, Helen,' she said.

'Me neither. But what else can we do?' Helen checked her watch. 'Come on, Sal, we can't sit here all day and worry about Jean when we've got the rooms to clean.'

Sally moved to the cupboard where the cleaning products were kept.

'Leave the vacuum cleaner for me to bring up,' Helen said. 'I don't want you straining yourself. I'll be up in a minute. I've just got something to do here first.'

Sally headed upstairs and Helen took out her phone. Within seconds, Rosie Hyde answered her call.

'Rosie, it's Helen Dexter from the Seaview Hotel.'

'Ah, Helen. Are you ready to talk about your murdered guest?'

'Perhaps,' Helen said guardedly. 'I might be persuaded to tell you what I knew about her if you're really interested.'

There was a silence at the other end of the line. Helen knew how ambitious and sharp Rosie was, and knew she'd piqued her interest.

'What do you want in return?' Rosie asked.

Bingo! Helen was in.

'A little bit of research on your part. My guess is that you journalists have access to resources that us mere mortals don't. I'd like you to find out as much as you can about the smashed glitter ball in Blackpool last year.'

'Blackpool? What does this have to do with Rosa de Wolfe's death?' Rosie asked.

'That's what I'm trying to find out.'

Helen gave Rosie as many details as she could about the glitter-ball smash, and about the rumours that it had been connected to the bribing of a judge.

'I'll do what I can,' Rosie promised. 'Now let's get back to talking about your murdered guest.'

Helen was guarded in her replies to Rosie's questions. Yes, Rosa had been an attractive woman, who'd seemed nice and who had been polite and respectful while at the Seaview. And that was as far as she went, telling Rosie that she'd been asked by DS Hutchinson and DC Hall not to reveal more. It was a little white lie, but she thought that if she kept mentioning the police, Rosie would soon get the hint that she wasn't about to say anything else. Then she impressed on the journalist that Rosa's murder had taken place in town and nowhere near the Seaview – not inside it, outside it, or even in the same street.

'You will mention this, won't you, Rosie? Otherwise I know my business will suffer again,' she pleaded.

'I'll do my best,' Rosie replied. She added that she would investigate reports about the glitter-ball smash as soon as she had time.

Helen ended the call and joined Sally upstairs, cleaning rooms, vacuuming stairs, dusting the hall. When all was done, they returned downstairs.

'Leave the vacuum cleaner, Sally, I'll put it away. It must be getting too heavy for you now.'

Deadly Dancing at the Seaview Hotel

Sally cradled her stomach. 'I have to be honest, I've found today difficult. The twins have started kicking. Want to feel them?'

Guided by Sally, Helen gently laid her hand on her friend's stomach. When she felt movement, a flicker beneath her fingers, she and Sally shared a look and tears sprang to Helen's eyes. The power of the moment caused her to step away, and she dropped her hand.

'I'm sorry, Helen,' Sally said. 'I didn't mean to upset you.'

Helen shook her head. 'It's all right. I'm fine. You know, sometimes the past just catches up with me. Losing my babies... well... It's a long time ago now. We must look to the future, and I'm overjoyed for you and Gav.'

Sally walked to her and Helen let herself fall into her friend's arms for a long hug. When she pulled away, she wiped her eyes on a tissue and tried to pull herself together before memories overpowered her.

'What are you up to today?' she asked as Sally took off her tabard and slipped on her denim jacket.

'I'm heading straight to the tanning salon to see Gav. The health and safety inspection is still going on. It's a nightmare. Gav's not himself. He used to be a creature of habit, Helen, always wanting the same food on the same day – you know, pie on a Monday, chips on a Tuesday. That's just the way he is. But with all the stress of Rosa's death, his harmless routines and habits are in danger of becoming obsessive. I've booked him an appointment to see the GP before his behaviour spirals out of control.'

Helen was distressed to hear this. She hugged Sally goodbye, offering her support, then sat on the sofa. Suki walked to her and nudged her hand with her head, her way of letting it be known she wanted making a fuss of. Helen willingly obliged. When her phone rang, she was surprised to see it was Rosie Hyde.

'Hi, Rosie.'

'Hi, Helen. I wanted to call straight away, before I leave the office to head to the seafront. My editor wants me to interview tourists who've had their chips stolen by seagulls. Anyway, I did some digging in the archives. We're part of a syndicate of newspapers, so I was able to access past editions of all our sister papers, including one in Blackpool. Anyway, I found a report that mentioned minutes from a meeting where the glitter-ball smash was discussed.'

Helen's heart began to beat wildly. 'And?' she said, desperate to know what Rosie had found.

'The minutes reported that the woodwork the glitter ball was attached to was rotten. The rafters were infested with woodworm, and the meeting discussed setting money aside for repairs to be carried out.'

Helen leaned forward. 'So the glitter ball fell because of the rotten wood?'

'So it seems. But there's more.'

'Tell me!' Helen urged.

'There was a report which was held back from the press, which means I'm taking a risk telling you. Also, the information has value.'

'You know you can trust me, Rosie. We've been here before after one of my guests died.'

There was silence at the other end of the line and Helen knew Rosie would be weighing up the risk.

'How about we barter, and you give me something in exchange?' Rosie said.

'Name it.'

Deadly Dancing at the Seaview Hotel

'A free week at the Seaview for my parents. They're coming to town later this year, and I can't have them staying with me. Mum nitpicks all the time, and Dad falls asleep on the sofa and snores so loudly that me and Mum can't hear the TV. If I can book them into the Seaview, free of charge, I'll tell you what I've learned.'

Helen didn't give it a second's thought.

'Consider it done. Now tell me what you know.'

'The builder who installed the glitter ball should have ensured that the rafter could take the weight. The woodworm infestation should have been spotted, and the glitter ball should never have gone up.'

Helen was intrigued. 'But why wasn't this reported or investigated further? Why wasn't the company fined? Someone could have been killed!'

There was silence at the other end of the line.

'Rosie? Are you still there?'

'Yes, still here. Sorry, Helen. I was just double-checking something. Ah, here we are. So the reason this wasn't reported and was kept out of the press was because the builder who installed the glitter ball was . . .'

Another silence.

'Rosie!' Helen snapped.

'Sorry, I'm going as fast as I can. The office broadband is playing up . . . Right, here we go. The builder who installed the glitter ball was the brother of someone high up in the dance world. It's nepotism at its worst.'

'That's shocking,' Helen said.

'Par for the course, I'm afraid. When you're in my business, you find out all kinds of nasty stuff that people don't want to have leaked. I couldn't find anything else other than a report of an injury to Beverley Cassidy, who fell backwards in shock when the glitter ball crashed down.'

Suddenly Helen's blood ran cold. It had been the mention of Bev's name in connection to a builder that had upset her.

'Rosie . . .' she began nervously. 'The builder who was negligent, what was he called?' She crossed her fingers. *Please don't let it be Mike Skipton*, she thought.

There was silence.

'Rosie?' she squeaked.

'Sorry, Helen, just waiting for the broadband to come back. Ah, here it is. The builder was Bob Stanley of Blackpool.'

Helen felt the tension drain away and her shoulders sank in relief. That was one less problem to deal with.

'Was there anything else you wanted to know?' Rosie asked.

'Yes, actually there is,' Helen said, thinking quickly. 'Did you receive a press release from Frankie and Bobby Tanner about the dance competition at the Spa?'

'Of course, and it went into *The Scarborough Times* to promote the event,' Rosie said. 'You should know by now that our paper covers everything going on in town. I remember the press release well because it was headlined "Curse of the Dance". That caught my attention as it's a great hook.'

'What did it actually say about the curse?'

There was silence again while Rosie searched online.

'It mentions a chap called Monty Curzon who was expelled from the dance world for six months for trying to bribe a judge. And it also mentions the glitter ball smashing to the floor.'

'Does the press release connect the two things?' Helen asked.

Deadly Dancing at the Seaview Hotel

'No. Monty's lawyer is quoted saying that his client was innocent of anything to do with the glitter ball. And of course there's no mention of woodworm or a negligent builder.'

'Thanks, Rosie, that's great. I'll ensure your parents are given our VIP suite.'

Rosie laughed out loud. 'Yeah, right!' she said and hung up.

Helen sank back on the sofa. Well, she thought, it looked like Monty had been telling the truth. The glitter ball hadn't been loosened deliberately to hit a judge on the head; it had fallen from natural causes. Then Frankie Tanner and his dad had used the incident to have the dance competition moved from Blackpool to Scarborough simply to get one over on Frankie's lifelong rival, Gav.

'What a mess,' Helen muttered.

Her phone rang again, and Jimmy's name appeared. Her heart did a one-two, and a smile came to her face. She was pleased and relieved that he'd taken the first step to reconciliation after she'd told him the truth about Graceland.

'Jimmy, hi? How are you?' she said, sinking further back into the sofa, relaxing for the first time that day.

'Is Jean there?' he barked.

Helen sat up straight.

'Jean? Why?'

'Helen! Tell me! Is she with you?'

'No, she's gone. She said something about meeting—'

'Bobby Tanner in town?' Jimmy asked.

'Yes, how do you know?'

'Meet me at Troost coffee shop on Huntriss Row as soon as you can.'

'Jimmy, what's going on?' she cried. But he had already hung up.

Helen jumped up and was about to fetch her car keys when she stopped. Parking in town was a nightmare; she could be driving in circles looking for a spot. Instead, she called Gav's Cabs and booked a car to arrive immediately. She settled Suki, locked the apartment, then waited at the back of the Seaview for the cab to arrive. She was shocked to see Gav in the driver's seat. His trademark sunny smile had gone.

'Gav, what are you doing?' she said. 'I thought you were at the salon with the investigators.'

'I'm back to driving my cab today, missus. It helps me feel calm. I've been through the wringer with all the questions they've fired at me about the salon. They're treating me like I'm suspect number one instead of a local bloke doing my best. Where can I take you?'

'I need to get to Troost coffee shop, quick sharp.'

He pulled the car around the corner of King's Parade onto Windsor Terrace.

'Hurry, Gav, please,' she urged.

'Gav doesn't speed, Helen,' he said.

Soon they were heading into town.

'Sally says that Frankie's offered to buy the salon,' Helen said.

'I'll never sell it, Helen. Not to Frankie or anyone, not after what happened. I couldn't live with myself if I did. I might turn it into a lock-up for my other businesses, but Frankie can whistle for it. Even if he was the last person on earth, I wouldn't sell it to him.'

'Gav, I've learned that Frankie might have deliberately moved the dance competition from Blackpool to Scarborough just to get one up on you. Do you really think he'd do such a thing.'

Deadly Dancing at the Seaview Hotel

'He absolutely would, missus,' Gav replied, carefully negotiating a roundabout. 'He always tried to beat me in business, but he hasn't got common sense, never mind business sense. Even when we were at school, he wanted to be better than me. I tried to help him, tried to be nice, that's the way I am, but Frankie went his own way in the end. He went off the rails and got involved with villains in town. The last I heard was that he and his old man were pulling scams with benefit fraud and the wills of care home residents.'

He pulled up outside the Palm Court Hotel. Ahead of the cab, parked illegally on double yellow lines, was Jimmy's car. A traffic warden was making his way towards it, ready to hand out a ticket. Jimmy never parked illegally. This was urgent business indeed, and her stomach turned over with anxiety.

'How much do I owe you?' she asked, leaning forward.

'Nothing, Helen. You brought Sally into my life, so I owe you everything.'

Helen leapt out of the car and ran across the road. Jimmy was waiting outside Troost.

'Jimmy? What on earth's going on?'

He pointed inside. Helen saw the back of Jean's head. She was sitting at a table opposite two men, one of whom was Bobby Tanner.

'I'll explain later. Right now, you and I are going inside to save Jean from losing every penny she's got.'

Chapter 34

Helen grabbed Jimmy's hand and pulled him into the café. Storming to the table where Jean was sitting with the men, she stopped dead, crossed her arms and glared at Bobby Tanner.

'What's going on?' she demanded.

Jimmy stepped forward and pulled his phone from his pocket. He began stabbing at the screen. Helen shot him a look.

'Must you look at your phone now, Jimmy? We're here to save Jean from herself!'

Jean slammed the palm of her hand on the table.

'You can't come barging in here, interrupting my meeting. I'm talking to my financial adviser, Mr Timms. This is my personal life. I'm not at work now, Helen. You can't order me about. And what do you mean about saving me from myself?'

She leaned across the table to the two men.

'I'm sorry about this. Helen's at a funny age.'

From the corner of her eye, Helen saw that Jimmy was still fiddling with his phone.

'Jimmy! Put your flaming phone away!' she barked.

'Wait a minute, Helen, there's something you need to see. Something Jean needs to see.'

The man sitting beside Bobby, who Helen assumed must be Mr Timms, was smartly dressed in a grey suit, white shirt and blue tie.

Deadly Dancing at the Seaview Hotel

He looked decent enough, she thought. But in her experience, which admittedly came from watching too much TV, most con men did. Mr Timms picked up his briefcase, then began to gather sheets of papers from the table. Helen looked at the sheets and was dismayed to see Jean's signature on the bottom of some of them.

'Oh Jean! What have you signed?' she asked, worried.

Jean lifted her chin and glared at her. 'It's none of your blooming business!'

The waitress walked over to the table.

'Is everything all right here?' she asked warily.

'We're fine!' Jean snapped, and the waitress walked quickly away.

'No, Jean, we're not fine. You need to take a look at this,' Jimmy said.

He turned his phone around so that Jean could see the screen. Mr Timms abruptly stood.

'I think I should be going,' he said, pushing his way from the table. Jimmy laid his hand on his shoulder to stop him.

'You're going nowhere, pal,' he said.

But Mr Timms was leaner, quicker and younger than Jimmy. He pushed him aside and ran from the shop. Jimmy gave chase, but before he left the café, his phone clattered to the table and Jean picked it up. By now, customers were staring. Helen looked at Bobby, nervous in case he was about to scarper too. She was relieved when he smiled at her. She'd read him wrong, she thought. But then he slid his chair back.

'Excuse me, dear. I need to use the facilities. At my age, coffee goes straight through.'

However, instead of walking to the back of the café, where

Helen could see the sign for the toilets, he legged it and ran outside in his Cuban-heeled shoes.

'Come back!' Helen yelled. 'Stop that man!'

She ran to the door, but Bobby had disappeared around the corner of Huntriss Row. Helen glanced right and left, looking for Jimmy, wondering where he'd gone. She turned back into the café and exchanged a look with the waitress.

'Sorry for the commotion,' she said.

When she returned to Jean, her heart fell like a stone. Jean was dabbing her eyes with a tissue. Her glasses lay on the table. When Helen sat down next to her, she put the glasses back on and picked up Jimmy's phone.

'Did you know about this?' she asked, indicating the screen.

'No, I didn't know anything. Jimmy just called me and asked me to meet him here.'

'It's a video, but I've seen enough.' Jean wiped her eyes again.

Helen took the phone and watched in horror as a man appeared on the screen. He was fresh-faced, clean-shaven and looked years younger than the man who had just run out of the café. He was also speaking with a shockingly bad American accent, but there was no denying it was Bobby Tanner. The video was an American TV show that revealed tricks that scammers and con men used to steal money and personal information, especially from older women. And there was Bobby, caught on camera by an undercover police officer, talking about how easy it was.

'It's like taking candy from a baby, man,' he boasted.

Helen switched off the phone and turned to Jean, who'd gone white as a sheet.

Deadly Dancing at the Seaview Hotel

'Jean, listen to me.' She gently placed her hand on top of her friend's. 'What where those papers you signed?'

Jean pushed her glasses up to the bridge of her nose.

'I signed my inheritance over to Mr Timms. He said he was going to invest it.' Her shoulders heaved.

Helen had to do something, and quick, but what?

'Right, we need to leave,' she said decisively. 'We're going straight to your bank. We need to stop money leaving your account and we need to do it now. Which bank are you with?'

Jean began to sob. 'The one on the corner of St Nicholas Street,' she said through her tears.

Helen calculated that if they walked fast, they could be there in ten minutes. She didn't dare suggest to Jean that they ran. She didn't think Jean's hips would take it. She dismissed the idea of calling the bank, imagining being put on hold, then trying to explain what had happened. Going there in person was the right thing to do.

'Come on. We've got to get there before Mr Timms and Bobby clear out your account.'

Jean wiped her eyes. 'Oh Helen, I've been so stupid. Why didn't I listen to you when you warned me?'

'There's no time for that now. Let's just concentrate on getting to the bank.'

As they walked out of Troost, Jimmy came running around the corner. He was out of breath and panting hard.

'Did you catch him?' Helen asked.

He laid his hand against the café window and shook his head.

'Bobby Tanner's done a runner too,' she explained. 'I'm taking Jean straight to her bank. We need to make sure nothing leaves her account.'

Jean swung her handbag across her body.

'That scoundrel's not getting a penny!' she cried.

'We'll go together,' Jimmy said.

Helen took Jean's left arm and Jimmy did the same on her right. Then, as quickly as Jean's chubby little legs would carry her, the threesome walked up Huntriss Row. Helen's heart was beating fast, and her own legs were shaking from shock. She could only imagine how Jean felt.

'How did you find out the truth about Bobby?' Jean asked Jimmy as they walked.

Jimmy cast a wary look at Helen, who nodded, encouraging him to tell Jean the truth.

'When I dropped you off at home the other day, I saw Bobby lurking at the end of your street. I figured he was waiting for you, to get you on your own to talk about money. Sorry, Jean, but Helen mentioned your inheritance to me; she was worried Bobby was after it.'

'I don't normally gossip about you, Jean, but these were exceptional circumstances. You've not been in your right mind since your mum died and you wouldn't listen to my warnings, or that of the police,' Helen added.

'All right, lass, don't fret. I'll let you off this time,' Jean said. 'Carry on, Jimmy.'

They reached the end of Huntriss Row and turned left onto Eastborough. The bank was still five minutes' walk. Helen could hear Jean's chest wheezing with exertion as Jimmy continued to talk.

'I figured Bobby wouldn't recognise me. As far as I knew, he'd never seen me before. So I parked opposite where he was waiting.

He never looked my way once; he was too busy speaking on his phone. I wound my window down, then took an old map book from the glove compartment and pretended I was looking at it. I heard every word Bobby said. He talked about getting you to meet Mr Timms, where they'd "do the deal", as he put it. He mentioned Troost and a date and time. I didn't think much of it then; I thought perhaps he was arranging to take you for lunch. But my instincts were telling me there was something more going on, so I took a picture of him. I thought I'd show it to Helen as proof, but with everything that's been going on, it slipped my mind.'

Jean had to stop for a moment to get her breath back.

'Come on, Jean, we can't slow down. What if Bobby and Mr Timms are at their bank now, or are banking online, and your money's already on its way to them? We've got to stop them!' Helen said anxiously.

They set off again, Jean still puffing and panting. They walked past charity shops and chocolate shops, souvenir shops and a bingo hall. The bank was three minutes' walk away now.

'I searched for Bobby's name online, because I was intrigued to know more,' Jimmy continued. 'And sure enough, up came details about the curse of the dance. Then about him and Frankie putting money into the dance competition to bring it to Scarborough. Then I found news reports about the fraud case that Bobby was sent to prison for. It involved a woman the same age as you, Jean. And there were more articles, court round-ups where Frankie Tanner was mentioned. He was in a young offenders' institute as a lad, for inciting violence.'

Helen could see the bank ahead, but Jean had stopped dead in the middle of the street with her hand on her heart.

'I can't take another step,' she said between breaths.

'Jean, you can. You must,' Helen urged her.

'Jimmy, tell me how you found the video about Bobby,' Jean said, gasping for air.

'Well, I couldn't find anything else about him when I searched for his name. But in last week's IT class at college, they showed us how to search using advanced methods. Using what I'd learned, I searched for his face, using the picture I'd taken. That's when I found the video, tucked away under layers of outdated links.'

Jean took a long, deep breath. 'All right, let's get my money back!' she cried, then she stormed forward up the hill to the bank.

Jean burst through the doors first, followed by Helen, then Jimmy. They marched towards a young woman and Jean flopped down in a chair.

'I need some help,' she said as her tears threatened again.

As quickly as she could, Helen explained what had happened. Immediately the young woman ushered them to a private, screened corner of the bank. Helen sat at Jean's side as the story unfolded. Jean explained how Bobby had tried to manipulate her, how he'd kept her from seeing her friends, even from calling them. He'd tried to control her and had firmly encouraged her to meet Mr Timms, wearing her down until she was too weak to resist. Helen tried to hold her hand, showing her support, but Jean snatched it back. This made Helen smile. The old Jean was still there.

Jimmy, standing behind them, tapped Helen on the shoulder.

'Isn't that one of your guests?' he whispered.

Deadly Dancing at the Seaview Hotel

Helen turned and peered around the screen to see the orange curled hair of Ballroom Bev. She was using a cashpoint machine inside the bank. *Nothing unusual in that*, Helen thought. But then she saw Bev counting out a large wad of cash, which she handed to Mike Skipton, the builder.

Chapter 35

'I confirm that no money has left your account, and we've put a stop on future payments coming out of there until this matter is resolved. We've alerted our fraud team about Mr Robert Tanner and Mr Tony Timms. And we'll refer the case to the police. Thank you for bringing this to our attention.'

Jean pushed her glasses up to the bridge of her nose. 'Am I free to go now?'

'Of course you are,' Helen said. 'You've done nothing wrong, Jean.'

She helped Jean to stand, all the while keeping one eye on what was going on in the corner of the bank. Bev and Mike were huddled together as Bev counted money into his hand. As Helen and Jimmy walked Jean out, Helen paused beside Bev.

'Hello there,' she said cheerfully.

Bev looked up, startled, and dropped a twenty-pound note. Helen ignored it, and looked at Mike.

'We meet again,' she said.

Bev glanced nervously from Helen to Jimmy and stood still with the wad of cash in her hand.

'I was just . . . er . . . Mike was in the bank, and I bumped into him and . . .' she stuttered.

Deadly Dancing at the Seaview Hotel

Helen held up her hand and smiled sweetly. 'There's no need to explain.'

She nodded at Bev, then Mike.

'It was nice to see you both.'

St Nicholas Street was busy with tourists heading to the funicular to ride the heritage tram down the hill to the beach.

'After what I've been through today, I need a stiff drink,' Jean said.

'Good idea,' Helen agreed. She looked around, wondering where the closest pub was that would suit Jean. But it was Jean who came up with a suggestion.

'Let's go into the bar at the Royal Hotel.'

The Royal Hotel was opposite the funicular, a short walk along the street.

'Would you like me to come?' Jimmy asked.

'Yes, Jimmy. I want you both with me. There's a lot to talk about. I need to get everything off my chest. Oh, I could kick myself for being so stupid.'

Inside the hotel bar, Jean chose a table by the window.

'Could I have a brandy, please?' she asked. 'You'd better make it a double.'

Jimmy did the honours and brought Jean and Helen a glass of brandy each and an orange juice for himself.

'To you, Jean,' he said, raising his glass.

Between sips, Jean began her tale of how Bobby had wooed her and complimented her and how she'd lapped up every word. She had to keep stopping to dab her eyes with a tissue or push her glasses up to the bridge of her nose. And then, with a crack in her voice, she told them how he had turned on her, threatening her with humiliation and intimidation to frighten her into signing over her inheritance to his financial adviser, Mr Timms.

'It sounds like coercive control,' Jimmy said bleakly.

Jean put her glass on the table, then reached across to hold Helen's hand, and Jimmy's.

'You were right, Helen. I wanted to believe him because I felt vulnerable. But you two saved me. You saved my inheritance, too. That nice girl at the bank seemed to know what she was doing. Thank you both for getting me there in time.'

'What will you do if Bobby or Mr Timms gets in touch with you again?' Helen asked.

Jean sat up straight in her seat.

'I'd be surprised if Mr Timms dares to contact me after being chased by Jimmy. And as for Bobby, well, if he turns up, I'll give him short shrift. I'll ring the police. I should have listened to their warnings.' She squeezed Helen's hand. 'More importantly, I should have listened to you. I'll have to chalk Bobby down to experience. There's no fool like an old fool, and I've been very foolish indeed.'

She picked up her glass and finished the brandy.

'Now, if you don't mind, I'd like to go home.'

'Let me drive you, Jean,' Jimmy offered. He held his orange juice aloft. 'My car's in town and I haven't had a drink.'

'Thanks, love, that'd be great,' Jean replied.

Helen looked out of the window at Jimmy's car, which now sported a parking ticket on the windscreen.

'You've got a ticket,' she said.

'It doesn't matter,' he said. 'It's a small price to pay for being here

Deadly Dancing at the Seaview Hotel

to save Jean. I had to get here as quickly as I could. The only way to do that was to abandon the car over there and run to the café.'

They stood, and Helen hugged Jimmy goodbye. She tried to hug Jean too, but Jean backed away.

'Steady on, lass. Least said, soonest mended.'

Helen suppressed a smile. The old Jean was returning.

'Take as much time off work as you need,' she said as they left the bar.

'No need, Helen, I'll be back tomorrow morning, bright and early,' Jean replied. She gave a cheery wave and turned towards the funicular station.

'Jean, the car's this way,' Jimmy called, pointing in the other direction.

Helen watched them go. She decided to walk back to the Seaview as it was such a warm day. She planned to walk the long way home, around the headland. But first, she needed to get down to the beach. The tram was at the top station. She paid her fare at the turnstile, then walked into the Victorian cliff railway and sat down on a wooden bench that lined the empty tram car. She was delighted that she might be on her own for the journey down. Then a woman entered, and her heart missed a beat. It was Bev.

'Mind your arms and legs now,' the operator called as he pulled the door closed. Bev sat at the opposite end of the car, as far away from Helen as she could, but there was no ignoring each other in such a small space.

'We meet again,' Helen said, smiling at her.

'We do indeed,' Bev replied, tight-lipped.

They travelled in silence as the tram car made its way down the hill. Halfway down, they passed the one heading for the top.

When they reached the bottom station, the door was pulled open and Helen stepped out. She waited for Bev.

'Are you heading off anywhere? Would you like to join me for a walk?' she asked.

She wondered if she'd gone too far. She never usually asked to spend time with her guests; it was the last thing she wanted to do. But there was something about Bev that intrigued her, especially after seeing her with Mike Skipton again, and with so much cash. Had this something to do with Rosa's death? Well, there was only one way to find out.

Bev glanced from left to right along the prom.

'Looking for something? Can I help point you in the right direction?' Helen asked.

Bev sighed. 'Sorry, Helen. I was checking to see if the coast was clear. Mike Skipton's after me for the rest of his cash. That's what I was doing in the bank when you saw me earlier. He's determined to get paid for the work that he's done.'

Helen indicated the beach, where the sun glistened on the sea like dancing diamonds.

'Let's walk to the Spa and have a coffee. My treat. Or we could even have a bite to eat. I don't know about you, but I'm peckish.'

Bev patted her stomach. 'I'm still full after eating your chef's wonderful breakfast. She really is a great cook.'

'Yes, she is,' Helen said, smiling as she thought of Jean.

'I can't stop, Helen. I'm due at the Spa to meet the others; we're rehearsing our show dance.'

They crossed the road and walked on the sand. Seagulls flew overhead, squawking. Children splashed in the shallows. There were deckchairs, blankets, buckets and spades. The tide was out on

Deadly Dancing at the Seaview Hotel

the crescent-shaped beach. Helen was tempted to take off her socks and shoes and paddle in the sparkling water as it gently lapped the bay. Questions formed in her mind as they walked, and she wondered how best to start asking them. There was only one thing for it, she decided, and that was to be direct. Well, Bev had been honest with her about looking for Mike Skipton when they'd left the funicular.

'How much more do you need to pay Mike?' she asked.

'Another five thousand should do it,' Bev replied. 'But I haven't got it. In fact, I've gone so deep into debt to pay what I owe him that I've had to take out a loan from a . . .' she paused and dropped her gaze, 'from a loan shark. I'm not proud of what I've done, but I had no choice. It was either that or return home to find my beautiful house smashed up. Anyway, that's how I had the money to pay Mike when he came to the Seaview, and it's how I paid him today. I'm being charged a fortune for the loan, but needs must. As for Tommy and his TV dreams . . . Oh Helen, it's such a mess.'

Helen kept her gaze ahead along the beach, where she could see the Grand Hotel.

'So the TV company still haven't given you their decision on the show?'

'No,' Bev replied.

Helen decided to press on.

'Not even with Rosa out of the running?'

'No. So you see, it's not looking good. They may be casting around for new, younger, cheaper talent,' Bev said. 'If that happens and Tommy doesn't get his show, I won't get my commission, which means I can't repay the loan shark. I'll end up having to sell my home. I'll probably go bankrupt. The production company told me they'd give me a final decision while I was in Scarborough. But Rosa's death has changed everything, and now I don't know when, or even if, I'll hear from them.' Her bottom lip wobbled, and tears sprang to her eyes.

The Spa came into view. Helen knew she'd soon lose Bev to rehearsals inside.

Bev pulled her phone from her handbag and glanced at the screen.

'The TV people have got all the power. They can keep me hanging on for as long as they need. They called twice while I was at the tanning salon, you know, on the day that . . . well, on the day Rosa died. I got very excited. I thought this was it, you know. Me and Tommy heading for the big time at last. But they gave me more platitudes, more stalling tactics.'

Helen clasped her hands behind her back as she walked. The steps leading to the Spa were ahead. Her time with Bev was running out. She had to act quickly.

'What time did they ring you that day?' she asked.

Bev put her foot on the first step. Helen reached for her arm.

'Bev?'

Bev hesitated, then sat on the stone step. Helen sat next to her, and they both looked out at the sea.

'The second time they rang, I was back at the Seaview with you and the others in the lounge. I was a mess, Helen, we all were, taking in the shocking news.'

'And the first time?' Helen probed.

Bev kept her gaze ahead, then swallowed hard.

'The first time they rang, I was in the tanning salon. I'd just gone in. I remember Elvis was singing.'

Deadly Dancing at the Seaview Hotel

'Yes, the gig went on for a while,' Helen said. 'There was quite a crowd around him.'

'I slipped out of the salon to take the call,' Bev said. 'There was no way I was going to miss the chance to talk to the TV people. Not even for a free spray tan. I moved away from Elvis and the music, but it was another put-off call saying no decision had been made on who they were going to give the show to. They were still choosing between Tommy and Rosa. Then I hung up and went back inside. Look, Helen, I must go, the others will be waiting.'

Helen said farewell to Bev but stayed where she was, sitting on the stone steps of the Spa, looking out over the beach, with spray tans and a dead woman on her mind.

Chapter 36

Helen's stomach rumbled, reminding her she hadn't eaten all day. She'd missed out on the bacon butty that Jean had cooked for her when she'd dashed upstairs to quiz Monty. She stood, thinking about the long walk back to the Seaview, and decided to grab a bite to eat before she set off. She saw dark clouds rolling in and so she also decided to change her plan and head home along the shorter route through town instead of around the headland.

Scarborough was a hilly town, and as the walk home was uphill, she'd need energy to get herself there. She thought about heading into Farrer's at the Spa, named after the woman who'd discovered Scarborough's natural spring water. It was the health-giving properties of the water that had first brought visitors and turned Scarborough into the country's earliest seaside resort. However, the tables outside the restaurant were full, and when she peeked around the door, she saw that inside was busy too. She decided instead to walk a little way up the hill to the Clock Café. She found a small table outside overlooking the beach and ordered a pot of tea for one and a cheese and pickle sandwich. Taking her phone from her pocket to check for missed messages, she caught sight of the beating heart emoji, ticking down the days to Graceland. She tried to ignore it and opened a message from Marie.

Deadly Dancing at the Seaview Hotel

Fancy an Italian meal tonight? x
She replied quickly.
I'd love to, thanks. 7 p.m. at Il Piatto? I'll book x
Then she pressed Jean's name on her phone.
As always, Jean answered on the third ring. 'Hello?'
'Hi, Jean, it's Helen.'
'Helen, love. Thanks for ringing.' She sounded tired. Well, Helen thought, it was hardly surprising.
'Just wanted to check you're all right.'
'Don't worry about me. As Jimmy would say when he's singing as Elvis, I'm a little shook up but I'm feeling fine. I've spoken to my solicitor for advice, too. This whole thing has given me a wake-up call. I'm sitting on a small fortune with my inheritance, and I need to put it somewhere safe until I decide what to do with it.'
'I'm sure your bank will give you solid advice,' Helen said, recalling the efficient and speedy way the bank had handled Jean that morning.
'I've already made an appointment to go and see them tomorrow, after I've finished work at the Seaview,' Jean said.
'I'm glad to hear it. Would you like me to come over to see you?'
'Helen, stop fussing,' Jean said firmly. 'Now, I'm going to hang up because my antiques show is on the telly and you've interrupted it. The auctioneer was about to bring the hammer down on a Ming vase.'
'All right, Jean, take care.'
After Helen had ended the call, she rang Il Piatto and booked a table. She was looking forward to seeing Marie again; it'd been a while since they'd had a good catch-up. Her tea and sandwich arrived, delivered to her table by a young waitress in a black frock

and white apron. It was details like these that made the Clock a wonderful Scarborough attraction.

'You look smashing,' Helen told the girl, and was rewarded with a big smile.

As she ate her lunch, Helen looked down the hill to the Spa. She thought of Bev and Tommy, brother and sister, dancing together now that Rosa had gone. Rosa's death meant that Bev had stepped back into the limelight. Also rehearsing inside would be Monty and Carla, the magnificent Curzons, with Monty taking the reins as choreographer. Again, this wouldn't have happened if Rosa had been alive. And Paul the podcaster would be recording music and voices to edit and broadcast to his listeners.

Sitting here in the sunshine, she began to feel mentally distanced from Rosa's death for the first time. It helped her think more clearly about what had happened. Had Rosa's murderer really been one of her guests, as DS Hutchinson had suggested? Or had someone else killed her? One thing she was certain of was that Gav was innocent. It hurt her deeply to know that he was still being quizzed by the police.

Once she'd finished eating, she headed back to the prom, fully intending to begin the walk home. But as she passed the Spa, she heard music floating from an open door. It sounded like music to waltz to. Following the sound, she headed upstairs to the Ocean Room, and stood in the doorway as couples whirled around in each other's arms. The floor was full of dancers, some in full ballroom attire, others in rehearsal leggings and Lycra.

The Ocean Room was a large hall with a bar at one end and windows overlooking the sea. Helen stepped gingerly inside, unsure if she was allowed to be there. She looked around nervously, expecting someone to throw her out. But as the outside door had been open, there'd been no signs to prohibit entry and no one had stopped her, she took heart and sat down at the side of the room. She watched the dancers, marvelling at how wonderfully they moved. How smooth and elegant their rise and fall. The waltz tune was one she recognised from an old movie she couldn't place. The dancers were moving in sequence, each couple following the one in front, twirling and turning, heads back, arms out. There were men dancing together, women too; older couples, younger ones, even teenagers.

And then she saw a face she recognised. Well, she saw the hair first. It was Bev, with her orange curls, dancing with Tommy. Their expressions were serious, deep in concentration, and they weren't looking her way. Bev was in leggings and a T-shirt with strappy sandals. Tommy was wearing sweatpants, but his shoes were shiny and black. Following them on the floor were Carla and Monty. Carla's bobbed red hair swung as she danced, and Monty smiled widely to the room as if the world's cameras were trained on his face. Both wore identical black leggings with tight black shirts. Helen remembered that she'd seen them wearing matching clothes before, on the day Rosa died, when Carla wore her sunny yellow dress and Monty complemented her beautifully in a gorgeous suit and yellow tie.

She looked around the room for Paul, wondering where he was. She spotted him sitting at a table by the window, facing the dance floor, his phone and a microphone in front of him.

The music ended, and couples pulled apart. Some went to sit down, some went to the bar, others checked their shoes, pulling at straps. Some stretched their arms to the ceiling; others spoke harsh words to their partners. And then the music started again. This time the beat was faster, livelier, and Helen recognised it as a jive. It was the only dance she knew. Her feet began to tap, and her hands began to clap; she couldn't help herself. The music was infectious and joyous. On the floor, some dancers were throwing their partner up in the air, twirling and pointing, kicking and flicking. Skirts were flying and knees and hips were shaking. It looked nothing like the jive that she and Tom used to dance. That had been basic, energetic and fun. What she saw on the floor now was physical, athletic, explosive, extreme. She'd never seen anything like it. It was exhausting just watching it.

Bev and Tommy looked incredible. Bev was a bundle of energy against Tommy's lean frame. Meanwhile, Carla and Monty were in a league of their own. Some of the other dancers even stopped their own rehearsal to stand in a circle around them, watching in awe as the Magnificent Curzons tore up the dance floor. Monty was pointing his fingers and stretching his arms, kicking his legs, working the room, winking at women in the crowd that had gathered around him. When the song ended, a round of applause filled the Ocean Room. Carla and Monty took a bow, then walked off to sit down.

Helen decided it was time she set off to walk home, before someone discovered she'd crept in. However, Paul was making his way across the dance floor, so she stayed where she was.

'Hi, Helen. I didn't see you come in. You know, you're not supposed to be here. Rehearsals aren't open to spectators.'

Helen stood. 'I heard the music outside and couldn't resist. The door wasn't locked,' she explained. 'Anyway, I'm leaving now.'

'How long have you been here? Did you see the Curzons dance the jive?'

Deadly Dancing at the Seaview Hotel

'Not long. And yes, I saw them. They were fantastic.'

'It's easy to see why people call them the Magnificent Curzons,' Paul said. 'Just wait until the competition takes place and you see them in their dancing clothes. For the ballroom dances, Carla wears a beautiful pastel blue gown. And for the Latin American dances, Monty wears the most wonderful shirt. It shimmers when he moves, and shines in the light, and it's covered in tiny red beads.'

Chapter 37

A bell rang in Helen's mind. Tiny red beads? Her mind whirled back to finding a red bead in the hallway at the Seaview. It had been stuck between the carpet and the skirting board.

'Sorry, what was that about beads?' she said.

'Monty's red shirt is sponsored by a designer who works exclusively for the Magnificent Curzons,' Paul explained. 'They get all their dance clothes for free in exchange for publicity for the designers, which Monty gives on Instagram and Carla provides when she's snapped by the press. Both also give lots of publicity to their sponsors on my podcast, it's expected. Look, Helen, if I were you, I'd scarper before you're discovered. Only dancers and people with passes like these are allowed in.'

He pulled a lanyard from under his jumper, where it was tucked away next to his chest, and pointed it at her.

'See you later,' he said as he walked back to his table.

Helen left the Spa thinking about the red bead she'd found. It had been shimmery and shiny, like the ones Paul had described on Monty's shirt.

Lost in thought, she walked along the prom, past Farrer's café, past fish and chip shops and fudge shops, ice cream parlours, candy rock shops and the Lord Nelson pub. At the corner of Foreshore Road and Eastborough, she turned left to head up the hill to St

Deadly Dancing at the Seaview Hotel

Mary's church. She took a deep breath. Not only was the street steep, but there were lots of steps and she needed to steel herself and get her legs into gear.

As she climbed higher, into the old town, she thought again about the bead. Something niggled her about it. She prided herself on the cleanliness of the Seaview and had instilled in Sally and Jean how important it was to keep the place shipshape. She knew it was unlikely that Sally would have missed the bead when she was vacuuming. So how long had it been on the floor? And why did it matter? She shook her head and tried to push thoughts away that didn't make sense.

She climbed more steps, heading higher into the old town with its narrow cobbled streets. Nearing the top, she noticed a group of women standing in the graveyard of St Mary's. It wasn't unusual to see people there, paying homage at Anne Brontë's grave. She forced herself on. No, she decided, if Sally had seen the bead, she would have vacuumed it up. But when had it fallen to the carpet? She struggled with this as she reached the top of the hill. From now on, it was all downhill, across the top of the North Bay and down King's Parade. She crossed the road, looking from the clifftop over the sea, with the mighty castle behind her. The Seaview was ahead, and in her sights. As she walked towards it, she saw Tommy standing by the gate. He waved, and she waved back.

'Hello, Tommy. I thought you were rehearsing at the Spa.'

'I've just finished for the day. I booked a Gav's Cab to bring me back here.'

He walked up the path, followed by Helen. As he put his key in the door, his phone began to ring. He opened the door, then pulled his phone out of his pocket. Helen walked into the lounge, arranging beer mats on tables that didn't need beer mats, anything to keep within earshot of Tommy to find out what was going on.

'Hello? . . . Yes. That's me,' she heard him say. 'The TV company. Really? . . . Oh. Yes. I understand. Of course . . . I see. I'll let my sister know. Is there any message I can pass on to her? . . . Right. Well, is there any news you can give me direct? . . . Of course, I understand, everything must go through my agent. Thank you for telling me. Bye now.'

He walked into the lounge and fell into the nearest chair.

'Everything all right, Tommy?' Helen asked.

He stared at the floor.

'Tommy?'

'Oh, sorry,' he said, looking up. He beamed a bright smile, but it didn't reach his eyes. 'No, everything's not all right. That was the TV company. Nothing will be right until I know for sure what's happening with my life. I can't sleep properly, Helen. The TV show is all I can think about. Well, that's when I'm not dwelling on poor Rosa's death.'

'Was it bad news you received just now?' she asked gently.

He shook his head. 'It was no news, actually. They were calling to let me know they can't get through to Bev. They've been trying to ring her but think there must be something wrong with her phone. I've tried calling her myself and had the same problem. I'll have to let her know when she gets back. Anyway, I'm done in. I'm going upstairs for a rest.'

'See you later,' Helen said.

Turning to the picture of Tom on the wall, she brought her

finger to her lips, kissed it, then gently placed the kiss on Tom's cheek.

'I miss you, love,' she said.

Downstairs in her apartment, she fussed over Suki. The dog raised her paw twice, and Helen inspected it.

'There's nothing wrong with it, Suki,' she chided.

She sat on the sofa and Suki stood in front of her, laying her head on the cushion, eyes flickering to Helen.

'I know you want attention, Suki, and that you need a W.A.L.K., but I'm worn out after my trek from the Spa. I'll take you in a while.'

The dog padded away to lie on the patio.

Later, after Helen had walked Suki around the block, she started to get ready for her meal with Marie. She wore her best black jeans, heeled shoes and a white lacy blouse. She picked her favourite silver hoop earrings and the silver bracelet that Tom had bought her for her fortieth birthday. After feeding Suki, checking her paw again, then ensuring she was settled, she headed out.

To reach the restaurant meant walking past Gav's Tans. She forced her feet forward, curious to see what was happening. The tanning salon was taped off with police hazard tape and the windows had been boarded up to stop prying eyes, but the door was open. Helen slowed down and looked in.

'Helen! Missus!' Gav shouted from inside.

Helen stayed where she was.

'Come in. It's all right. The police are finally finished in here,' he called.

She gingerly stepped inside and looked around. The salon had been equipped to a very high standard and the reception area had a warm, calm, peaceful vibe. The fittings inside were high-end, luxurious. There was a polished wooden floor and plush pink armchairs. She noted a rack full of glossy, expensive women's magazines. It was exactly the type of reading material that Marie liked and Helen didn't.

'Forensics have left, they're done with the place,' Gav said.

Helen noticed dark circles under his eyes. Where before he used to look fit and lean, he now looked gaunt and thin.

'Do the police still suspect you had something to do with the death?' she asked gently.

Gav nodded. 'I'm what they call a person of interest. But they haven't charged me with anything . . . yet.'

'Do you know a good lawyer, in case you need one?' she asked, concerned.

He leaned against the reception desk. 'I know five, if I need them.' He held up his right hand and crossed his fingers. 'Which I'm hoping I won't, of course. I wish the police would hurry up and find the killer. I can't have this hanging over my head. I can't eat, I can't sleep. I can't be a husband to Sally, and she needs me now more than ever. Neither can I be a decent dad to Gracie with all of this on my mind. It's all I can think about. My insurance company won't answer my calls. Plus, there's a whole load of expensive stock in here that I don't know what to do with.'

He looked around, and Helen saw opened boxes full of tanning solution. There were other items too, salon equipment that she didn't recognise.

'I hate to ask, Helen, but would it be all right if I drop off some of these boxes at the Seaview tonight? I'll collect them first thing in the morning, I promise.'

Deadly Dancing at the Seaview Hotel

'Why can't you leave things here overnight?' she asked.

'After what happened, I want the place emptied as soon as I can. I've got a lock-up I can leave stuff in, but the more expensive things... well, I'd rather they were somewhere more secure. I wanted to take these boxes home, but Sally says she doesn't want anything from here in the house, and I can't say I blame her.'

'I'd love to help, Gav, but I don't have my car with me. I'm on my way to meet Marie for dinner,' Helen said.

Gav's eyes filled with tears, and Helen's heart went out to him. She offered him a compromise.

'Look, Sally's got her keys for the Seaview. Borrow them and bring your boxes to the hotel tonight. Put them inside my door, out of my way so I don't trip over them when I stumble home after a few glasses of wine.'

Gav hugged her tight. 'Thanks, Helen, you're a star. I'll come to collect them first thing in the morning.'

'No problem, Gav. I want to do everything I can to clear your name.'

His face clouded over. 'You know, missus, Gav usually knows what to do, I'm a creature of habit, but I'm struggling now and confused. My other businesses are suffering. I've had to subcontract my Gav's Gardens work. The only thing I can manage is driving a cab. I'm ruined, Helen. Ruined.' He hung his head.

'The police will get to the bottom of this, you'll see. It'll be over soon,' Helen said. She knew how hollow her words sounded, but she didn't know what else to say. 'Gav, I'm so sorry. I wish this hadn't happened to you.'

'Gav's sorry too, Helen,' he said.

Glenda Young

He pulled a set of keys from his pocket, walked to an alarm panel and punched in a four-digit number.

'Let's go. Gav wants to get home to Sally and Gracie and a big cup of tea. I'll come back here later to pick up the boxes and leave them overnight at the Seaview.'

Chapter 38

Helen walked into Il Piatto to find Marie sitting at the back. Typical Marie, she thought, finding the most secluded table so that they could gossip without being overheard. Marie stood, and they hugged and kissed.

'My word, you look gorgeous . . . again,' Helen said admiringly. She took in her friend's well-cut black trouser suit, short-sleeved pink blouse and matching black waistcoat.

Marie did a twirl. 'I bought it in York. Isn't it lovely?'

Helen agreed that it was, noting that Marie hadn't complimented her on her lacy blouse, but then she must've seen it a hundred times.

They picked up their menus and Marie glanced at Helen over the top of hers.

'Your hair looks nice,' she said, and Helen felt a faint blush of pride. To receive a compliment from her most glamorous friend was a real treat, something she never took for granted.

They ordered their food: pizza for Marie and pasta for Helen, with a carafe of iced water and a bottle of red wine to share. Once the waiter was out of earshot, Marie leaned forward and spoke in a whisper.

'Come on then, tell me your news. Have the police found Rosa's killer?'

Helen leaned forward too. 'Not yet. DS Hutchinson's asked me to keep an eye on my guests. He thinks one of them might be the murderer.'

Marie leaned back in her seat and sighed. 'Crikey, Helen. You could be housing a killer under your roof.'

Helen shuddered. 'Don't remind me. I'm trying not to focus on that too much because it's too scary for words. What I'm doing instead is quizzing my guests.'

'Oh Helen. DS Hutchinson shouldn't be asking you to do his job for him. He's a detective, let him detect. You're a landlady, so you should . . .' Marie shrugged, 'landlade.'

Helen smiled. 'I wish it was as easy as that. You don't know what it's like having guests living under your roof. You feel responsible for them, and when one of them is killed, well, it's put suspicion on them all. It's a horrible feeling and one I want to get rid of as soon as I can. Can we change the subject, please?'

'What else is going on in your life, then?' Marie asked, leaning forward again. 'How's Miriam next door?'

Helen grimaced. 'Don't mention that woman! I gave her bed and breakfast while she had the pest control people in, and she's never once said thank you.'

Marie arched an eyebrow. 'Pest control? Has she got mice?'

'No, it's bedbugs,' Helen whispered.

Marie pulled a face. 'Have you got them at the Seaview?'

Helen held up her crossed fingers. 'Not as far as I know.'

'And how's Mr Dish of the Day? I still follow him on Instagram.'

'Oh, you mean Monty. He and his wife tell each other lies. They've got an open marriage; they've both told me about it, and I know both of them are lying to each other.'

Deadly Dancing at the Seaview Hotel

'Do you think they're trying to pull you in for a threesome?' Marie smirked.

Helen shuddered at the thought of Monty and his warm sausage.

'The short woman called Bev – the one with the orange hair – well, she's got a builder who's followed her all the way to Scarborough to ensure he gets paid for work done on her house. Don't you think that's weird?'

'Definitely,' Marie agreed, then her eyes lit up with glee. 'Oh, Tommy Two Shoes has been into Tom's Teas a few times for coffee. He signed autographs for everyone who asked. He's got a really sweet tooth. He's eaten me out of peach melbas.'

Helen sat up straight in her seat. 'Peach melbas? He said he was buying one of those in Bonnet's around the time of Rosa's death.'

Their wine arrived, and Helen and Marie sat back in their seats. The waiter opened the bottle at the table, then poured a little wine into Helen's glass. She tasted it and announced it acceptable. Once he had filled their glasses and walked off, Marie leaned forward again.

'What about the woman with the red hair, Monty's wife?'

'She's called Carla. She goes sea swimming each morning; that's about all I know, as she's managed to stay out of my way. I could do with more guests like her who keep themselves to themselves. Mind you, her room is a tip. You should see the mountain of clothes she leaves all over the floor.'

'Do you reckon she's the killer?'

Helen shook her head. 'No, but she's now giving the performance of her life in a show dance at the competition that she wouldn't have done if Rosa had been alive. Monty's choreographing the dance. Again, it's a chance for him to shine in the spotlight that he wouldn't have had . . .'

'If Rosa had still been alive,' Marie said.

'Exactly. Maybe they all had a hand in her death, because they all stand to gain in one way or another now that she's gone.'

'What about the groupie?'

'You mean the podcaster. Well, Paul follows the dancers around the country, at his own expense. He earns money from sponsorship of his podcast. But it seems like he's in the clear. He was podcasting live from outside the salon at the time of Rosa's murder.'

Their food arrived, and there was silence for a few moments while Parmesan was grated onto pasta. As they ate, Helen brought Marie up to speed on Jean and Bobby Tanner, and how Jimmy had helped stop Jean's inheritance from going into Bobby's account. Marie raised her glass and clinked it against Helen's as they made a toast.

'To Jean!'

Marie continued eating, then looked up at Helen.

'So, how are things with you and Jimmy?'

Helen chewed her pasta for a very long time before she replied.

'They're all right,' she said, then she stuffed her mouth with another forkful.

'Come on, Helen. This is your oldest, best friend you're talking to. Tell me the truth.'

Helen laid her fork on her plate.

'He wants me to go on holiday with him.'

Marie's face lit up. 'Well, that's great.'

'No, it's not. He wants me to go to Graceland, but I can't.'

'Why not?' Marie asked, then she gave a knowing smile. 'Oh, I

Deadly Dancing at the Seaview Hotel

get it, it's the Seaview keeping you from leaving Scarborough and having a life . . . again.'

Helen pulled her phone out of her handbag and swiped it into life. There, flashing on and off, pulsing red, was the beating heart emoji, counting down the days to Graceland. She peered at it. The days had counted down to zero. There was now less than twenty-four hours left.

'Why can't you go?' Marie demanded. 'I've lost track of the number of times Jean and Sally have offered to look after Suki and the Seaview. And you know I'd help out too.'

'I just can't go, Marie. Now can we change the flaming subject?'

'You *can* go,' Marie said, reaching across the table and taking Helen's hand. 'And you should. If you feel for Jimmy what he feels for you, you should take him up on his offer. You've got to find out if what you have between you is real. If it's going somewhere. This is your chance to determine your future with an amazing man.'

Helen slammed her knife on the table. Other diners looked their way.

'You know fine well that Tom and I promised to celebrate our silver wedding anniversary there! I can't go to Graceland without Tom!' she cried.

The waiter bustled over. 'Everything all right, ladies?'

'Everything's fine, thank you,' Marie replied sweetly, and the waiter walked away.

'You don't have to go without Tom,' Marie said gently.

Helen looked at her as if she'd gone mad. 'What do you mean?' she demanded.

'Well, you've still got some of Tom's ashes in your apartment at the Seaview. You could take them to Graceland.'

Helen sank back in her seat, stunned. She'd never once considered this. Suddenly, everything began to make sense. It was as if a fog had lifted.

'Are visitors to Graceland allowed to do that?' she asked.

Marie nodded. 'A friend of mine did it when her brother passed away; he was an Elvis fan too. She sprinkled his ashes there discreetly and privately. Mind you, if you take ashes across borders you need a document from the funeral director, but I'm sure it's easy enough to arrange. A friend of mine at the funeral parlour owes me a favour. I'll ring him now and get it sorted for you.'

Helen felt an excitement building.

'No, I couldn't . . .' She looked at Marie. 'Could I?'

Marie raised a perfectly manicured eyebrow. 'You could. And you should.'

Helen looked down at her plate, her heart beating fast. Then she pushed her chair back and stood.

'Marie, would you mind if I don't finish my pasta? I need to go home. I've only got a few hours left to pack, grab some sleep, then brief Jean. I need to book a cab to get me to Leeds Bradford airport in time to meet Jimmy in the VIP lounge.'

'I could drive you,' Marie offered, but Helen shook her head.

'You're too busy with Tom's Teas. I'll be fine in a cab.'

Marie pulled the bottle of wine towards her.

'Then run like the wind, Helen. Give my love to Jimmy, and send me a postcard from Memphis.'

Helen tried taking Marie's advice about running, but realised she was out of breath by the time she reached Eastborough. She settled on a fast walk instead. All the while, her heart was bouncing and her mood was high. Marie was right. But then, she was rarely wrong. She *should* give Jimmy a chance. How would she ever know how happy she could be if she didn't take this leap of faith? She *could* take Tom with her, even if it was in a strange way.

Of course, there was a lot to sort out in the short time before she left. She'd have to speak to DS Hutchinson, whatever Marie said, and she'd need to run through the Seaview's upcoming bookings with Jean and Sally. She felt uneasy about leaving them with what could be a murderer at the Seaview. She was also worried about Sally, who was starting to struggle with the heavy work, though she could always ring the agency to send help if needed. Her heart fell. Perhaps Graceland wasn't on the cards right now.

She was see-sawing all the way home. On the one hand it seemed the perfect time to jet off with Jimmy and forge a future with him. On the other, there was an ongoing investigation into the murder of one of her guests. And so it went on, Helen thinking one thing then the other, twisting her mind this way and that. All she wanted to do was get home, take Suki for a quick walk then collapse into bed.

When she walked into the apartment, she expected to find Gav's boxes from the tanning salon, as they'd agreed earlier. However, no boxes were there.

Chapter 39

The next morning, Helen woke earlier than usual with a lot on her mind. She knew she had to ring DS Hutchinson to talk to him about the possibility of going away on holiday while a murder investigation was under way. She heard Marie's voice in her head telling her not to ask, but to demand the time off. However, she didn't think she had the courage to do that. If DS Hutchinson agreed she could go, then she had her suitcase to pack and the Seaview's affairs to get in order before she left for the airport that afternoon.

She reached for Suki's lead hanging on the back of the door, and as she did so, her phone rang on the kitchen worktop. She swung around to answer it, and the lead in her hand flew out and connected with her glass fruit bowl with a metallic clang. The bowl shifted precariously, teetering on the edge of the bench.

'Oh no!' she cried as she leapt into action. Her phone continued to ring. Paper clips, pencils and loose odds and ends from the bottom of the bowl fell to the floor. However, the bowl itself, along with two apples and a banana, was saved. Suki padded around with her teeth chattering, a sure sign she needed to go out. Helen pushed the bowl back onto the bench and swiped her phone into life, just as the caller hung up. She recognised the number of the local butcher. Nothing to be concerned about, she knew, as he

Deadly Dancing at the Seaview Hotel

sometimes called to ask if he could substitute her breakfast order of pork sausages for beef.

She clipped Suki's lead to her collar and went outside. The morning was calm and bright, and Helen breathed in the soft sea air. However, she didn't get far. She stopped when she saw Carla at the front door of the hotel. Carla was wrapped in the robe she wore when she went for a swim. She had her back to Helen and seemed to be having trouble getting through the door. As Helen walked towards her, she noticed that Carla's hair was dry, and that she carried a small handbag instead of her beach bag. She also wore a pair of scarlet stilettos. How odd, she thought. She walked up the path with Suki at her side.

'Been for a swim?' she asked innocently.

Carla turned sharply, and her red bob swung around her face, but she didn't answer. Suki lifted her paw to Helen.

'Suki, no, not now,' Helen said.

'I can't seem to get the door open,' Carla said.

Helen stepped forward, unlocked the door and pushed it hard. She almost fell over three cardboard boxes.

'What the . . .!' she cried.

The boxes were from Gav's tanning salon. Bottles of lotion and spray tan guns poked from the top of each one.

'Gav! I meant leave them in my apartment, not here,' she grumbled. She bent down and began pushing the boxes along the corridor, out of the way of the door. When they were lined up against the wall, she dusted her hands together then stood back to let Carla inside. She noticed that Carla's changing robe was completely dry. Something wasn't right.

Breaking her own rule about not taking Suki in through the

Glenda Young

front door, she followed Carla along the hallway. A warning bell rang in her mind as she tried to think back and remember. She'd seen Carla in her robe twice before. The first time had been on the beach, when Carla had been in the sea, red hair slicked back, her skin wet. The second time had been on the morning of Rosa's death. She'd spotted Carla returning to the Seaview after her swim, or at least that was what she'd assumed.

Think, Helen, think! She attempted to focus, her head spinning as she forced her mind back to that morning. She remembered she'd walked Suki early as always, and when she'd reached King's Parade, she'd seen Carla outside the hotel with dry, styled hair. She remembered thinking at the time how that contradicted what Carla had said about never wearing a bathing cap.

She marched forward. 'Where had you been on the morning of the day Rosa died?' she demanded.

Carla turned, and her bobbed hair swung. 'What?' she said.

'I saw you enter the Seaview that morning. You were wearing your changing robe, as you are now.'

'I'd been for a swim,' Carla said quickly, defiantly.

'Yet your hair wasn't wet; it was styled just as it is now.'

Carla tilted her chin and narrowed her eyes. 'My word, you're a nosy old bat. Do you spy on all your guests?'

Helen knew she'd rattled her and so she carried on.

'I don't think you had been for a swim.'

Carla's demeanour changed. Her shoulders slouched, her dancer's posture disappearing as she slowly walked to the stairs. Helen was quicker and got there first. She stood guard at the bottom with Suki.

'You're going nowhere. I want to talk to you in the lounge, now,' she ordered.

Deadly Dancing at the Seaview Hotel

Carla laughed out loud. 'This is ridiculous, darling. Now, kindly let me pass.'

Helen refused to move.

'Go and sit in the lounge,' she repeated.

'This is ridiculous!' Carla protested again. But Helen stood firm, and Carla reluctantly walked into the lounge, keeping her robe closed. Helen followed, her heart beating fast.

'Sit by the window where I can keep my eye on you,' she said.

'Darling, what's going on?' Carla said, less confident now. Helen drew strength from the crack in the woman's charming facade.

'Sit down, Carla,' she said firmly.

Carla sat down. Helen took a seat by the door, in case Carla turned nasty and she had to run out. Suki lifted her paw to her.

'Suki, no,' Helen said, annoyed, but the dog pawed her knee.

'I want the truth, Carla. Where had you been on the morning Rosa died?'

Carla turned and looked out of the window. Suki pawed Helen's knee again. Helen looked from Carla to Suki. She hated to see her beloved dog in distress. Quickly she took Suki's paw and inspected it, stunned to see the tiny piece of blue sea glass and the red bead that had fallen from her fruit bowl. She took both out of the pad and laid them on the table, letting Suki's lead drop to the floor. Suki walked across the room and stood beside Carla.

'Get your mutt away from me,' Carla snapped as she shifted in her seat and crossed her legs to distance herself from the dog. That was when Helen saw the sparkling dress under the changing robe. It was a Latin American dance dress, covered in tiny red beads.

Suddenly, horribly, pieces of a red-beaded jigsaw began to slot together. Helen's heart pounded. Sweat broke out on the back of her neck. She picked up the bead from the table, the bead that had been in Suki's paw, the bead that she'd picked up from the hallway on the morning Rosa died and kept in her fruit bowl since. She looked from the bead to Carla's dress, from the dress to the bead. She held the bead aloft.

'This is yours!' she cried.

Carla shifted in her seat and pulled the robe tight, hiding the dress again.

'You were wearing that dress under your robe on the morning Rosa was killed, weren't you? I found this bead in the hallway before breakfast that day. I knew it hadn't been there the night before, because I'm fastidious about keeping the Seaview clean.'

'So you found a bead. So what?' Carla snarled. 'It could be any bead. Monty's got a matching shirt. It could have fallen off that.'

'My guess is that on the morning of Rosa's death, you hadn't been for a swim in the sea. Had you?'

'It's none of your business!' Carla said defensively.

'Where had you been?' Helen demanded. She pulled her phone from her pocket. 'I've got DS Hutchinson's number here. It's about time I gave him a call. I'm sure he'd be interested in hearing what you have to say.'

Carla shrugged. 'I'd been out all night, dancing. Are you happy now that you know? I always take my robe because it keeps me warm.'

'Seems a strange thing to wear for a night out,' Helen said.

Carla narrowed her eyes. 'It hides a multitude of sins,' she said, glaring at Helen. 'This is my favourite dress. The robe is the only thing I've got that's big enough to hide it.'

Deadly Dancing at the Seaview Hotel

'Why would you want to hide it?'

'Because I'm not supposed to wear it in public unless I'm dancing with Monty in his matching red shirt. It was a condition imposed by the designer who sponsors us.'

'Where did you go dancing?'

Carla turned away again. 'Just out. Stop bugging me! What is this? The Scarborough Inquisition?'

Suddenly she leapt to her feet and barged at Helen, pushing her off her chair and against the door. There was a scuffle, and red beads went flying from Carla's dress. Suki began barking. Helen pulled herself to her feet; she felt dazed and dizzy, and it took her a moment to get her balance. Carla was running for the front door, and Helen knew she had to stop her. She forced herself along the hallway, reaching the door just as Carla put her hand on the lock. With every ounce of her strength, she grabbed the back of Carla's robe. With her other hand, she yanked a spray tan gun from one of Gav's boxes and poked it hard against Carla's back.

'Freeze. I've got a gun.'

Carla froze.

'Put your hands up.'

Carla put her hands up. 'Don't hurt me, I'm too young to die!'

'Get back in the lounge,' Helen ordered.

Keeping the spray tan gun pressed hard against Carla's back, she marched her back to the lounge. Through the window, she spotted a bright orange Gav's Cab pulling up at the kerb. Gav bounded up the path and let himself in with Sally's keys.

'I've come for my boxes, missus,' he said as he walked into the lounge. But when he saw what was happening, his face darkened.

'Gav, call the police!' Helen yelled.

She watched as Gav took his phone from his pocket and dialled.

'Sit down,' she told Carla.

Carla sat, and Helen threw the spray gun on the floor.

'It was just a plastic toy!' Carla said, outraged.

'Gav, stand next to me and don't move until the police arrive,' Helen said.

Standing in front of Carla, she looked her hard in the eye.

'Tell me everything. I want Gav's name cleared and I want him to hear every word. You've put the poor lad and his family through hell.'

'Helen, what's going on?' Gav cried.

Helen wasn't sure where she was going next with her madcap theory, but she had to make sense of it. For Gav's sake, for Sally's sake, for her own sanity and her beloved Seaview. Coolly and calmly, she turned her attention to Carla.

'Gav, if I'm right, we're looking at the woman who murdered Rosa de Wolfe.'

Chapter 40

'Bitch!' Carla spat.

Helen shook her head. 'How dare you call me that! I'm protecting Gav, my livelihood and my hotel.'

'I didn't mean you, I meant Rosa,' Carla hissed. She was staring wildly from Helen to Gav. 'Do you know how many times I should have won trophies for being the best dancer, how many times I lost out to that woman? I've been bitter about this for years!'

Helen inched closer to Gav, and he took her hand. Suki stood between them, watching, as Carla continued, rambling now, words tripping over themselves in the rush to come out.

'She used every trick in the book to ensure she won all the competitions she entered. And it wasn't because she was the best dancer. She tried to bribe judges, Helen. She even pulled Monty into her corrupt world at Blackpool, but it didn't work out. He was suspended from the dance world for six months. And there's more.'

She seemed to shrink in the chair, her robe gaping open. The red beads on her dress were losing their shine now, hanging lank against her bony knees.

'Monty and I were sponsored by an Italian designer; we had our dancing clothes made specially, we didn't need to spend a penny. But then Rosa stole our contract. Can you imagine how that felt, to have everything taken from us after we'd worked so hard to earn prestigious sponsorship? We were the envy of the dance world before that happened. Since then, our clothes have been made by a sweat shop in Gateshead. Now it's second-rate stuff and the beads keep falling off.'

Gav squeezed Helen's hand as Carla ranted on.

'I was sponsored by a make-up company too. I didn't have to buy any of my own cosmetics as long as I mentioned the brand when I was interviewed on Paul's podcast. Then Rosa stole that contract too. She took everything I had. Everything. Except Monty. He wasn't interested in her in that way; she wasn't his type, although that didn't stop her from trying it on with him each time they met.'

Her face darkened.

'This went on for years, Helen. Years. And I smiled through it all. I gritted my teeth and I smiled. But I hated her, oh, I can't tell you how much I wanted her out of my life. And then the final straw came after we arrived in Scarborough and I found out that she'd been having a fling with Frankie Tanner. Well, that was her business, but then I was summoned to see him. He told me that I wasn't going to be opening the show with Monty, even though we'd worked for months to prepare our exhibition tango. That was bad enough, but then he said Rosa had been given the top spot instead of us. It was too much.'

'And so you killed her,' Helen said calmly.

She heard Gav gasp, but she ignored him and carried on.

'How did you do it?'

Carla pulled her changing robe around her, as if she wanted to disappear inside. 'I seduced Frankie Tanner,' she said. 'I wanted to get even with Rosa. I thought if I got Frankie on my side, he'd change his mind about giving her top billing at the competition. It

Deadly Dancing at the Seaview Hotel

was a lot easier than I expected. He had no qualms about being unfaithful to her after I'd plied him with half a bottle of gin. Neither did he shed a tear when she died.'

'So the night before Rosa died, you got Frankie drunk,' Helen said.

Carla ignored her.

'He told me about a tanning salon in town that was being opened the next day by an old school friend of his called Gav. Frankie said that Gav was a creature of habit and that he could guess what the salon's alarm code would be. He said it would be the same four numbers Gav always used: his birthday, which was the twenty-fifth of September. So the code was 2509.'

'Damn!' Gav muttered under his breath. Helen squeezed his hand.

'After a night's dancing, we decided to break into the salon for a laugh. I didn't think for one minute we'd get inside. I'd drunk the other half of the bottle of gin, so I wasn't thinking straight. I thought it was a giggle, a way to impress Frankie, to get what I wanted, which was Rosa off the top spot at the dance.'

'I can hear the police, I can hear sirens!' Gav cried.

Helen heard them too. She crossed her fingers and hoped they were headed to the Seaview.

'What happened next?' she asked.

Carla remained silent as the sirens got louder.

'You might as well tell us, Carla. The police are on their way.'

She pulled up the hood on her robe and sank inside it.

'Frankie broke into the back of the salon. By some miracle, he'd guessed the alarm code right. Turns out your friend Gav here really is a creature of habit.'

Gav shifted at Helen's side.

'Carry on,' Helen said sternly.

'Frankie wasn't interested in anything inside the salon except for seeing how Gav ran the place. He was looking for paperwork, details of suppliers, that kind of thing. While he was doing that, I messed around in the tanning booths, and that's when the idea struck. I'd used similar booths before. I knew how they worked as I've used more tanning salons in my life as a dancer than you'll have hot dinners. I've seen the same mechanism before. I knew I could break it so that the tanning solution wouldn't stop when the timer went off. All I had to do was steer Rosa into the correct booth the next morning when we went for our spray tans.'

'Wasn't Rosa suspicious when you ushered her into the doctored booth? And didn't Bev spot you trying to steer Rosa into that particular booth?' Helen asked.

'Bev was too busy taking a phone call outside about her stupid brother's TV show,' Carla said. 'As for Rosa, luck was on my side. She chose the tampered booth herself. She walked straight into it. I didn't need to use my powers of persuasion. It was too easy. Once she was in, I simply jammed the door shut.'

'Were you with Frankie again last night?' Helen asked, looking at Carla's scarlet shoes.

Carla shrugged. 'Might have been. What's it to you?'

A police car and van pulled up outside the Seaview. Helen was heartened to see DS Hutchinson and DC Hall climb out of the car. Uniformed officers got out of the van.

'Gav, go and let them in,' she said, not letting her gaze waver from Carla.

Deadly Dancing at the Seaview Hotel

The two detectives entered the lounge. Carla retreated further into her changing robe. Helen looked at DS Hutchinson.

'She's confessed to killing Rosa de Wolfe.'

DC Hall read Carla her rights, then led her away.

DS Hutchinson looked at Helen. 'Are you all right?'

Helen shook her head, then collapsed into a seat. 'No.' She looked into his eyes. 'Do I need to come to the station to give a statement?'

He nodded and helped her to stand, then looked at Gav. 'You'll need to come too.'

'I need a minute to take Suki down to my apartment,' Helen said.

Downstairs, anxiety filled her as her thoughts turned again to tiny red beads. She breathed deeply, trying to calm her mind. She thought about Graceland. Should she really go after what had just happened? Could she?

Two hours later, DS Hutchinson drove Helen back to the Seaview. She was relieved to see the Gav's Cab no longer outside and assumed Gav must have returned home.

'Forensics found matching red beads from Carla's dress inside the tanning salon and finger prints that match Carla's all over the tanning mechanism that she broke,' he explained as she opened the front door. 'We have enough evidence to convict her. Take care, Helen, and thank you for all you've done.'

'Do you need me for anything more?' Helen asked, keeping her fingers crossed.

'No, you've done all you need to,' he replied.

She breathed a sigh of relief. Then she pulled out her phone and looked at the beating heart emoji. The countdown for Graceland had just a few hours left.

'Now then, which room is Mr Curzon in? I need to speak to him,' the detective said.

After directing the detective upstairs to Monty's room, Helen walked into the lounge on shaking legs. She was surprised to see Tommy, Bev and Paul there so early in the morning. They were ashen-faced, motionless, in shock.

'Carla called Monty from the police station. He told us about her confession,' Tommy explained.

Helen sat down, exhausted, as Bev began to speak.

'Monty's leaving today. He won't dance without Carla. No one wants to see one Magnificent Curzon; they always dance as a pair. He sees no reason to stay and wants to leave as soon as he can.'

'I understand,' Helen said. 'Are you all leaving?'

Bev sat up in her seat and glanced at Tommy. 'No. Tommy, Paul and I will stay for the dance competition tonight and leave tomorrow. We've agreed with Monty that Tommy and I will do the show dance; we're going to do one of Tommy's old routines from his Two Shoes days. It'll act as both a homage to Rosa and a celebration of Tommy's future.'

'A celebration?' Helen asked.

Bev beamed at her brother and took his hand in hers.

'Oh Helen, it's wonderful news. We found out that Tommy's getting his TV show! The TV company called him last night. They tried calling me but couldn't get through because my phone was cut off. I was so far in debt I couldn't afford to pay my bill. Filming begins in three months, which is enough time for me to whip my brother into shape and get him dance fit. No more cream cakes and peach melbas for Tommy. I'll finally be able to give Mike the rest of his money and pay off my loan.'

She cast her gaze to the carpet.

'Nothing seems real after what happened to Rosa, though. We've had two awful shocks.'

'Can you manage breakfast?' Helen asked, looking at each guest in turn.

'Yes, but no marmalade for Tommy. He's back on his diet,' Bev said, shooting her brother a stern glance.

Chapter 41

When Helen walked into her apartment, she heard a pop song on the radio. Then she heard Jean's voice, happy and singing along. In the kitchen, Jean was scrambling eggs in a bowl, shaking her hips side to side. When she saw Helen, she placed the bowl on the kitchen top.

'You look done in, love,' she said.

'I'm fine, but tired. Sit down, Jean, I need to speak to you.'

Jean looked around her, aghast. 'Sit down? Me? Now? I can't. I'm making breakfast.'

'Then listen to me carefully,' Helen said.

Without missing a beat, or a stir of the eggs, Jean leaned forward as Helen told her about Carla's confession. Her eyes widened in horror, then she shook her head.

'My word, those poor guests upstairs,' she said.

'Monty's leaving today, and the others are going tomorrow. Then we've got a couple of quiet weeks with only weekend guests booked in.'

Helen's phone pinged. She walked to the dining table, where her handbag was slung over a chair. She pulled out her phone and saw that the beating heart emoji for the Graceland app was larger than it had been before. It was redder, pulsing faster, and there was text underneath that read: *Six hours to go, cat, go to Graceland! Don't forget to pack your blue suede shoes.*

'Jean?' she said carefully.

'What, love?'

'I know Jimmy's already asked you and Sally about looking after Suki and managing this place if I go away on holiday with him . . .'

Jean pushed her glasses up to the bridge of her nose. 'Yes, love?'

'Well . . . would you still like to do it?' She bit her lip and waited for a response.

Jean placed the bowl and spoon on the worktop and looked at her. 'No.'

Helen's heart dropped. Then she saw a mischievous smile make its way to her friend's lips.

'I wouldn't like to do it, Helen, I'd *love* to. On one condition.'

'Name it,' Helen said.

'That I can move in here with Suki while you're away.'

Suki walked to stand beside Jean. Jean looked around the kitchen and living room.

'If I could stay here, it'd be perfect. It'd be a change of scene that might help me cope. Plus, I'll have the dog to keep me company. As you say, we've only got weekend guests coming in while you're away. I'm sure me and Sally can manage, and Marie has offered to help if we need her.'

Helen scribbled the name of the staff agency on a Post-it note.

'Ring the agency if you need more help. I don't want Sally doing too much. She's got to look after herself and the twins.'

She walked around the worktop to Jean, intending to hug her, but Jean backed away, holding up a wooden spoon as a warning not to come closer.

'When's your flight?'

'This afternoon.'

She pointed the wooden spoon at Helen.

'Then you'll need to pack. After you've taken Suki for her W.A.L.K.' She looked at the dog. 'By the way, is her paw all right or do I need to keep in touch with the vet while you're away?'

Helen stroked Suki's ears. 'Her paws are perfect. If she raises one, she's attention-seeking. However, it's best to check in case anything's in there and she's trying to tell you something.'

She sat on the sofa and rang Sally.

'Morning, Helen. I'm on my way to work now. I'll be about half an hour,' Sally said.

'It's all right, Sal, I'm not checking up on you. I'm ringing to ask if you and Gav are all right.'

'Gav's great, Helen. The police called first thing this morning and told us they've charged Carla Curzon. He's gutting the salon today, taking everything out. And he's going to change the alarm code on all of his businesses. Carla's arrest will be all over the news, so you'd better brace yourself for more mentions of the Seaview.'

'Ah, about that,' Helen said. She glanced at Jean, who was now slicing mushrooms. 'I'm hoping to miss the news in the next few days. I'm going away with Jimmy.'

At the other end of the phone, Sally squealed so loudly that Helen had to pull her phone away from her ear.

'If you and Jean need me for anything, ring me. And don't overdo things, you hear?'

Deadly Dancing at the Seaview Hotel

'Loud and clear!' Sally said, and then she squealed again.

Helen showered, dressed, then pulled a black suitcase on wheels from the back of the cupboard under the stairs. Meanwhile, the beating heart app pinged every half-hour to remind her she had little time left. She laid the suitcase on her bed, ready to pack, then thought better of it and headed back to the kitchen, where she snapped Suki's lead to her collar.

'Be a good girl for Jean,' she told the dog as they walked.

On the beach, she stopped and turned her face to the sky.

'Am I doing the right thing, Tom?' she breathed into the wind. When there was no reply, she knew there was only one way to find out. And so she walked on, one foot in front of the other, back to the Seaview, to her suitcase, her passport . . . and Tom's ashes.

All packed, with the beating heart emoji now in danger of cardiac arrest, warning her she had less than five hours before her flight, she presented herself in front of Jean with her suitcase.

'You look nervous,' Jean said.

'I am,' Helen replied.

Jean handed her a plastic container.

'There are two slices of coffee and walnut cake in there. I made it fresh this morning before you woke up. Take them to the airport to enjoy with a cuppa. And don't worry, I didn't forget anything this time. It's a perfect cake, if I say so myself.'

Helen took the container and placed it in her flight bag.

'Thanks, Jean, for everything,' she said.

'Thank you too, lass, for saving Mum's money.'

Helen swiped her phone into life.

'Good morning, Gav's Cabs!' a woman's cheery voice answered.

'Good morning. It's Helen Dexter at the Seaview Hotel on

King's Parade. Could I have a taxi, please, straight away? I'm going to Leeds Bradford airport.'

When the taxi arrived at the back of the Seaview, Jean walked towards Helen with open arms. Helen collapsed into them, feeling warm and secure, as though she wanted to stay there for ever. Finally she pulled herself away, knelt beside Suki and snuggled her dog. Tears filled her eyes.

'I'll miss you both,' she said, looking from Suki to Jean.

'Here, girl,' Jean called, and Suki padded away to her side.

'Have a wonderful time, and don't worry about us,' Jean said.

Helen wheeled her case to the back door of her apartment and was both delighted and surprised to see Gav standing beside the bright orange cab, holding the passenger door open for her.

'Morning, missus!'

He placed her case in the boot, and Helen turned to wave to Jean and Suki. As she climbed into the passenger seat, her phone pinged, with the beating heart emoji almost bursting from the screen. She texted Jimmy to tell him she was on her way to the airport, and immediately received three heart emojis, a smiling face and a thumbs-up in return.

As the cab sped along the A64, Helen began to talk about Carla and the police, but Gav shook his head.

'Hope you don't mind, missus, but Gav wants to put the past behind him. He's looking to the future.'

'I understand, Gav, no problem,' she replied.

Her phone rang, and she saw it was a call diverted from the Seaview's landline. She made a mental note to ring Jean to tell her how to undivert calls while she was away.

Deadly Dancing at the Seaview Hotel

'Good morning, Seaview Hotel,' she said politely.

'Ah, good morning,' a woman's voice replied. 'I hope you can help. I'm the executive personal assistant to a singing artiste who'll be performing a gig at the Open Air Theatre. She'll have her musicians with her, and I need somewhere for them to stay that's discreet and nondescript. Somewhere that's tucked away and blends in, that's even a little bit dull. Your hotel fits the bill.'

Helen was aghast. 'Dull?'

'We don't want her fans to know where she's staying,' the woman continued. 'If we put her in one of the big hotels, like the Crown, or in a showy apartment at the Sands, the chances are her fans will find her. What we need is something less . . . obvious, where she can rest. And she needs a lot of rest. She's fresh out of rehab after a . . . personal problem and is now planning the comeback gig of her life. She hasn't performed in public since 1982, when she was top of the charts. I'm afraid I'm not at liberty to divulge her name until we sign a contract. Her anonymity is of the utmost importance.'

'I see,' Helen said, although she wasn't quite sure that she did. 'Well, when would she and her band like to come in?'

RAISING READERS
Books Build Bright Futures

Dear Reader,

We'd love your attention for one more page to tell you about the crisis in children's reading, and what we can all do.

Studies have shown that reading for fun is the **single biggest predictor of a child's future success** – more than family circumstance, parents' educational background or income. It improves academic results, mental health, wealth, communication skills and ambition.

The number of children reading for fun is in rapid decline. Young people have a lot of competition for their time, and a worryingly high number do not have a single book at home.

Our business works extensively with schools, libraries and literacy charities, but here are some ways we can all raise more readers:

- Reading to children for just 10 minutes a day makes a difference
- Don't give up if your children aren't regular readers – there will be books for them!
- Visit bookshops and libraries to get recommendations
- Encourage them to listen to audiobooks
- Support school libraries
- Give books as gifts

Thank you for reading.
www.JoinRaisingReaders.com